THE
RAVENOUS

Also by Amy Lukavics

Daughters unto Devils
The Women in the Walls

THE
RAVENOUS

AMY LUKAVICS

HARLEQUIN®TEEN

ISBN-13: 978-0-373-21260-6

The Ravenous

HARLEQUIN® TEEN
www.HarlequinTEEN.com

Printed in U.S.A.

To Roxie, Jamie and Chelsea:
How could I ever write a book about sisters without dedicating it to you?

CHAPTER 1

Before the birthday balloons, and before the accident, before the broken mirrors and the black veins and the dismembered bodies in the basement, there was only the Cane sisters.

If only it could be like this all the time, Mona Cane thought as she and her four sisters crowded the reflection of the store mirror. They stood in a row, smiling and tilting their heads back and forth in unison as if they were all a part of the same organism. *If only what people thought about us was the truth. "The Cane sisters are so great!" "They love each other so much!" "What a wonderful family the Canes have!"*

But really, Mona knew it was all a lie.

The other customers at the boutique let out passive-aggressive sighs and begrudgingly made their way through the narrow aisle left by the sisters, who were crowded in front of the entire sunglasses section at Lily Lu's, leaning into each other to fit in front of the mirror as they tried on several pairs. Some people tried to hide their stares, flit their eyes up in between browsing the brightly colored scarves and fashionably-thinned T-shirts from the racks nearby, but others just stared openly.

While their family moved around frequently according to the whims of the army, there seemed to be a general sentiment shared about the sisters wherever they went, a hushed sort of intrigue, an envy that bloomed from the knowledge that no matter what happened in the world, the girls would always have each other.

How nice, Mona thought, trying not to let the bitterness creep in.

Although it *was* kind of nice on days like this, she knew as she took in the shared joy between herself and her sisters, so rare these days. Even Juliet, nineteen years old and the hardest of them all, couldn't help but laugh as their youngest sister, Rose, picked up a pair of hot-pink-framed sunglasses, slid them onto her face and struck an enthusiastic pose.

"Those were made for you," Juliet said, her smile warm as she addressed the baby of the family. But her smile hardened and chilled when she turned to look at Taylor, her constant shadow since the age of one. "Can you step back, please?"

Taylor flinched at the unexpected sting. "Me? Why?"

"You're *hovering*." Juliet pulled her shoulder dramatically in. "Jesus, Taylor, you're so close that I can smell your breakfast! Can't you breathe through your goddamn nose every now and then?"

Taylor backed away immediately, not changing her facial expression as she reached forward and picked up another pair of sunglasses to try on. It was like she had simultaneously heard Juliet and not heard her at all. None of the other sisters reacted, either. Mona let her eyes fall away from the mirror.

Letting out an irritated sigh, Juliet gently took the glasses out of Taylor's hands and put them back. "I think we should all get the same ones Rose did, but with different colored frames."

And just like that, Mona knew that the decision about the sunglasses was made, all because Juliet had said so.

"Everybody pick a color!" Rose squealed in delight as she grinned at her reflection through her new shades. "Obviously, I call pink!"

Beside her, their middle sister Anya shot forward to claim the pair with the emerald green frames. Mona knew that Anya was choosing them because they were the same color as the beloved weed that she was always packing into her starglass pipe and smoking in their closet.

"Best color," Anya said to herself with a wicked, confident little smile that Mona both resented and coveted. Even though Anya was only sixteen, a year older than Mona, the difference felt enormous at this point in their lives. Especially in the past year, since they'd stopped spending so much time together, right around the time things at home had gotten worse.

"I can't decide," Juliet said, studying herself in a pair of sunshine-yellow-framed shades. "These, or..." she quickly replaced the sunglasses with ones that were framed with bright bloodred "...these."

"Ooooh," Rose cooed, and all the other sisters nodded in quiet agreement. "I think the red looks so good on you, Juliet, and it even matches your lipstick!"

And your uncontrollable temper, Mona thought, wishing she could whisper it to Anya so they could share a laugh. *What a perfect match.*

"I think you're right," Juliet said, carelessly letting the yellow sunglasses fall back crookedly onto the holder on the table in front of them. She barely had time to pull her hand away when Taylor snatched the yellow frames and eagerly put them on. She stared at herself in a way that showed how shamelessly she wanted to be just like Juliet.

In fact, Mona happened to know that Taylor usually hated yellow things, and that the only reason she'd chosen the glasses was because Juliet *almost* did, which meant that Taylor would be *almost* as cool for getting them instead. Ever since Mona could remember, Taylor was always right behind their oldest sister, eager to please her and be accepted by her and, as far as Mona could tell, somehow transform herself into Juliet's clone.

"Hurry up, Mona," Juliet urged, turning her head toward the cash register, obviously over the thrill of the search and eager to leave. "Just pick already. Blue or orange are all that's left."

Without hesitating, Mona reached out and took the blue pair. Blue was calm. Blue was cool. Blue was…sad, which was embarrassingly reflective but oh well. She slid the glasses on her face and studied her reflection with those of her sisters, the lot of them like one long, fucked up rainbow.

Once the glasses were paid for, the Canes got ice cream cones across the street. This was a sisterly tradition that they had taken with them to every town they'd lived in:

ice cream. Everywhere had ice cream. Juliet and Taylor got coffee flavored, Anya got butter pecan, Mona got cookie dough and Rose got rainbow sorbet. As they strolled down the sidewalk downtown and licked the cones that were already melting in thick drips down the waffled sides, their likeness was so strong it nearly looked manufactured: auburn hair and freckled skin and very thin upper lips that, much to the sisters' dismay, revealed their slightly buck front teeth if they didn't remember to hold their mouths right.

They walked in a group with Rose in the middle, surrounded like a baby elephant in a herd that was anticipating lions. The other people on the sidewalk were forced to step aside as the girls pummeled through, licking their cones and letting out shrill bursts of laughter as Rose told a joke she'd heard at school.

If only it could be like this all the time, Mona thought again, *but with Mom and Dad with us.*

But "Mom and Dad" wasn't really a thing, not for eighty percent of the year anyway, since Dad was always away for work.

When the cones were gone and their fingers were sticky and the sky became heavy with clouds, the girls reluctantly made their way back to the vintage Mustang convertible at the curb two blocks back, which was a guilt gift from their father when Juliet turned sixteen. Even though Taylor had her license and Anya had her learner's permit, Juliet was the only one with a car, and she *always* drove. Mona suspected it was her way of claiming the spot closest to their father, since she might as well have been a third parent herself.

Even with their combined stories, the girls felt like they hardly knew their dad. They'd never seen him long enough to get past the awkward, always-smiling stage of the relationship, where at the sign of any sort of conflict or situation requiring discipline, he'd slip away to clean the grill, or fix the gutter, or anything that would allow him to slink out the back door and drink a few beers alone.

But having a father as dedicated to the army as one could possibly be, the girls also knew that there was no chance of change, ever. Mona had faced this fact maybe five years ago, when she had to stop reading her favorite book series because of how envious she was of the main character. Instead of finding escape in the books like she always had before, Mona's heart began to hurt at the carefully crafted descriptions of a family that had lived in the same town for their entire lives, descriptions of family dinners and Saturday outings and showy holidays that the main character didn't seem to cherish at all, at least not in the way that Mona thought she should. One day after finishing the most recent book, Mona mumbled under her breath that the main character was a dry bitch.

She never read another book in the series again.

But now, five years later, Mona thought she'd done a good enough job of internalizing those feelings—what good were they, anyway? She stopped having fantasies about setting down roots somewhere with her parents and sisters, stopped imagining what it would be like to have sleepovers with a best friend that you'd known since kindergarten, stopped believing that there could ever be such a thing as "home" to her. Not a real home, anyway. There were only houses and houses and houses, across states, across the country, back and forth, never staying long enough to develop any real bonds with anyone else. New ideals were thought up and embraced.

Mona's situation was hardly extraordinary, there were plenty of military brats that grew up to be just fine, better than fine even, happy, *fulfilled*. "Home" could supposedly be attained through people instead of houses, *home is where the heart is* and all that, but Mona didn't feel like she had a home in any of her sisters.

She used to, in Anya.

But like so many other things, Mona had lost that, too.

Once all the Cane sisters had piled into the convertible, with Taylor in the front seat and Rose tucked securely in between Mona and Anya in the back, Juliet reached overhead to close the roof of the car. She secured the last latch just as raindrops started to dot the windshield, and with an irritated sigh, she cut away from the curb and made her way back to post, where their two-story house with a large wraparound porch and big windows sat in one of the designated housing neighborhoods.

Between the size of their family and the seniority of their father's rank, they were always placed in especially nice houses wherever they were stationed, although their current house had only three bedrooms and therefore required the girls to share. Mona was bunked up with Anya and Rose. Taylor and Juliet had the bedroom down the hall.

They entered through the kitchen to discover the

house just as quiet as when they left it; Mom must've still been in bed, where she spent the majority of her recent days. All of the lights were off, the blinds were closed, and, with another one of her signature irritated sighs, Juliet made the rounds to wake the house up.

Their mom was always home but never in sight; she lived like a snail, retracted beneath the covers of her bed, sleeping or peeking out at the television that was always playing the cooking channel. The shades on the windows were always drawn shut, and the paper pharmacy bags of prescription pills and empty wine bottles formed quite the spread over her nightstand.

Mom had once told Juliet that having children ruined her life. That was eleven years ago, when Rose had been only a newborn. Dad was overseas, as he'd been for all of their births. Juliet was eight. A little young to become Mom Number Two, but as Juliet loved to point out, life was not only a bitch, but a goddamn raving mad bitch who loved to point and laugh and kick and claw.

What a wonderful family the Canes have!

After the windows were open and the television was on and the younger girls had plopped evenly over the couches to get caught up with their shows, Juliet checked the sink for thawing meat and found none, although she did discover an empty bakery box that had contained an entire banana cream pie when they'd left for downtown earlier. When Mona checked over her shoulder from the couch to see what Juliet was cursing under her breath about, she saw the white and yellow box for just a second before her sister pushed it deeper into the trash can and closed the lid.

No, Mona thought, desperate to keep the mostly-jovial mood the girls had shared at the boutique and the ice cream shoppe. *No no no no.*

But it was too late. The discovery of a stagnant, sleeping house and the missing banana cream pie that was meant for Rose's birthday in two days was apparently enough to force Juliet back into what Mona thought of as her dark place. When Juliet was in her dark place, you had to be especially careful not to piss her off in any way, which wasn't as easy as it sounded. Anything from a too-loud speaking voice to leaving a piece of trash on the kitchen counter was enough to make Juliet yell or hit, or both.

Mona thought of the joke she'd made to herself at the sunglasses shop, about Juliet's uncontrollable temper, but it had lost any glimmer of humor by now. Mona remembered the awful time when she was eight and Anya was nine, and Juliet needed to use the bathroom, so she told them to watch Rose. The girls had been right in the middle of a video game, and weren't too excited at the prospect of stopping it to keep an eye on Rose, who was only four, so they sat her down on the couch behind them and went back to it without a second thought.

After the game came to an end, the girls realized that Rose, who had been quietly sitting and watching before, was nowhere to be found. Juliet came downstairs before they could find her, and made a heart-stopping discovery: the baby gate that usually blocked Rose's access to the doggie door in the kitchen had been down the whole time.

The girls had run outside in pure panic, only to find

Rose barefoot in the middle of the street, waving her little arms frantically at a truck that was speeding past. Juliet had screamed at the sight, sprinted down the driveway to scoop Rose up in her arms, before turning to Mona and Anya, fire in her eyes.

"How would you like it if Rose had been hit by a car?" she screamed, grabbing a handful of Anya's hair and pulling her down to the ground. Then she came for Mona, shoving her hard onto the pavement. "In fact," she whispered, leaning down so that only Mona could hear her, "how would you like it if I pushed *you* into the road the next time a car came by? How do you think it'd feel to get hit? Do you want to find out? Because I can make sure it happens, Mona, trust me."

The look in Juliet's wild eyes had turned Mona's blood to ice. That was the first time she had felt true, real fear at the hands of her oldest sister. But like so many other things in life, Mona had forced herself to stop thinking about it. She didn't want to face what it might mean for Juliet to be so willing to threaten her like that.

"Mona and Taylor, get off your asses and help me make dinner," Juliet screeched from where she stood in the kitchen, her voice deadly sharp. "Now."

Both girls scrambled over themselves to comply.

Because, despite the fact that they were all old enough to take care of themselves, and despite the fact that they argued so much over everything under the sun, if there was one thing all of the Cane sisters could agree on indefinitely, it was this:

When Juliet told you to do something, you listened.

CHAPTER 2

The day after the ice cream cones, Mona woke to the sound of the vacuum running at six in the morning. It roared from the living room on the floor below, back and forth, back and forth, bumping into things, the wall maybe, or perhaps the sides of the bookshelves. Mona sat up and clenched her teeth. She knew right away that their mother had finally come out of her bedroom, for better or for worse. It always happened like this.

"Goddamn it," Anya yelled from beneath the black comforter piled on her bed across the room, a single arm hanging over the edge of the mattress. From the next bed over, Rose moaned and pulled her pillow around to cover her face and ears.

"This has been building up for a long time," Mona said, slowly bringing her legs over the side of her own mattress. Her stomach was starting to twist around itself, dread laced with anxiety at what awaited them downstairs. "We knew she'd come back to us eventually."

When their mother was in one of her checked-out

phases, it was like she didn't exist at all, like the girls lived in the house by themselves. But when she came out of those spells, the transition was always something that was heard, seen and felt by everyone. Mom made sure of that.

"That doesn't mean I have to accept her little tantrums." Anya sat up, her hair in a remarkable state of bedhead. "You guys just love to go along with this shit, like it's normal and okay. I'm going to ignore it, because that's the opposite of what Mom wants, and screw her."

Below them, there came another hard *thump* as the vacuum ran into the wall again. Anya peered across the room at Mona, and her eyes narrowed just the slightest bit. "You're all just enabling her to keep acting like this when you trip over yourselves to ask her what's wrong. She needs to use her words, like a goddamn big girl."

Mona thought back to when she and Anya, her older sister by one year, were great friends. They even used to pretend they were twins. But then their differing opinions over Mom had driven them apart. Anya started ditching Mona more and more often, always leaving to hang out with the school friends she never had a hard time making, and it hurt like hell. Suddenly, they weren't the counter team to Taylor and Juliet anymore.

Now, the year of distance in age seemed enormous to Mona: Anya had her learner's permit, and a girlfriend, and a real, paying job at the day care across from the high school. It was like a whole other level of existing. Mona didn't have anybody special, a boyfriend or a girlfriend or even just a *best* friend, besides Lexa, anyway.

Thank goodness for Lexa. Mona had started talking to her a little while after a big fight with Anya, one where their relationship had gone from swinging on a hinge to full-blown fallout. It'd been the most alone Mona had ever felt, but then she'd met Lexa online. Talking to Lexa was like talking to the old Anya, before she'd started disagreeing so strongly with Mona about how to "handle" Mom. Finally, she had someone to talk to again.

Lexa's family couldn't have been more different than Mona's. Her parents were happy, crazily in love, and she and her siblings all got along just fine. Maybe it was because of this that Lexa was able to so confidently tell Mona that it wasn't normal to be afraid, truly *afraid*, of her oldest sister, or that it didn't really sound like Mom was okay, or that what had happened with Anya was awful. And while these were all hard things to hear, Mona couldn't help but feel a touch of relief that somebody, anybody, not only understood her but had concern for her, as well.

Still, at the end of the day, Lexa wasn't a real-life friend, and could only do so much from the internet. So when Anya acted like this about Mom, like she was some unfeeling monster hell-bent on ruining their lives, it pissed Mona off. *You don't have to care because you have other people in your life*, she wanted to scream. *This home is all Mom's got. This is all I've got.*

"Wow," Mona said to Anya instead of yelling at her. She couldn't stop the sarcasm from weighing her words down, couldn't help but stare coldly at her sister with unblinking eyes. "What a great way to look at it. It's not like Mom is clinically depressed or anything, she's just 'acting' this way, right?"

"Guys," Rose interjected, finally pulling her pillow down to uncover her face. "Stop."

It was this very thing that ended up driving Anya and Mona apart in the first place. Every few days came yet another reminder, it seemed. Mona wondered if it would ever stop.

Down the hallway, Mona heard the sound of Juliet and Taylor's bedroom door opening, followed by moody stomping footsteps that let her know things were about to get even louder at this ungodly hour.

"Turn it off," Mona heard Juliet's voice screech from downstairs. *"Turn it off!"*

Another crash as the vacuum ran into the wall, followed by the shatter of breaking glass. *A picture must have fallen*, Mona thought. Anya lay back down and pulled the covers over her head again.

Rose sat up and stepped into her slippers, biting her lip, her dark eyebrows furrowed. Mona watched her with a frown. She remembered how Rose had recently cut her hair short, how Mom had yelled at her until she'd cried, convinced her that she'd made some sort of awful, hideous mistake.

"Nobody at school wants to be my friend," Rose had admitted to the sisters afterward, as they were gathered in her room to provide comfort after Mom's stress-induced tirade. Rose pulled at the ends of her hair with such intensity that Juliet had to physically stop her. "Now I'll go from being the new freak to being the *ugly* new freak."

"It's okay, Rose," Mona said now as her sister shrugged into her baby-pink robe. "You don't need to go down there." The vacuum finally turned off downstairs and was followed by eerie silence.

"Yes I do," Rose responded simply. She looked up at Mona, her lips pursed together. "Juliet shouldn't have to face her alone."

Mona hated conflict and would do almost anything to avoid it, even if that meant being a total coward and letting Juliet be their mouthpiece, as she so often was on days like this. The problem was, Juliet's opinions on Mom fluctuated depending on her mood; she could go from Anya's cold apathy about the situation to Mona's more pitying approach in a heartbeat. You never knew how situations like this would turn out.

Rose stood and left the room, offering Mona a weak smile before she stepped out. Mona glared at the lump of blankets and limbs on Anya's bed, then threw a stuffed animal at it.

"Ugh," the lump grumbled without moving. "Don't be a bitch."

"No," Mona answered, forcing herself to stand. "You've got that part down pat."

There was some guilt when she said it, and the knowledge that things wouldn't get better with Anya unless she tried a little harder, but that was mostly washed away by the unease that settled in her mind when she realized how weirdly quiet it suddenly was. *Too* quiet after the angry vacuuming and Juliet stomping downstairs.

Mona left her bedroom and made her way down the

hallway, passing Juliet and Taylor's empty room. The hallway was dark and cramped; Mona deeply wished there was a skylight to make it less murky. She always went up and down the carpeted stairs with a bit of urgency, to spend as little time as possible on them, to escape the invisible arms she always imagined were reaching for her ankles.

The bottom of the stairs opened up into the living room, where Mona spotted a small vase in pieces on the floor. It must have fallen from the shelf it had been sitting on and hit the corner of the coffee table. A few feet away from the jagged pieces, Mona's mother was standing with her hands on her hips, clearly upset.

"Let's ask Mona what she thinks," Mom said when she noticed her. "Mona, why do *you* think I missed a call from your dad this morning?"

The word *dad* set off a whole new series of anxious feelings. Mom's inability to consistently parent the girls and live without struggling seemed to revolve around Dad's absence. Whenever he came home, Mom was a completely different person, or at least she seemed to be. She got up every morning, she showered, she made coffee and breakfast and suggested fun day-outings where they could be together as a family.

Those times always felt like a surreal sort of heaven-on-earth to Mona, even though she never got to spend real quality time getting to know Dad. Everything was always a rush, an enthusiastic attempt to do as many things as possible before he inevitably had to return to being a colonel. Mom never seemed to be able to get enough of him while he was home, always pulling him into their bedroom for an hour at a time, always taking his attention during conversations by talking over the sisters. He only ever called late at night or early in the mornings, depending on where in the world he was. Missing a phone call from him was not a small deal.

"I don't know," Mona said, her eyes darting around the room to see where Rose was, eventually spotting her sitting on a bar stool at the island in the kitchen. Standing beside her was Juliet. "Why did you miss a call from Dad?"

"Because Juliet didn't remember to take my phone off silent after you all came home from your little outing yesterday." Mom took her hands off her hips to pace around the room, picking up random pieces of discarded clothing and some magazines left behind from last night.

Juliet let out a frustrated sigh and crossed her arms. Mona could tell she was having a hard time staying quiet. During her "napping days," Mom constantly set her phone to silent, and any unwanted stimulus was grounds for a meltdown.

Mom looked with dismay at the coffee table, which had a mixing bowl lined with unpopped corn kernels and salt sitting on top of it. "Do you girls even know what it *means* to clean up after yourselves?" she asked. "Goddamn it!"

"We *have* been cleaning," Mona said defensively, remembering all the times Juliet had assigned them chores, the dishes and the trash and the vacuuming. "Every day." *And you haven't been doing anything.*

She hated the toxic feeling she got whenever her mother acted like this. She would not give in to it like Anya did, would not let the feeling turn into hate or resentment, that wasn't how family was supposed to work. She had to support Mom if there was any hope of the depression receding, even just a little bit. She had to be strong. She had to be loyal.

Where Anya saw a one-dimensional villain, Mona saw someone who *wanted* to do better, but just…couldn't. Mom's mopey demeanor, combined with her short temper, hardly ever made for a pleasant exchange, but Mona refused to forget the times when her mother had worked so hard to hold on to a consistent routine, before it inevitably fell between her fingers like sand and everything collapsed again. Mona didn't want Juliet to be the family's backbone, she wanted Mom to be, and she needed to do whatever she could to help her mother get there.

"I'll do it," Mona said, stepping forward to take the clothes and magazines from her mother's arms. "I'll clean this stuff up. Just try to rest. I'm sorry about the missed call."

"I'll do it myself," Mom nearly yelled, jerking her arms away roughly and dropping a magazine, and that was when Mona realized that she was drunk. She felt stupid for not noticing before.

"Calm down, for Chrissakes," Juliet sniped from where she stood near Rose. "I said I was sorry for forgetting. Don't you think it's kind of ridiculous for you to get mad at us over one little mess when you can't even change the volume on your phone yourself?"

Mom glared at Juliet, and Mona took the opportunity to step away, back toward the stairs. She spotted Taylor hiding around the corner, sitting on the last few steps, listening. "What are you doing?" Mona whispered.

"Just let Juliet take care of it," Taylor replied, twirling her long hair around the end of her finger and biting at her lower lip. "The fewer of us that get involved, the better." Typical Taylor to hide behind Juliet. And Mona hadn't even wanted to get into the argument in the first place.

"How dare you!" Mom screamed at Juliet, but her face reddened in embarrassment. "You understand more than anybody what I go through, with my chronic pain. It confines me, Juliet. Do you think I *want* to be in my bed for days at a time?"

Again with the chronic pain, Mona thought. Mom brought it up whenever she wanted to defend her behavior, which Mona hated. There was no reason Mom should have felt like she had to defend whatever it was that she was going through. The pain was unreliable, and manifested itself in a different way each time, often conveniently close to whenever something especially stressful or tiring was happening. Mona just wished her mom would admit that she needed more help than she was letting herself accept. She deserved more than pain and bad feelings.

And so did Mona's sisters.

"*Weeks* at a time," Juliet corrected. "And you keep saying it was your stomach that was hurting, but you were somehow able to eat an entire pie while we all went into town yesterday? That was supposed to be for Rose's birthday."

Please don't push her, Mona thought. She glanced back to Taylor, who was sitting on the stairs and looking as though she was trying to shrink into herself. As much as Mona hated confrontation, she knew it affected Taylor even worse.

"I…needed the sugar," Mom spurted, not quite slurring her speech but nearly there. "I was having a crash. None of you realize how very much I've done for you, the things that I've sacrificed—"

"Yes, sacrifice," Juliet said, her eyes narrowing even more. "I would know nothing about that."

The room went deathly quiet for a brief moment. Once, Juliet had been a magnificent pianist. She still was, Mona figured, but you'd never know it because she'd quit playing. She had been offered a full ride to Juilliard, but when she realized how ill-equipped Mom was to handle her absence, she'd turned the scholarship down.

After all those years, talking about escape and independence and concertos. Just like that, Juliet's dazzling future burned to ashes. When she gave it up, something inside of her changed, *died.*

"Of course we realize, Mom," Rose cut in, her tone with far less edge than Juliet's. "And we appreciate it."

"I really don't think so," Mom snapped back, again turning her attention to cleaning up the living room. She couldn't just pick something up or set it down; she had to snatch it up with a huff, or slam it down hard against something. Her anger radiated throughout her every movement, and her breathing, and her profanity-laced mumbling.

Mona was considering her options when Juliet made a dramatic movement to the trash can and yanked the bag out, causing a few pieces to spill and slide across the floor.

"Don't you start too," Mona mumbled as she made her way past Juliet to help pick up the spare bits of trash. She thought of Mom, and of Anya upstairs. "We don't need a house full of angry women."

"Oh, get over yourself," Juliet replied with enough bite to make Mona flinch. "You should have stayed upstairs if you weren't gonna do anything but set her off even more."

"You're the one who insulted her about the phone," Mona grumbled under her breath. "And you're the one who brought up the pie, we could have just gotten another one—"

"Please," Rose cried out suddenly, putting her hands over her ears. "Everybody, please just stop it!"

Why did they always have to fight? Why couldn't all days be like yesterday, when they actually got along for a few solid hours. *Even dinner went better than usual*, she thought. She had hoped it would last a few more days, or at least through today. As much as she didn't want to admit it, she knew the root of why things went wrong so quickly.

"I'll stop it," Mom said, "when Juliet stops being a bitch." Mona could see the regret in Mom's eyes as soon as the word fell out of her mouth, but it was too late. It was always too late.

Juliet stopped dead in her tracks from taking out the trash and turned toward Mom. She raised the bag of trash up in front of her before purposefully letting it go, sending it to break open over the tile of the kitchen floor.

Mona felt ill and afraid at the same time. These arguments had gotten pretty out of hand before, but now they were starting to get worse with every fight. *Mom just called Juliet a bitch.* Juliet, the one who had taken care of them all for years when Mom couldn't.

Rose kept her hands over her ears. Juliet stormed away from the mess, and Mona and Rose followed her, despite their mother's demand that somebody stay behind to help her clean it up. *Must get away,* Mona thought urgently, desperately. *I can't handle seeing her like this.* Maybe Anya was right for hiding in bed after all. Maybe if they left Mom alone, she'd have some time to calm down and realize that she needed to apologize to Juliet.

When Juliet saw Taylor cowering against the wall of the stairs, she exhaled sharply and snapped, "Didn't I tell you to stay in our room?" Instead of defending herself, or saying something that Mona wished she would say like *I'm a part of this family, too,* Taylor bubbled over with apologies as she scrambled to keep up with Juliet, immediately trying to comfort her with insults about Mom and what just happened.

The two older girls reentered their bedroom at the top of the stairs, and Juliet slammed their door shut. Mona reached out for Rose, a lump in her throat, but her little sister scurried ahead. They entered their bedroom, and Anya was still in the same spot beneath the covers of her bed. Rose sniffed and rushed into the shared bathroom that connected their room to Juliet and Taylor's, then shut and locked the door. Mona could hear her crying from the other side.

"I told you," Anya said glumly from where she lay hidden.

"Just shut up," Mona snapped, almost beginning to cry herself. She got back into her bed, curled up into a ball, squeezed the sheets between her fists until the cartilage in her fingers popped. The vacuum started up again downstairs.

Mona's anguish made her bones hot, but she somehow forced herself to go back to sleep, after all, it wasn't even seven yet, and today was Sunday. She woke up a little later to the sound of Rose moving around the room carefully, obviously trying to be quiet. The smell of something deeply sweet was heavy in the air. Mona heard Anya snoring across the room. She listened to Rose but kept her eyes shut.

After a few more minutes, somebody gently pulled the covers back, exposing Mona to the sweet-smelling sunshine of her bedroom. A cool finger ran down the bridge of Mona's nose, then again, then again.

"Wake up," Rose said without whispering, and her breath smelled like frosting. From the other side of the room, Anya's snoring stopped. "Welcome to New Sunday."

Mona opened her eyes, and saw that Rose had constructed an impressive fortress of some kind using tapestries and clothespins and string lights. She'd cleaned the entire room around it, even the sections around Anya's and Mona's beds, and it looked lovely. Laundry that was once piled on top of the desk now hung in the open closet the three girls shared.

"How'd you do all this?" Mona asked, her voice still a little groggy from sleep. "And so fast?"

"You guys have been asleep for hours," Rose said, straightening up and admiring her work with pride. She had changed from her robe and pajamas to basketball shorts and a T-shirt. "This tent is the coolest thing, Mo, just you wait and see."

"What did you mean by New Sunday?" Mona sat up and rubbed her eyes. She was also curious to know what was causing that delicious smell, which added an especially magical touch to the vision of the room.

"You'll see," Rose said. "Just get up and get dressed. Wear something comfortable, though. We're staying in today. Meet me in the tent in ten minutes."

And with that, she turned on her heel and walked across the room through the open bathroom door, going straight into Juliet and Taylor's room, likely to wake them up and tell them the same thing she'd told Mona.

"Did you hear that, Anya?" Mona asked, standing and heading to the tall dresser beside the closet for some sweats and a tank top.

"Mmm-hmm," Anya grumbled from her bed. "Stay out of the bathroom. I have to piss and smoke a bowl."

Mona found it outrageous how little Anya tried to hide her weed-smoking habit, and even more outrageous that Mom had never brought it up once, even when the halls were heavy with the skunky scent. Though, Mona did have to admit that Anya was much more pleasant to deal with when she was high.

Fifteen minutes later, the sisters had finally finished sorting out who had to pee and who wanted to brush their teeth or hair over their double-sink counter. They all gathered in the tent Rose had constructed, sitting in a circle, a plate piled high with canned cinnamon rolls in the center of them. There was a bottle of orange juice and five short glasses.

"Welcome to New Sunday," Rose announced as she looked around the circle of faces, none of them quite as cheery and bright as hers. "As most of you know, this morning got off to a little bit of a rough start. But honestly, screw that!"

Mona thought of everything that had happened earlier with a frown.

"Tomorrow is my twelfth birthday," Rose continued. "It also happens to be the first official day of spring break." She paused for dramatic effect. "Coincidence, or magic?"

Juliet smiled. It acted as somewhat of an icebreaker, a blessing for the other girls to smile, too.

"The real question," Juliet said, reaching forward to grab a cinnamon roll and take a huge bite. "Who's gonna make Rose's new birthday pie?"

"Mom needs to make it," Anya said, keeping her glazed eyes down as she also reached for the plate before them all. "In fact, I vote she should make two. One banana cream and one Oreo."

"I don't need a pie," Rose insisted, but Mona knew how much she preferred it over cake, especially on her birthday. "All I need is all of you."

"You are so cheesy!" Juliet said, passing a cinnamon roll to Taylor. "But I like it."

Anya rolled her eyes at Mona, who poured juice for everybody and pretended not to notice. *Why can't you just go along with anything?* Mona wanted to ask Anya, but not as bad as she wanted to keep the peace, so she bit her tongue.

"It's settled then," Rose announced, gulping her orange juice gratefully. "Tomorrow is going to be the best birthday of my entire life. Agreed?"

"Agreed," Mona said, and the other girls nodded, as well. "It'll be the best day ever."

CHAPTER 3

Mona had a strong and often stressful desire to be Rose's favorite sister. Rose was nice to all of them so it was hard to tell if she even *had* a favorite, but if she did, Mona liked to believe it'd be her. They were the closest in age, after all, and Mona was never short with Rose, like she so often was with Anya. And she never argued with Rose, like she so often did with Juliet. And she never thought that Rose was pathetic, like she so often did with Taylor.

For those reasons, Mona felt like she had a good chance at being the favorite, especially if she could manage to secure the new birthday pie before there was time for another fight to break out about it.

After the girls had spent a good hour in Rose's makeshift bedroom tent the day before, giggling and exchanging memories about houses they used to live in, Mom had knocked on the door, asking in a level voice if any of the girls knew where the laundry detergent was. The girls had looked at each other in shared discomfort; they all knew they'd run out a few days ago, and surely this would give Mom yet another reason to yell at them about something now that she was out of her cave. After a few moments of hesitation, Juliet announced loudly that they didn't have any. The girls braced for impact.

Somehow, though, Mom didn't get mad at all, a stark contrast to the way she'd been acting that morning. She even announced that she'd drive herself to pick up more, like it was no problem. She also mentioned that she'd get a new pie for Rose while she was out.

Rose had grinned at them then, beneath the twinkling string lights of the fort. "See?" she said to her sisters, collecting the empty juice glasses and stacking them in the center of the sticky plate. "Things are turning around already."

But when Mom had returned home three hours later, she was fuming over some mail truck that had cut her off, and the only thing in her shopping bags were bottles of wine, a few refilled prescriptions, a bag of foiled white chocolates, and a magazine full of slow cooker recipes that Mona knew her mother would never even try. No laundry detergent.

No birthday pie.

Rose had acted like she didn't care, but her disappointment showed itself in her every movement, and set the tone for the rest of the day. So Mona had made sure to get up and going much earlier than her sisters today, so that she could take her bike to the post's commissary to remedy the situation before it got worse.

Her little sister shouldn't have to worry about stuff like this with all the stress she went through at school. Mona couldn't understand why Rose didn't have a gaggle of friends, but in a sick way, it made her feel a little more secure, a little less vulnerable to losing another sisterly connection like she had with Anya. She and Rose had never even been that close.

It seemed that no matter where they moved, Rose was picked on by her peers. Mona wondered if it was because of how sweet she was about everything, maybe she was too cartoonlike for most people. If that was the reason, then they didn't deserve her, anyway.

Once Mona tied the laces of her sneakers and slipped into a thin blue hoodie to protect against the slight chill in the air, she headed downstairs for the garage, making sure to hurry down the steps of the darkened hallway like she always did.

"Be back in a bit," she told Taylor, who was eating a bowl of cereal and watching television alone. None of the other sisters had come downstairs yet, and neither had Mom. Mona figured there was plenty of time to get the pie and laundry detergent and be back before Rose's birthday had a chance to get started.

"Whatever," Taylor answered without looking away from the screen, not bothering to ask Mona where she was going. Her eyes widened as an especially loud argument broke out on the reality show she was watching. "Bye."

"Bye," Mona replied, then opened the door beside the refrigerator, the one that led down to the basement.

The wooden steps creaked as Mona carefully made her way down. The rough grain of the railing threatened to leave splinters in her skin if she pressed down too hard. Mona always resented the fact that the light switch was at the *bottom* of the crudely made staircase—who decided that was a good idea while this house was being built? Her breath was held uncomfortably in her chest until she felt her sneakers hit pavement, then her hand instinctively reached out for the switch, filling the room with light.

Mom's car took up a good portion of the basement, which was also the garage. Even though it didn't fit Juliet's car, there was still enough room left over for storage boxes and a large meat freezer that Mom tried to keep loaded for months at a time, as well as the washer and dryer and open space underneath the stairs. Mona pulled her bicycle away from the wall next to the car and opened the garage door with a grunt, tugging upward on the thin rope that was tied to the bottom.

The weather was cool but there wasn't any wind, which Mona was thankful for as she pulled her hood over the short brown-red pigtails that sat low on her neck. She slipped her earbuds in and pedaled hard toward the corner of the block, toward the post's commissary. She thought back to yesterday when Mom had returned with her bags of booze, booze that she most definitely drove off post to get at a real grocery store so that she wouldn't be seen by any of the other military wives. The commissary was where Rose's favorite pie was, anyway. Mona wondered if her mom ever had any intention of getting it in the first place.

Don't think bad about Mom like that, she scolded herself. *Focus on what can be done today.*

It only took her ten minutes of biking before she pulled off the sidewalk and into the parking lot of the commissary. After showing her military ID to the people at the door, she hoofed it straight to the baked goods, hoping with everything inside of her that there would be more banana cream pies today. Relief filled Mona when she saw that there was just one left, in the chilled panel beside the cookies. She grabbed it and headed straight for the checkout, nearly forgetting the laundry detergent and having to backtrack after a few seconds.

When she was finally at the counter to pay, she heard a little squeal of delight coming from behind her. Mona looked over her shoulder and forced a smile at the woman next in line, whose name was Sarah something-or-other.

"Hi there, Anya!" Sarah grinned wide and rubbed Mona on the arm. "Long time no see, honey."

"I'm Mona," Mona said, turning back toward the cashier. "Anya is the one who's a year older than me."

"Of course," Sarah gushed, blushing. "You both look so alike, forgive me. Hey listen, how's the old colonel's wife doing, anyway?" Mona could tell instantly that Sarah was digging for gossip material for the mutual "friends" she shared with Mom. "It's just that it's been an awful long time since we've seen her at our weekly coffee dates. We sure do miss her!"

You don't even know her.

"She's fine," Mona answered, loyal despite her distaste over the current Mom situation. Loyalty is everything when it comes to family, Mona believed. It didn't matter what they do or put you through: at the end of the day, they were the only family you had. "She's just been insanely busy taking care of us all."

"That's right—five daughters, what a blessing!" Sarah said as the cashier was handing Mona the receipt. "You all are the definition of wonderful."

We sure are, Mona thought bitterly as she let out a phony smile and "thank you!" and headed back out carrying her bags. *Truly fucking wonderful.*

To think of how the people at the post perceived them versus the actual truth was bewildering to Mona. What would they think if they knew how dysfunctional everything was? Mona realized that it didn't even matter, not really—her family would no doubt be moving again before too long anyway, since they'd been here for nearly a year. The thought made a lump form in her throat.

Maybe, just maybe, they would get to stay for a long time, long enough for her to turn eighteen and graduate high school and live wherever she damn well pleased. Preferably the same town where Lexa lived.

Mona paused to pull her phone out. Top 'o the mornin, she texted Lexa. Won't be around so much during the day because Rose is turning twelve! But I can chat later tonight if you're free.

Less than a minute passed before Lexa replied. Awww, happy bday Rose! And yes, chat we will. Have fun today, lovely.

The girls exchanged a few emojis and Mona replaced her phone in her pocket, smiling. It was a small exchange, but knowing she had someone who was always excited to hear from her always cheered Mona up. She was so fucking grateful for Lexa.

It took twice as long to get back home as it did to get to the commissary, because balancing a boxed pie on her lap with a bag of laundry detergent looped around one handlebar wasn't exactly easy. She was buzzing with nerves over the idea of crashing her bike and dropping everything all over the sidewalk. Eventually, she turned back onto her street, then into the garage. She carefully climbed off her bike, leaned it against the wall beside the car, and pulled the garage door down.

Mona set the laundry detergent on top of the washer that sat against the back wall. She flipped the light switch off and headed up the stairs in the pitch dark, hardly trusting herself not to trip and fall and make all of this effort for nothing.

She entered through the kitchen and kicked the basement door closed behind her, only to see that Juliet had somehow acquired a bright bouquet of foil balloons, stars and hearts and a big colorful birthday cake. She must have gone out in her car late last night to get them. The numbers *1* and *2* floated side by side amongst the other balloons, shining in chrome. Mona realized once again, like she did upon first waking up this morning, that this was Rose's last year before she became a teenager. *Welcome to hell, baby sister.*

Behind the balloons, all four of Mona's sisters sat in the living room, their faces anything but celebratory. "I got the pie," Mona said, setting the box down on the counter triumphantly. "Who's ready to party?"

"Me," Rose said, but Mona could tell her enthusiasm was a little forced.

"What's wrong?" she asked, confused.

"We were talking about what to do today," Anya answered, looking especially unhappy. "We thought it'd be cool to catch a movie at the drive-in."

"That sounds great to me," Mona said. She crossed her arms as she studied their faces. "So what's the issue?"

From somewhere upstairs, a door slammed.

"Mom got mad that we didn't invite her." Taylor bit her lip and looked to the ceiling. "It turned into a whole thing. We're waiting for her to get ready now."

Mona closed her eyes and took a deep breath. *Of course it turned into a whole thing.* How could it not? Mona wanted her mother to feel supported and loved, but sometimes she wondered at what point the support became submission. She wondered if there was any point in knowing the answer either way.

Rose hopped up and made her way to the pie, taking a spoon from the drawer beneath it and digging in without hesitation. "Best birthday breakfast ever," she said in between mouthfuls of whipped cream and pudding. "Have some, guys."

Juliet watched Rose with a bit of sadness on her face. "Don't you want us to put candles on it and sing to you?" she asked. "We always sing to you."

Rose grabbed more spoons and started tossing them at each sister. "Forget the singing," she said, sinking her utensil into the center of the pie to scoop up another bite. "This year I'm starting a new tradition—we eat pie for breakfast while we're waiting on our grouchy-ass mom to get ready to go to the movies."

They finished the pie within ten minutes, then sat piled over each other on the couches while they waited for their mother to emerge. Anya pulled out her phone and started texting somebody on it, probably her girl-friend, Everly. For some reason, it irritated Mona beyond reason that Anya wasn't paying attention to the shitty sit-com the rest of the sisters were watching. It didn't make a difference really, but Mona just wanted Anya to be present. It was like she couldn't go ten minutes without her Everly fix. Was life here that bad? Mona already knew the answer, even if she didn't let herself admit it.

"What's Everly up to?" Mona asked after Anya failed to put the phone away for twenty straight minutes, almost constantly typing up a message or giggling behind her hand at a response. Anya's face darkened at the question.

"Nothing," she said. "Why do you only care when you want me off my phone?"

The response embarrassed Mona because it was true. She'd never really had any true interest in getting to know her sister's girlfriend, and had only ever viewed Everly as someone to distract Anya from the short time they would be in this town. Anya didn't date in every town they lived in, but this relationship hit hard and quick. Mona had even overheard Anya during late-night Skype sessions, whispering about somehow finding a way to stay behind if their family got relocated before she had a chance to graduate.

Fat chance.

Didn't Anya understand that there were things like laws? The longest they'd stayed anywhere was two years. She had better get used to the idea of life without Everly, and fast. Then Mona remembered how just this morning she'd been fantasizing about somehow staying in town herself, and in actuality she was just holding on to her grudge against Anya.

Mona let out a little huff and felt her cheeks go hot. "Forget about it, geez."

"That's what I thought," Anya said under her breath, and shifted her attention back to her phone.

Rose sighed from beside Mona, and it made Mona feel bad. *Don't mess up her birthday even more than Mom already has.*

"So excited to go to the drive-in!" she said, and everyone but Anya and Juliet nodded in agreement. "We haven't been to one in ages. That one in Illinois was so fun."

"The barbecue they served was amazing!" Rose exclaimed, and Mona was happy to see her smile a real smile. "All drive-ins should offer barbecue, I mean really."

Taylor checked the clock on her phone for the tenth time, and the corners of her mouth turned down. "If we don't hurry, we'll have to do the evening showing, and I know Rose wanted to go star-gazing tonight."

"Mom needs to hurry her ass up." Juliet stood up and walked over to the bottom of the stairs. "Mom!" she called. "It's time to go!"

The sisters assembled in the kitchen, huddled around the island counter that housed the stove. After a minute of silence, there came the sound of footsteps descending the stairs leading to the living room; a moment later, Mom stepped into the kitchen. She wasn't dressed, her hair wasn't brushed, and Mona could see that she wasn't wearing a bra.

"I was about to get ready when I realized that I forgot the pie yesterday." The sadness dripped from her voice, spilling, diluting Mona's irritation into something that made her stomach heavy. "Rose baby, I am *so* sorry." Her voice started to crack a little, like she might cry. "I don't know what's been happening in my head lately—"

"It's okay, Mom," Mona said gently. "It's been taken care of."

"It's not okay," Mom insisted, offering a tired, empty smile as she reached out to rub Rose's back. When nobody said anything else, Mom took a deep, shaky breath. "I think I'm too tired to go with you today after all," she said. "Take my car, though. It needs gas and I was hoping you could stop and get some on the way."

She held a ten-dollar bill out toward Juliet without meeting her eyes. Mona, Anya, Rose and Taylor all nodded and started making their way to the door that led to the basement, each giving a small wave or goodbye to Mom as they went. Juliet stayed right where she was standing. Mona opened the door, and Rose's birthday balloons swayed in the breeze that blew in from the darkness below.

"Are you serious?" Juliet asked, without taking the ten-dollar bill. "After the fit you threw this morning over not being invited, now you're refusing to go?"

Please no, Mona thought, and could tell from her expression that Rose was thinking the same thing. *Please let's just go.* Anya looked up from her phone. Taylor nervously twirled a lock of hair around her finger.

"It wasn't a fit," Mom said defensively. "I didn't mean to yell like that before, it's just—"

"It's Rose's *birthday*." Juliet's eyes were slightly widened, and it unsettled Mona. "You can't even get yourself together enough to come out this once?"

Mona was overcome with the urge to flee down the basement stairs behind her, already waiting, no longer scary but welcoming, *calling*. She could see that her mother was trying. She could see that her oldest sister had run out of patience. Mom just needed to rest, but now Juliet wanted to push her. She thought back to yesterday, when Mom called Juliet a bitch, the first sign that the snowball had finally reached hell, and now came the part where they all started melting away.

We need to leave, she thought in a rising, unfamiliar panic. *We need to get the hell out of here right now. Something bad is going to happen, it can't, it's Rose's birthday...*

"Put gas in the car when you leave," Mom snarled suddenly, stepping forward to press the ten-dollar bill into Juliet's hand. "Get the fuck out of here before I decide you're not allowed to go at all."

"Get your own gas," Juliet replied coolly, and threw the bill directly in Mom's face. "I'm taking the car Dad bought for me."

Mom reached out and slapped her on the cheek, hard. All the other girls froze, and Rose let out a little yelp. *No*, Mona thought, her feet heavy on the kitchen floor. *No no no no...*

"I hate you," Juliet yelled, and shoved Mom, hard. She staggered backward, nearly falling over her own feet but just managing to stay upright.

Mona watched in what felt like slow motion as her

44

mother launched across the kitchen, stumbling, toward the sisters and the open basement door. Everyone instinctively stepped out of the way—everyone except for Rose. *THE BASEMENT DOOR IS OPEN*, Mona's mind screamed. Mom collided with Rose, who caught Mona's eye for an awful split second, scared and confused, as her hair floated up and she fell, full-force, down the basement stairs.

The Cane sisters at the top of the stairs all lifted their hands quickly, abruptly, as though they were all con-nected to the same puppet string. Small groans of dread escaped their lips.

Rose flew backward into the dark before anybody could reach out and grab her. Everybody was yelling her name, as if that would stop it somehow, but all they could hear in return was the impact of her body tumbling down the wooden steps to the concrete floor of the basement.

Everybody stopped screaming Rose's name and shut up in order to hear if she was making any noise, but there was only silence in the dark basement. Mom was panting on the floor of the kitchen, crawling for the stairs, her face twisting around and shimmering with sweat. Juliet stumbled over her, her hands trembling, and ran down the wooden steps to turn on the light below.

When she did, and they were all faced with the severity of what had happened, everybody started screaming or crying at once. It was total chaos. At the bottom of the steps, twisted at a funny angle with blood streaming out of her ears, was Rose, her neck bent, her lips parted, her eyes staring ahead into eternal nothingness.

Mona knew instantly that her little sister was dead.

CHAPTER 4

Mona Cane stood still while the rest of her family beelined for the basement steps, going down them in a single, monstrous mass. Mona wondered vaguely if the old wooden stairs were structurally sound enough to hold them all without collapsing. She wondered if she was about to hear a sound even louder than their wails: the sound of splintering wood, followed by an awful rush of crunches and pops and cries before the dust settled into ultimate silence.

Rose is dead.

She's dead on her birthday.

There's blood coming out of her ears.

"Fuck you!" Juliet was shrieking now, at their mother. "She's fucking dead, you killed her, what were you fucking thinking you stupid fucking—"

"Shut up," Anya bellowed. "Mona, call an ambulance or something! Why are you just standing there?"

Because I can't move, Mona thought, her lips parted, her mouth dry. "An ambulance won't help her."

Mom started mumbling something, ignoring Juliet completely as she lowered her face over Rose's. Mona saw Taylor shoot Anya a look, clearly shaken by whatever their mother had said.

"No shit it's her birthday," Juliet said in response, her voice wavering as it devolved into weeping.

Mona needed to find her feet, she realized. She needed to go down and be with her family and hold Rose's hand. The urge to do it was sudden and strong, but also scary, because Mona couldn't understand why she'd want to hold a dead person's hand. Maybe she should have been scrambling for an ambulance all this time like Anya said. Maybe there was still a chance baby Rose could pull through it.

No. Mona knew despite the temporary flicker of hope. She thought of Rose's eyes, how completely lifeless they were. *There's no chance that she's alive.*

"This isn't happening," Mona said, going quickly down the stairs, startling Taylor and Anya with the desperate intensity of her steps. Everybody was crying except for Mona. She knelt down on the ground and took her sister's hand, still warm despite the glassy gaze in Rose's eyes. "Please wake up."

"She can," Mom said after an awful pause, and just like that she stopped crying. Her eyes were wide, as though she'd just remembered something very important, something amazing, and the relief on her face terrified Mona. "She can get up again!"

She's completely lost it, Mona thought in horror. *Being*

responsible for Rose's death has broken her and now she's gone completely goddamn batshit.

For a second, her mind tripped over itself—had it truly been Mom's fault? No, it was an accident, that's all. A freak accident that they were all a part of in some way. Using Mona's logic, Juliet would have been responsible for throwing the ten-dollar bill in Mom's face and pushing her temper over the edge. Anya and Taylor would have been responsible for standing by without intervening before things went too far.

Oh, my god.

The center of Mona's chest suddenly felt like it had been crushed in.

I was the one who opened the basement door.

"What are you talking about?" Juliet snapped at Mom, her face red and wet. "She's fucking *dead*, Mom!"

"But she doesn't have to be." Mom dropped Rose's other hand, the one Mona wasn't crying all over, and stood. "I know a way to bring her back!"

"Mom, I think you should come upstairs," Anya said, speaking as though she was talking down some sort of wild zoo animal that had just escaped. "Come sit down, I'll get you a glass of water, we'll call the emergency line on the base."

"You don't understand." Mom started going up the stairs, quickly, not bothering to wipe the snot from beneath her nose. "Don't call anybody. I mean it. Listen to me, girls, listen…"

Suddenly, Mona couldn't stand to be there anymore, holding Rose's dead hand in the dark while her mother lost her mind and her sisters called someone to come and take her baby sister away forever. Would her mother go to jail? Would Juliet? Mona had heard of freak accidents before, people being killed by faulty roller coasters and plane crashes and stingrays that jumped randomly out of the water only to strike some poor boater on the head. But this felt different, somehow. Rose's death was so… avoidable.

There *had* to be some sort of punishment for it.

Mona stood silently and went up after her mother, giving Rose one last suffering glance. She felt like there were knives stabbing her from the inside, a rabid humming-bird ready to gouge its way through the fleshy prison of her heart, racing, breathless.

Let her sisters take care of everything that had to happen next, let Juliet. Mona couldn't stand to live like this for another second. When she reached the kitchen, she could see that her mother was sitting on the couch in the living room, dialing someone on her cell phone. Her face was still shiny with tears, but it was also calm, eager. She didn't have a wild glare in her eyes, no noticeable instability. She simply rubbed the hem of her shirt between her fingers while she waited for whoever she was calling to answer the phone.

Mona kept walking, through the living room, up the dark twisted staircase despite the fact that Anya was crying her name out desperately from the basement. This time, Mona didn't hurry up the stairs to avoid the invisible hands. She went slowly, willing for them to grab her ankles and pull her under and never let her go, make her live a tortured life under the stairs for all eternity. But soon enough she was at the top stair, and no such favor had been given.

When she reached the hallway she cut through Juliet and Taylor's room to get to the connecting bathroom that the girls all shared. She closed the door behind her and locked it, then went to the other door, the one that led to her own bedroom, and locked it, as well.

Mona pawed through a big wicker basket beneath the sink until she found a screwdriver. The handle was cool and calming under her palm, and already she was happy with her decision to leave the nightmare down-stairs behind. But still, her breath was quick, ragged, un-controlled. Mona knew she needed to relax or she was going to hyperventilate and pass out.

She hurried over to the toilet and stood on it, not caring that she was still wearing her sneakers that were muddy from being outside. The commissary felt like months ago, years, grabbing that cheerily boxed pie and wanting to punch Sarah something-or-other for asking about her mom. None of it was relevant now. None of it mattered. *Will anything matter again?* Mona wondered as she stabbed the tip of the screwdriver between the vent above the toilet and the metal grate that covered it.

She pried the grate up and reached inside without hesitation, too practiced in this act to fear spiderwebs or rats. They were never there, even though the vent didn't work and should have been a prime hiding place for creepy crawlies. What her hand *did* find, however, was the cool glass of the half-empty bottle of vodka that she'd shoved in there late last night.

Hypocrite.

"Oh well," Mona whispered aloud, hardly realizing she was doing it. She already felt like she'd had a few swigs—maybe that was what happened when you watched your baby sister die, saw her final gaze of pure panic and horror before she tumbled backward into the darkness of the basement. You got death-drunk. Either way, now was the time to get drunk-drunk.

She took five long, careless chugs, crisply screwed the lid back on, then replaced the grate and the screwdriver. The entire act, from start to finish, was complete in well less than a minute. Mona brushed her teeth and tongue with enough vigor to draw lots of red when she spit into the sink. Afterward she retreated to her bedroom, only feeling a tiny touch of warmth in her stomach, eager for the rest of the vodka to kick in so her head could go for a little swim.

I'm going out to sea, Mona said in her head, talking to Rose. *I'm going to turn into a mermaid and never return.*

Mona peeled her T-shirt off and replaced it with a tank top, then kicked off her muddy sneakers and pants and crawled into her bed. *No wait, this is Anya's bed, duh.* She let out a sharp tick of breath in irritation, as if moving to the bed three feet away was the hardest task in the world. Once she was in though, she pulled the sheets over her head and lay facedown on her pillow, final, safe.

She wasn't sure how long it was before she felt the alcohol warm her. She changed positions, relishing the fuzziness of how it felt, the unsteady air. *And nobody even knows*, she thought as she heard the muffled sounds of her sisters talking to Mom downstairs.

"I can't believe you guys are even talking about this when she's still down there!" came Anya's voice, and Mona turned over again and put the pillow over her head completely, blocking out the noise.

I'm in the dark now, Rose, Mona thought from the shadows. *I'm in here and I'm waiting for you, come join me, won't you?*

That was when Mona started crying again, and once the tears started they wouldn't stop. She clenched her teeth together hard to keep from making too much noise, her arms slithered like drunken snakes around her torso, and she held herself as she rocked back and forth through her tears. Without the support of her hands the pillow got pushed up, letting in cruel, betraying light from somewhere behind the sheet. Mona burrowed her head back beneath the pillow and used it to stifle her pained wail.

She tried to remember the moment that she realized she was exactly like her mother, with her desperation for things she couldn't have and her pitifully short sense of patience with life, but failed, as she always did when she was drunk enough to revisit this topic in the more spiderwebbed corners of her mind.

The idea of growing up as colossally unhappy and damaged and drunk as her mother haunted Mona like a ghost, a persistent, gnawing ghoul that hung from her shoulders like a backpack full of rocks. Deep down, Mona knew that the ghost was the reason she was so willfully forceful about the idea of Mom getting "better" on her own, naturally. Whenever Anya spoke of their mother like there wasn't any hope unless something drastic was done, Mona knew it meant that there wasn't any hope for her, either.

Mona never wanted to do anything to "handle" Mom. Anya wanted them all to come together and push her into wellness somehow. And that was where the rift between Mona and Anya had begun and it grew and grew and grew, until it was deep enough to leave them separated. It hadn't been until then that Mona started drinking. It hadn't been until then that the self-fulfilling prophecy *really* began.

There has to be a way out, she believed. *There has to be some way to change fate.* But then again, as she was thinking it, she was drunk; what hope did that show for a change of fate?

If only Dad would come home, Mona thought for the millionth time in her life. *If only he would decide that he hates working in the military, if only he'd get a job where he comes home every night, and stays home on weekends and holidays, if only our family could settle down and set down some roots somewhere, anywhere, like in those stupid Jesse books.*

Frustration caused Mona to kick her foot against the mattress, and she realized her head wasn't swimming but flailing, *drowning*, being tossed around by choppy waves that only got bigger and more violent by the second.

But he will get to come home now, she realized. *A death in the family has to be reason enough to give someone a significant leave of absence.*

Mona always dreamed of this moment, but not like this, why did it have to happen like this? Rose wanted Dad home just as badly as Mona did, as badly as they all did, even if they never talked about it. But when Dad came home this time, Rose wouldn't be there, she'd never be there again, and all Mona could do to keep from screaming was give in to the dark fuzzy depths in the back of her eyelids and slide, agonizingly, into a most troubled sleep.

CHAPTER 5

When Mona woke up, the house was silent.
Her mouth tasted rotten, and her head was a little heavy from the alcohol, but she felt significantly more sober and knew that she must have been sleeping for hours. Why hadn't anybody woken her up? She thought back to before, to chugging the vodka in the bathroom and then crying herself to sleep over Rose.

Rose.

Mona reached out from under the sheets to grab her cell phone from the nightstand. She saw that it was just past four in the afternoon, which meant that she'd been asleep for six hours. That fact scared her so much that she stayed still in bed, the sheet over her face as the light from the phone glowed in the heavy silence.

Six whole hours, and no one came to wake her up even once? Where was everybody if it was so quiet in the house? Was Rose's body still down in the basement, sprawled over the bottom of the stairs like a broken doll with bloody ears and teeth?

Mona wondered how on earth she could have slept through officials coming to the house to gather Rose's body. A thought turned her stomach: what if they *did* try to wake her up, but she was too drunk to respond? She scoured her mind for evidence supporting the theory, but found none. It wasn't like she'd drunk enough to completely black out. She never straight up forgot things, she was much more careful than that.

It was as if nobody had come into the bedroom at all.

Something else came back to her: the fact that her mother had been acting insane, saying something about how Rose didn't have to be dead, like she'd be able to "come back" somehow. The memory caused Mona's spine to tingle. Mom was acting so sure about it, so calm after her initial hysteria when Rose died. Did her sisters have to take Mom to the hospital to get sedated or something? Even if that was what happened, why the hell wouldn't they wake her up to tell her?

Maybe it was an emergency.

Still too scared to move from her bed, Mona opened the messenger app on her phone, found the name she was looking for, and opened the thread. She typed:

Lexa, are you there

She waited nervously, begging the universe to prompt just one of her sisters to make noise from downstairs, or from the bathroom, or from under the bed for all she cared. The level of quiet made her feel as though she might be trapped in an alternate dimension, where something was very wrong.

hey. at little bro's tball, sorry. what's up?

Mona's fingers trembled as she entered her message: Rose is dead.

She saw the little check mark indicating that Lexa had read the message then the little dots indicating that the reply was coming.

WHAT?! the text said. How? Oh, my god I'm so sorry Mona, I am so so sorry...

And I can't find anybody, Mona typed in reply, ignoring Lexa's question, refusing to allow the sorrow to drown over her again, her breath quickening. She realized that she'd crossed into melodramatic territory, now. She hadn't even gotten out of bed yet. She added on: I mean that I think my house might be empty.

This time, the response took a little longer to come: What do you mean? What's wrong? Have you looked for them everywhere?

Just then, there came a sound from downstairs. It was muffled, but recognizable as a cough. Then some voice, in a low tone that lifted at the end as if asking a question.

Mona flung the sheets off of herself and sat upright. She spied some pajama shorts on the floor in front of her bed, a pair of used skull-and-crossbone underwear still inside. She tossed the underwear into the hamper across the room, wiggled into the shorts and headed downstairs.

In the living room, her remaining sisters were sitting

on the couches, staring mundanely at the television as some movie played. Juliet's eyes were red and raw, and Taylor looked like she was sleeping with her eyes open. Anya had her hood pulled up, and her bare feet hung over the side of the couch. Mom was nowhere in sight. Someone had taken Rose's birthday balloons away.

"Where's Mom?" Mona asked, her throat thick, and she cleared it to make herself sound less groggy. "Is she in her room?"

"She's gone," Juliet said without looking up from the TV. "She took Rose's body and left."

Mona blinked, not understanding. Took…Rose's body? "What?" she said, and Taylor shifted her weight uncomfortably from where she sat perched beside Juliet.

"Don't ask about it." Juliet's voice was deadly still. "She promised us she'd take care of all the arrangements, whatever that means in her sick head. I wouldn't be surprised if we never saw her again."

"She really was losing it," Taylor chimed in, meeting Mona's eyes with hesitation. "She kept saying she was going to bring Rose back…"

"Enough," Juliet emphasized, her eyes growing wet again. "I can't take that shit anymore. She's gone to make the arrangements, that's all."

Today was supposed to be a special, fun day. Mona remembered yesterday, when Rose gathered them all in her makeshift tent for New Sunday, with cinnamon rolls and orange juice and sticky-sweet promises about her magical birthday. Mona wondered what Rose would have said had she known she'd be dead in less than twenty-four hours.

Where in the hell is Mom?

"So she didn't say specifically where she was going?" Mona tried to ask with the least amount of urgency possible, as to not upset Juliet any further.

"She's going to Danwin Cove," Anya answered, pulling out her phone and knitting her eyebrows together as she stared at the screen, then typed something. *I wonder how Everly reacted to the news that Rose is dead*, Mona thought blankly. *I wonder if she's planning on sneaking out to see her tonight. I wish I had someone to run away to. If only Lexa lived here...*

"Wait," Mona said suddenly, Anya's response finally sinking in. "Danwin Cove? But that's a five-hour drive!"

Danwin Cove was a tiny beach town on the East Coast, where the Cane family had lived two houses ago. Mona remembered the grit of sand between her toes from always wearing flip-flops, and the fishy smell of lobster in the air at the restaurant they all used to love. Why on earth would Mom go there with Rose's body?

"We're done talking about this," Juliet said loudly, cutting off Mona's train of thought. "The plan is that we're waiting here until Mom gets back. If she's not back by morning, we call the police, just like I told her I would if her crazy ass went missing with Rose."

Suddenly Mona wished she had stuck around, instead of dousing her panic in vodka and then sleeping through the entire day. The idea of Mom driving all that way— and did she really have Rose's body in the car? Was that even legal? With every question, the situation made less sense.

"I mean it," Juliet continued, sensing Mona's upset. "Just push it out of your mind until morning."

Yeah, okay.

Mona tried to convince herself that for some reason, Mom wanted Rose to be buried in Danwin Cove. Rose had loved it there, after all, the clouds and the chowder and scouring the beach for shells and sea glass. Maybe Rose had said something about it feeling like home to Mom. Maybe this was just a big misunderstanding, and what Mom was doing was right.

The lie burned like salt on the wound that was Mona's mind. If it was right, why wouldn't she have it done the official way, without a dead body in the car?

She headed to the kitchen for a soda, on autopilot, forcibly avoiding the sight of the basement door. Mona wondered if she'd ever be able to use the basement steps again. As of now, it was looking like a definite no. She cracked open her soda and scurried over to sit beside Anya on the second couch, which had significantly more room without Rose on it.

Would everything remind her of Rose from now on? Mona felt like she couldn't escape it.

She chugged half the soda in one go, desperate to dull the headache and nausea left over from her spontaneous drinking binge in the bathroom earlier. She considered checking the fridge for leftover fried rice, but for some reason, eating something felt like a betrayal of Rose. She sipped the cold, bubbly liquid from the can and lost herself in the reality show marathon her sisters had chosen.

The rest of the day went by like something out of *The Twilight Zone.* The girls functioned independently of each other while still remaining close by, like a group of toddlers too nervous to interact with one another. With every passing hour that went without a phone call from Mom, things felt more and more off.

Bedtime came within the same hour for everybody. Mona stayed sprawled on her back in the dark, staring at Rose's empty bed and the open window above it, which showed many twinkling stars and brought in swirls of fragrant night air that was soothing to breathe in. Mona pictured a million different scenarios in her head, of her mother driving her sister's corpse all the way to Danwin Cove.

Mona had read all about what happened to a dead body as time progressed. All these hours after Rose's fall and her body was likely in an awful state. She imagined her mother rolling down the window in the car to try and air out the stink. She imagined the car pulling up to Danwin Lobster Shack by the pier, the window still down, her mother pushing her sunglasses to the top of her head as she brightly exclaimed, "We're here, Rose! Did you want me to just bury you or did you want to get some crab cakes first?"

The vision was so clear that Mona realized she must be dreaming. She watched her mother get out of the car, seagulls squalling overhead, as Rose's bare foot stayed pressed against the backseat window, blue and green with rot. Mona tried to walk to the car but couldn't. When she called out for help, her mother turned toward her, sharply, the brightness draining from her eyes as she stared at Mona in cold, bitter anger.

"Why did you open the basement door?" her mother hissed, reaching into her blouse and retrieving a bloody fishing hook. Behind her, Rose's birthday balloons sailed away into the sky above.

Her mother lunged for her, but before the nightmare could finish, Mona snapped awake in her bedroom, sitting up in nearly perfect synchronicity with Anya in the next bed over. Daylight filtered through the blinds. Rose's bed looked the same as it did yesterday. Mona's heart pounded in her throat, the nightmare still fresh, as she became aware of why she and Anya had awoken at the exact time.

Downstairs, Taylor and Juliet were screaming.

CHAPTER 6

"What in the hell?" Anya managed to cry out, as both girls hurried to stand and make their way to the door. Mona ran ahead in the hallway, too fast to allow herself any logical thought as to what might be awaiting her downstairs. Juliet and Taylor weren't screaming anymore, but one of them was sobbing.

"Be careful!" Anya hissed as Mona nearly tripped down the curved staircase, ever shrouded in shadow. Mona could nearly feel her sister's breath on her neck. She jumped down the final three steps and bounded into the living room, where Taylor was on her knees, bawling.

Behind Taylor was Juliet, standing with her hands in her hair, her mouth a quivering O of shock.

Behind Juliet was Mom, a wild grin on her face, her face filthy with streaks of dirt.

Behind Mom was—

Rose.

Everything paused when Mona looked into her baby sister's eyes. Mona replayed the events from yesterday in her head, over and over in flashes; Mom and Juliet's fight, Rose's face when she got shoved backward, Rose falling, Rose screaming, Rose *dead*, she was dead, *she was fucking dead...*

"Mona," Rose said, her voice frail, her neck upright and straight and unbroken. She shifted in her seat, looking around self-consciously. "Why is everybody so upset?"

Mona let her eyes take in her sister's every detail, from her severely mussed hair to the same clothing that she had died in, which was now wrinkled and darkened with grime. Her neck may have been upright, but there was some ghastly green and black bruising that bloomed from the collarbone up, blending into the skin like spilled watercolors. Thick veins spiderwebbed up through the bruises, angry and dark. *Just looking at it hurts*, Mona thought, but then Rose turned her head to look around at everyone and didn't even flinch.

How on earth is this possible?

"Everybody's fine, Rose honey," Mom cooed, and Mona's legs began to feel wobbly and weak. "They're just emotional now that they know you're okay. I called them about the accident when it happened, of course, so naturally they've been worried."

The "accident"? Mona felt sick. She couldn't remember the last time she'd heard Mom talk to Rose so gently, so tenderly. Taylor hiccuped from where she knelt on the floor.

"How did you do this," Juliet asked, looking at Mom

with widened eyes. "Tell me what you did to her right now or I swear to god…"

"Juliet," Mom interrupted, her tone blushing with an underlying intensity. "Not now. Rose doesn't need to hear all the details…"

"I do, though," Rose cut in, clearing her throat of something thick. Mona sensed Anya stiffen beside her at the sound, heavy and ugly and unnatural. "I don't understand what happened, Mom. If we were in an accident, how come the car is okay? And so are you. And why did I wake up in the car and not the hospital? You won't even let me look in the mirror, I feel fine, I don't feel like I was in an accident, I don't even remember leaving…"

Mona realized that Rose had no idea she was dead. She really was alive again through some morbid miracle. Mona was eager for her mother to fill them in on how this happened, what she did in Danwin Cove that could possibly have resulted in…this. But what *was* this? Who was this pitiful little bruised thing sitting at Rose's spot at the breakfast table, wearing her shirt that was still covered in darkened drops of blood from the real accident, the *fatal* one?

"Why were the mirrors the only thing broken in the car?" Rose asked. "Something feels wrong. Something feels different."

The words were horrifying. Mona took a deep breath and held Rose's stare, weirdness be damned. She searched and searched for even the slightest sign of mishap; evidence that there was some demon from hell dwelling within her sister's body, evidence that the real Rose was gone like she had been before.

But there came no evidence. As Mona looked into Rose's eyes, she only saw what she had always seen whenever her little sister needed her. Pleading. Trust. Desperation.

Taylor stood up, her face shiny with snot and tears, and took Juliet's elbow as she stepped forward. Anya's breath trembled in the quiet. They all seemed to realize it at the same time as Mona: this was really, truly Rose.

"Oh, Rose," Mona managed, and all of the sisters rushed forward to circle around her, sniffling and leaning their heads down, and Rose began to cry.

"Please let me see a mirror," she begged, strained, her fingers tightening around themselves. Her hands looked as healthy as they ever did, Mona noticed. Rose hadn't seen the bruising all over her neck, she probably had no idea it was even there. Mona imagined Mom busting all of the mirrors in the car and goose bumps flourished up her sides and back.

"We need to get you into bed," Juliet answered when nobody else did. She straightened, pulling the other sisters away from Rose. "Do yourself a favor and wait to see a mirror until you've had a shower. But first, rest."

Juliet wrapped her arm around Rose's shoulders and led her toward the stairs. "I'll be back in a minute," she said to their mother, her eyes narrowed. It was implied: *and you're going to tell us what the fuck is going on.* Mom didn't say a word, just stared at Rose and Juliet as they passed, biting her lip nervously as they went.

"We need to get rid of all the mirrors," Mom whispered right away, walking across the living room to remove a small decorative one from the wall. "Keep all the televisions on, all of the time, so they never go dark and show reflections."

"Mom," Anya tried, her face crumpled up. "Please..."

"When Juliet comes down," Mom promised, rushing around to collect all the glass picture frames on shelves and on the wall. "I will tell you all about it. But first, help me girls, I'm not kidding. If she sees her own reflection, she'll *know*."

Mona couldn't believe that they were all going along with the command like it was the only thing to do. She realized they were all scared of what might happen if they didn't listen to Mom now.

Clearly, she was not the same person they thought before. Clearly, there was more to their mother than forgotten birthday pies and empty bottles of painkillers. Somewhere in there, there had been a person who knew things. Who could achieve the impossible.

The world looks different now, Mona thought as she pulled the powder compact out of Rose's purse and threw it into the trash. *It feels different.* Maybe that was what Rose meant when she said that something was wrong. It was like nothing was absolute anymore, nothing was strong enough to act as an anchor. There were no more anchors in their lives now, there was only chaos and fear and a little girl who was once dead but was now alive again, as well as the terrifying thought of what might happen if she saw herself in a mirror.

Would the bruising ever go away? What about the thing with her throat—it sounded so grotesquely clogged when she tried to clear it. The memory of her rotted dishevelment when she first came home, combined with her deer-in-the-headlights stare, was bone-chilling.

Within fifteen minutes, they'd cleared the entire first floor of anything reflective. Mona found herself grateful beyond words that the oven door was white and low to the ground, otherwise her mother would have broken it with the same hammer that she used to shatter the mirror in the downstairs bathroom. On the television screen, some reality star cried over an earring that had been lost in the ocean.

Mona wondered how Juliet was doing with Rose upstairs, if everything was okay, but how *could* it be, really? She felt a little stab of guilt for wishing that she was just a little tipsy to help make this unknown new world a bit less terrifying and awful. The intensity of the situation was electric, settling into her skin, her blood. Still, despite all that, she couldn't deny the flicker of excitement deep down: *Rose is back! You have her back!*

Mona realized that Rose being back also meant another thing: her father definitely wouldn't get sent home now that there hadn't been a death in the family. *Fuck it,* she thought. *I would rather have Rose any day.*

Mona felt a hysterical, gleeful giggle start to rise in her throat, but she pushed it down. *Where is my mind,* she sang in her own head, wondering if her brain was producing some sort of chemical reaction as a survival tactic.

Then she remembered something sobering: she'd already told Lexa that Rose was dead. How could she ever take that back? *Sorry, I was kidding?* Or maybe *One of my sisters was playing a joke on me?* It was the only thing Mona could think of. Even though one of those opinions made her look like an asshole and the other would further encourage Lexa's wariness regarding Mona's family, she would have to choose something.

After all, Rose was alive.

Finally, Juliet came down the stairs. She was alone. "It took some convincing to keep her out of the bathroom," she said, her eyes gazing ahead into nothing as she ran her fingers through the ends of her long hair. "We can't let her see herself like that."

"She'll know that she was dead if she does," Mom said, looking to the garbage bags filled with mirrors and picture frames and shiny metal surfaces. "We have to give her time to adjust, at first. Harlow told me that."

The name *Harlow* made Mona remember things she hadn't in a long time, back from their short time at Danwin Cove: a too-small living room with a person standing still in the shadowy corner. Mom going out overnight and coming back the next morning, run-down and red-eyed, as turned up as if she'd taken a shot of adrenaline. *Harlow took me out,* she'd say, swirling around in the middle of the tiny living room, her arms out. *She's dangerous, that one. She's magical.*

Mona remembered that figure again, the one standing in the corner draped in a long floral dress, wearing a grin that was careless and cold. Blond hair, pasty skin that was dotted with little scabs. She remembered the figure leaning forward, whispering wickedly as she passed along a cellophane-wrapped candy into Mona's hand: "Don't tell your mother."

That was the only time they ever met. She heard her mother talk only a few more times about Harlow before she stopped mentioning her at all, becoming stone-faced and rattled if someone asked about her. And so Mona forgot all about her. They all had, based on the looks on her sisters' faces.

This was the first time they'd heard Mom say Harlow's name in years.

"Harlow told you?" Juliet repeated, her eyebrows furrowing together. "That weirdo meth-head from the beach? *Harlow* is responsible for bringing Rose back from the dead?"

Mom shushed Juliet, motioning at the staircase behind them. "We need to take this conversation to the backyard, where we know Rose won't hear." Without waiting for confirmation from any of the girls, she walked past them all through the kitchen, to the mudroom, and out the sliding glass door leading to the yard. The girls all followed in uncomfortable silence.

When the door was shut, Mom turned to look at them, her face still dirty like she'd been gardening all day. Mona wished she would take a shower and put on new clothes.

"The mirror thing isn't permanent," Mom said, finally breaking the silence. "But she can't look into her own eyes. If we can get her to go even a week without seeing her reflection, her soul should have enough time to resettle itself."

Resettle? The notion caused a chill to run through Mona. Did that mean that Rose was currently...unsettled? *Of course she's unsettled, she was* dead!

"What did you have to do to make this happen?" Juliet demanded, her eyes narrowed. "What did Harlow make you do?"

Mom looked down to her shoes, kicked at one foot with the other. "It's a ritual of sorts. You can call the dead back from the place beyond. You can...command them back."

"But how?"

"You don't have to know everything," Mom snapped. "After I just moved heaven and hell to get Rose back for you, not a single one of you has thanked me! All you care about is how, how, how?"

"You got her back for *us*?" Anya cut in, her expression matching Juliet's. "Are you sure you didn't get her back so *you* wouldn't get in trouble for pushing her down the goddamn stairs?"

"How could you even imply that?" Mom opened her mouth and then closed it again. "Jesus Christ, what is the matter with you all? Why aren't you happy to see Rose?"

"Don't turn this around on us," Juliet said, stepping forward, the skin on her neck and chest flushed in anger. "You always said that having children ruined your life, Mom, so let's not pretend you did this for us or Rose or anybody but yourself. You are insane. You are ridiculous. And now you've gone and—"

"Rose may not be herself for a little while," Mom went on, ignoring Juliet's insults. "There are a few things I still have left to do to bring her back completely." She held her hand up to stop Juliet from interrupting her. "But I *will* do them, girls, and then you'll see that this was for the best. Rose will get to live out her life as she deserves. No matter how you feel about me."

There was silence as the girls digested everything. So Rose wasn't even "completely back" yet. In that moment, Mona understood that what had been done was unnatural and wrong. Rose had been pulled from...wherever she was, against her will. Against *nature's* will. Mona remembered back to when Rose had died, how she felt certain that there would be a punishment in store for them.

If there wasn't a punishment coming before...there was absolutely one coming now. Or maybe this was it.

"You're selfish." Juliet said what Mona was thinking, and judging from the looks on their faces, it looked like Anya and Taylor were thinking it, too. The girls were so very used to being let down by their mother, but this was a whole new level of fuckery. Mom somehow felt like it was her place to "command" Rose's soul back into her body? What if Rose never felt right or okay again?

"Don't you all start on me again," their mother shot back right away, clearly ready for an argument. "How dare any of you imply that I've done something wrong? Would you rather Rose stay dead? Would you rather her be gone forever because of something as stupid and insignificant as a freak accident on her *birthday*?"

Mona agreed with Juliet, but she also couldn't deny

that deep down, she *was* happy that Rose was back. At least…she thought she was, anyway. The hope of things resembling anything close to normal had seemed straight up impossible this time yesterday, and now, well, at least there was a chance. According to Mom, Rose would be able to come back to herself soon enough.

"But she's suffering," Anya added, and Juliet nodded. "She can't even handle being in her own skin without panicking, and we won't be able to keep her away from mirrors for a whole week. In fact, once she wakes up and realizes we've taken away or broken all the mirrors in the house, she's *really* gonna wig, and what are we gonna tell her then?"

"We'll tell her eventually," Mom said. "But right now it's important that we keep her as stable as possible."

"Why?" Mona blurted out, remembering the other things Mom mentioned she needed to do in order to help Rose get back to normal. "What could happen otherwise?"

Mom paused at this, which sent Mona into a fresh spiral of anxiety. She was still worrying about the repercussions of this ritual, whatever it was…and whether it had some sort of price that needed to be paid for having their baby sister back from the dead.

"Nothing will happen," Mom insisted finally. "But we don't want her going through any more stress than necessary after what she's already been through, alright?"

In the next yard over, the Canes' neighbor, Mrs. Tully, appeared on her back porch, heading to the deck railing before lighting a cigarette and blowing the smoke downwind. She saw all the Canes looking at her and waved awkwardly.

"I'm going inside," Anya said, pushing past Mona to go back through the sliding glass door. Juliet and Taylor followed, so Mona followed, too. They left Mom outside to deal with the awkwardness of exchanging pleasantries with Mrs. Tully and made their way back to the living room. Upstairs, there was silence. The idea that Rose was up there felt just as unreal to Mona as the memory of watching her die yesterday morning. For a brief moment, she considered that perhaps *she* was the one who died, and was now living in her own personalized version of purgatory.

"I'm going upstairs," Juliet announced, the first of them to break the silence. "There are still some mirrors in our bedrooms, not to mention the bathrooms. We need to take care of them before she wakes up."

What will happen then? Mona wondered, trying to imagine what their new life with Rose would be like. At least it was spring break, and school would be out for a week. Maybe by then, things could start to feel somewhat normal again.

Still, Mona resented the fact that Rose felt like a stranger to her now. *It's still her, it's still Rose,* Mona reminded herself angrily, willing herself to get it together. *Be happy that she's back. Be grateful.* But underneath it all, she couldn't deny the gut feeling blooming inside her stomach like a poppy of dread:

Something was wrong with Rose.

CHAPTER 7

R ose didn't ask about the mirrors again.
     She didn't ask about the accident, either—after
her initial burst of scared concern when she first arrived
home, she was now eerily quiet all the time, something
that was very unlike her, but Mona figured there must
have been some sort of trauma inflicted during the ritual. How could there not be? Mom said it herself, her
soul hadn't resettled yet. Either way, it made it hard to
act natural around Rose. Especially when her person-
ality was so different than it had been before her death.

There was a lot of walking around aimlessly, a lot of
staring, a lot of head-scratching, so much so in fact that
Mona started hearing the frantic sound in her sleep, in
her dreams. She dreamed that she was scratching her own
head, so hard and so fast that warm, soggy chunks of scalp
started falling onto her shoulders, smearing her hands and
arms with slicks of blood. When she woke up in a cold
sweat, there was Rose, scratch-scratch-scratching away
in the dull blue darkness of early dawn.

In general, sleep was becoming an issue. It wasn't easy to relax with the knowledge that the body in the bed right across the room not only used to be dead but was now wide awake, staring unblinkingly at the ceiling as if there was something up there that nobody else could see.

Even after Rose had changed out of her death clothes and cleaned up and brushed her hair, the vivid bruising that ruled over her neck was viscerally startling. Taylor was the only sister who couldn't keep her gawking under control, until Juliet knocked her on the head with her knuckle and muttered *cut it out* while Rose wasn't looking. On the flip side, Anya seemed to be hesitant to look at Rose at all, and spent way more time than usual in their closet, settled in the corner with all the pillows, turning the pages of library books in between puffs from her glass pipe. Mona understood the reasons for why it was happening, but wished Anya would get over it for Rose's sake.

The idea that upsetting Rose could cause something bad to happen made it feel like the whole world was covered in eggshells.

For the first four days after her resurrection, Rose got up, took a shower, combed her hair back in front of the bare wall over the twin sinks, then brought her pillow downstairs to lie on the couch, like she did when she had the flu. Her energy was impossibly low, and Mona was starting to wonder if Rose would be able to return to school once break was over in a few days.

Mom swore that she'd be able to, that she'd perk up after a bit and everything would be fine, but Mom's word wasn't exactly golden, and Rose's sluggishness seemed to only get worse with time, not better. The nasty gurgling sound that happened whenever she cleared her throat didn't go away, like whatever was in there couldn't be cleared, was too thick, too sticky.

Juliet aggressively rose to the occasion and took care of Rose's every need, like she always had, except now Mom was usually in the room to see it, which put a weird sort of damper on things. Instead of spending her days locked in her room drinking, Mom had taken to lingering downstairs with the girls, sitting on the corner edge of the couch while she bounced her knee with an intensity that caused the whole cushion to rumble.

"Jesus, Mom, go smoke a cigarette or something," Anya said dryly from beneath her hood on the next couch over. "You're making me anxious."

Mona shot her sister a glare, but Anya just flipped her off and continued texting Everly and avoiding eye contact with Rose. Mom took Anya's suggestion and went to smoke on the stairs, as if that was any better than smoking in the living room.

"Are you unable to step outside for that?" Juliet asked from where she was painting Rose's toenails, and Mom pretended not to hear her. Rose blinked slowly and continued staring through the television, seemingly unaware that anyone was speaking.

Mona was glad that she was buzzed for this. She'd taken to getting her secret swigs from the liquor bottle in the bathroom vent whenever she wanted a short break from everyone, particularly Rose. This amounted to several sips throughout the day that left Mona's head heavy and ready for sleep by six in the evening.

It occurred to her then that disagreeing with Anya about Mom's habits only ended up making her even *more* like Mom. When they used to argue about how to handle Mom, Mona hadn't even started drinking yet, although she did share Mom's tendency to avoid things. Was that why she was so opposed to Anya's suggestion of having a sit-down with Mom and laying out how they all felt?

No, she reminded herself. What Anya wanted to do wouldn't have helped at all. It would have just caused a lot of unnecessary drama and made things worse.

Worse than losing Anya?

So, of course, she took a few more sips from the bottle, pushed Anya out of her mind. There were more important things to deal with right now.

At meals, Rose didn't eat much. She looked hungry as she poked around her plate, but if she tried to chew and swallow anything, she vomited it back up, right onto her plate. Mona was starting to worry that before too long Rose would just die again of starvation or exhaustion or whatever it was that was making her skin such a sunken gray-green color and her eyeballs look like they were sinking into her skull. After a while she started holding her hands to her stomach, writhing around and letting out little moans every now and then. "I'm hungry," she cried. "Then eat," Juliet begged, her eyes wide and scared.

At the beginning of the fifth day, Mom brought up a package of meat from the basement that was wrapped in brown paper, and Mona barely registered the fact that the meat from their local butcher was always wrapped in white paper. She did find it odd that Mom was cooking though, and in the morning no less. She watched as Mom hastily chopped an onion and a few stalks of celery, then added it all to a stew pot along with a big handful of baby carrots. A few minutes later, when the whole downstairs was fragrant with the smell of softened vegetables, Mom added the meat, which was cut in haggard chunks and strips, and a few cans of beef broth.

"That smells really good, Mom," Taylor said when she came down from her room and plopped down beside Mona, who was up early after going to bed before the sun was even down yesterday. "What is it?"

"It's for Rose," Mom murmured, staring into the pot as she stirred with an odd sort of glazed expression on her face. "I only made enough for her. I need to get her strength up for school on Monday."

Mona knew why Mom was doing this for Rose—to prove a point to Juliet, she was sure of it. Mom seemed hell-bent lately on trying to somehow reclaim her role as the head of the household, the *matriarch*, which wasn't really possible after all these years of leaving Juliet in charge.

"Well, I hope she eats it," Taylor said as she turned back toward the television, biting her lip and looking nervously to Mona. "Have you noticed how awful she looks lately? Juliet said it's like watching her die all over again."

Mona looked at Taylor through the softened lens of

having had too much sleep and not enough all at the same time, took her in like she hadn't in quite a while. It was all too easy to overlook Taylor, Mona realized with a bit of sadness. She had been a watered-down shadow of Juliet's for such a long time now, maybe forever, and it was long past the point of just being a phase—Taylor was *eighteen*, for Christ's sake! And yet here she sat, wearing a T-shirt with Juliet's favorite band on it and wringing her fingers around each other while she eagerly waited for her beloved big sister to wake up.

If Taylor wanted to, she could have left the house tomorrow, taken her small bit of savings and found some roommates to crash with, started working regularly and built a life for herself in a stable place. But of course, since Juliet sacrificed going to her dream college, Taylor had to sacrifice too, for reasons Mona couldn't comprehend without becoming angry. Taylor was probably just waiting for Juliet to leave before she did, so she could make sure to go to the same place, the same damn *house* if possible.

Nonetheless, Taylor was right to share Juliet's concern for Rose. Something needed to be done for her, Mona could feel it.

"Maybe we can just make her eat it," Mona said, and the words felt wrong as soon as they came out of her mouth. "I mean, like, strongly encourage her to, without throwing up. Tell her that it could help her feel better."

"It *will* make her feel better." Mom was still stirring, even though Mona was pretty sure you were supposed to let that sort of thing simmer instead of stirring it to death. "Homemade soup makes everything better."

Her voice was weirdly distant, like she'd gotten lost in her mind a bit, and Mona figured she must be high on one prescription or the other. At least the sobriety lasted a few days, anyway. If only Mom hadn't been so strung out during those few days, but Mona knew not to be picky. Dad's next visit wasn't scheduled for another seven months.

That was a long time to spiral, Mona thought with a shudder. She couldn't even imagine how much worse things could get in that amount of time. It was unfathomable.

You should be grateful that Rose is alive! she thought to herself. *At least you still have her, in a way, at least…*

It was the "in a way" part that had pushed Mona to drink today. It seemed like there was a different reason every day, or sometimes it was the same reason several days in a row, but either way she'd been discovering to her total horror that even when the reason had disappeared or passed the point of being relevant, the urge to drink was still there.

Mona left Taylor downstairs, heading up to the bathroom for just one swig. She was up on the toilet, about to unscrew the vent, when she heard a fluttering sound behind her. She turned and nearly screamed at the sight of Rose standing there, the circles under her eyes heavy and dark, peering at her like a curious raccoon. Mona dropped the screwdriver and stepped off the toilet and fumbled to act natural.

"The door was open," Rose said slowly. She bit at some loose skin on her lower lip, her expression unchanging. There was blood on her lip, staining her front teeth. "I didn't mean to scare you."

Mona forced a smile, put her hand over her chest. "I'm fine, I'm fine! I just thought I'd locked the door behind me, is all." She didn't attempt to explain what she was doing with the screwdriver. There was not a single answer that would be remotely believable, so Mona decided to leave it, talk past it as quickly as possible to make it all go away. "Mom made some special soup for you."

"I can smell it," Rose said, and wrapped her arms around herself. Her hair was static-ridden and tangled from bedhead, and she wore an old softball T-shirt and a pair of black basketball shorts. Her little toes moved impulsively along the edge of the bathmat on the floor. She looked like she was seven years old again like this, and it made Mona's heart ache. "I want to eat it."

Mona made a point not to let her eyes linger on the green and purple bruising all over her sister's neck, which was as vivid as ever. Still, it was hard not to see it out of the corner of her eye, even when she focused on Rose's face. The veins were just so *dark*, like they were filled with ink instead of blood.

"The smell woke me up," Rose continued. "It smells... good."

Mona forgot all about the bruising and the vodka in the vent, and her fake smile became a real one. It was the first time Rose had expressed interest in food since she'd been back. "Yeah?" She wrapped her arm around Rose's shoulders. "Let's go downstairs and get you fed, then."

"Okay," Rose agreed hesitantly. "I'm so hungry, Mona. I'd eat a dog if we had one."

The bluntness of her tone was startling. Mona forced a weak chuckle, but Rose didn't even crack a smile. The two walked down the hall together, and Mona noted that there was more urgency to Rose's step than yesterday. *She must be really hungry!* Was it possible she was finally starting to come around, just like Mom said she would? The idea was so cruelly promising that Mona had to struggle not to prematurely bask in her relief.

Downstairs, Mom had finally stopped stirring the pot and was now standing at the kitchen sink, staring vacantly out the window with her back to the living room and the rest of the girls. Taylor told Rose good morning and looked anxiously to the stairs, clearly still desperate for Juliet to come down. Juliet and Anya were always the ones who slept the latest.

"That smells good, Mom," Rose said, eagerness evident in her tone, and Mom turned quickly away from the window. "What is it?"

"Oh! Hi honey!" Mom said with such a burst of excitement that Mona decided she must certainly be high. Why else would she be so wound up? Unless the ritual had scarred Mom for life, too. Who knows what sort of weird shit was involved? "Let me make you up a bowl."

Mom ladled the thick, chunky stew into a white porcelain bowl and motioned for Rose to sit at one of the bar stools alongside the island. Mona watched with widening eyes as Rose stood over the first stool and pulled the bowl across the counter. Without hesitation, she took a huge bite that spilled down the front of her chin and dripped back into the bowl. She sat as she chewed, her eyes closed, and took a deep breath through her nose after swallowing.

Mona braced herself for Rose to vomit, but it didn't happen.

"Mom," Rose said, almost like she was in disbelief. "It's so good I can't even stand it."

Mom looked pleased as punch with herself. "I know what my girl needs."

It was an annoying thing for her to say, but Mona realized that she didn't really care. Mom had somehow broken Rose's no-eating spell; this could mean everything for her recovery. Already some color had returned to her cheeks. Mona sat at the stool next to Rose and breathed another sigh of relief. Mom looked on, her face dirty and smudged, her eyes exhausted, then excused herself and headed upstairs for a shower.

"You've gotta try this, Mona," Rose gushed as she continued to shovel the soup in. She chewed on the meat with a ravenous intensity, almost to a point that was startling, but Mona reminded herself that it was the first time Rose had really eaten in days. It must have just taken her stomach a bit of time to come back around after dying. Mona shivered a little, even though she wasn't cold.

"You should eat it all," Mona answered, her stomach queasy at the sight and sound of Rose eating. "I'm not the one who needs all those nutrients."

"I want you to try it," Rose insisted, pausing for just one second to lick gravy from her lips. "It's too good for me to enjoy alone, Mona, seriously, please."

Rose was looking and sounding so much perkier than what Mona would have dared believe was possible a few days ago. Not wanting to put a damper on things, Mona hesitantly took the spoon, even though she wasn't even close to hungry.

Just one bite, she thought. *And then she'll be content enough to eat the rest.*

Mona got a piece of the beef and a chunk of onion in her spoon, along with a small pool of the dark, fragrant broth. The beef looked a little different than the stew meat they usually used for stuff like this—lumpier, more raggedly cut. With the bite still steaming, she carefully lifted the spoon to her mouth. Rose hadn't finished chewing yet, which told Mona the meat must not have been very tender.

Mona took the bite all at once, the broth sliding down her throat as she worked her teeth over the tough, weird-tasting meat. It wasn't the best soup she'd ever tasted, in fact, there was something off about the meat specifically.

The meat was unique in both flavor and texture, porky but tough, although the presence of garlic and onion helped make it more manageable. Still, it had the sour flair of beef that'd been sitting out for too long or something. Mona remembered how roughly cut the meat chunks were, and wondered if it was possible the butcher who provided it to Mom was new to the job. Mona chewed and chewed, bile rising in her throat, wondering when the meat would break down, wondering how long it would take to floss strings of it from her teeth later. Hopefully it wasn't spoiled; she would hate for Rose to get sick after finally being able to eat something.

"See?" Rose said, not even waiting for Mona's reaction before grabbing the spoon back. After a minute, the meat was all gone from the soup, and Rose tossed the spoon aside and started gulping the broth straight from the bowl. "It's the best thing I've ever tasted in my whole life."

She finished the entire pot, and was sad when it was all gone.

CHAPTER 8

"Hold still," Juliet commanded as she stood over Rose, a bottle of pasty foundation in one hand and a cosmetic sponge in the other. "This is gonna take a few minutes at least."

Rose was sitting at the vanity chair in the girls' shared bathroom with her chin tilted up and to the left, exposing the darkened area of bruised skin on her chest and neck. After finishing the soup Mom made for her, Rose was noticeably more herself than she'd been since coming home, and begged her sisters to take her out somewhere, anywhere. It happened just like Mom said it would. But what were the "other things" Mom had mentioned before, that she needed to do to help Rose along? What else had she done besides just make some soup?

"There's a barbecue celebration happening somewhere on post," Rose insisted when she saw how hesitant her sisters were. "I saw a post about it on the community forums. Can we go? Please?"

"But…" Mom faded away mid-answer, clearly scrambling for a way to talk around what was obvious to everyone but Rose: the bruising was too dramatic and unnatural-looking to be seen in public.

"Of course we can go," Juliet cut in, making Mom's eyes widen and Mona's heart skip a beat. "But you've got to do us a favor in exchange. You have some bruising left over from your accident. You know how nosy the people around post are... Let us cover it up for you. With makeup."

And that was how they all ended up surrounding Rose in the bathroom while Juliet sponged the thick liquid foundation meant for covering up tattoos onto the skin of Rose's neck. Juliet used to use the makeup on the scorpion tattoo on her forearm when she worked at In-N-Out Burger, but ended up getting fired anyway, for refusing to take off her nail polish and bloodred lipstick. The thick formula only lightened the bruising after the first coat; by the fourth coat, it was nearly completely covered.

"There you go," Juliet said with a smile, dusting the entire area with some loose powder to set the makeup in place. "Just be careful not to rub it off, and definitely stay out of the pool."

The community barbecue was happening at the post's recreation center, somewhere the sisters had gone often when they'd first moved in but had gotten tired of quickly. Mona thought about all the people who might be there, Mom's old group that she used to drink afternoon wine with until she fell off the social wagon hard, other military brats with deployed parents who were all too eager to prove how well they were handling not

knowing if their moms or dads would still be alive tomorrow.

Mona knew it was unfair to look at the situation
that way. Really, she was just jealous of those kids who
seemed to do fine with all the moving and worrying. It
was something she should have gotten used to by now,
after so many years of not knowing anything else. And
yet, here she was, wishing her dad would just quit, get
a job that only ran from Monday through Friday, and
move them to their first real hometown.

The idea of going to the barbecue was exhausting to
Mona, but the fact that Rose was so hyped up on the
idea gave enough of a reason for all of the Cane girls to
at least pretend to be excited about the outing. *We almost
weren't a family anymore, but now we are again, look at us!*

Taylor put on a bikini top that had been handed down
from Juliet, along with a pair of high-waisted shorts and
an oversized black sun hat. Anya put her phone down
long enough to smear sunscreen down her arms and
along the bridge of her nose. Mom and Juliet scoured
the fridge and freezer for some sort of snack to bring
along, and ended up bagging a Tupperware container
of hard-boiled eggs and a two-liter of cola into a paper
sack. Mona went upstairs to find her flip-flops only to
discover a text from Lexa waiting for her:

how you doing? I am so sorry for your loss. :(

Shit. Ever since Mona first texted Lexa about Rose,
there had only been silence between them. Mona knew

it was because Lexa was giving her space until she wanted to talk, but it'd been long enough to worry her. Mona knew she'd have to address this at some point, might as well get it over with now, and besides, she really missed her daily chats with Lexa.

She sat for a moment on the bed, biting her lip and staring at the screen, not wanting to start typing until she knew what she was going to say. Finally, after a minute:

You won't believe this. Rose was in a car accident, and one of her friends died. At first we didn't know who had died and who was alive, and at one point things were miscommunicated and we thought it was Rose. But it wasn't. She's alive. Everything's totally fine.

She nearly tossed the phone back to her nightstand, not wanting to keep it on her during the barbecue, not wanting to worry and fret over the possibilities of Lexa's response. She started to become seriously uneasy about how she'd chosen to word the end of the text—*everything's totally fine*. If it happened like Mona claimed it did, things wouldn't be totally fine, not at all. Rose would be devastated with the loss of her friend, and the family would be shaken from almost losing Rose. It nagged and nagged at Mona, because Lexa wasn't dumb nor would she pretend to be if she suspected something was off, but it was too late now to go back and change the text.

It'll all blow over, she promised herself, leaving the bedroom and heading down the stairs. *Rose is back and she's fine and soon we'll be able to forget all about this week from hell.*

Downstairs, the sisters were waiting in the living room. Mona saw that they all had on their matching sunglasses, the ones with the same frames but in different colors, and rushed back upstairs to grab her blue ones. She saw the notification light on her phone flashing, surely Lexa's response to her lie, and ignored it. Mona didn't blame herself for the lie, but still couldn't help but feel like her one solid friendship in life had been tainted.

Until now, she'd never been anything but honest with Lexa. Now she had this enormous, life-changing secret that she'd never be able to reveal. It made her feel disconnected and alone, like nobody would ever really know her fully, like she'd never be able to truly be herself around anyone she liked or even loved.

Get over it, Mona scolded herself as she slid her sunglasses over her face. *It's worth it to have Rose back.*

Rose's pink frames looked especially cheery on her smiling face today. Mona couldn't help herself; she planted a big kiss on the top of her sister's head and pulled her into a hug.

"I'm so glad you're feeling better," she said, a little embarrassed at first, but then Juliet and Taylor and Anya came over and took turns doing the same thing.

"Guys!" Rose squealed, wriggling away from them as she turned on her heel to dash into the kitchen, toward the wooden door that led to the basement. "Let's go already! I was so tired of having to be in bed all the time, I can't wait to feel the sun on my skin…" She put her hand on the doorknob and pulled, the breeze from the basement below blowing her hair back.

"Wait!" everybody screamed, even though Rose was standing motionless at the top of the steps, looking down into the dark. Mona and Juliet rushed forward at the same time, nearly bumping into each other, and linked their arms through Rose's before she could take another step.

"I feel weird looking down there," Rose murmured, the previous glee from her face gone and replaced with something more disquieting. "What...what's..."

"Close the door now, girls," Mom commanded boldly from behind them, speaking quickly. "There's...we should ride in the Mustang. It's parked on the curb, not in the garage."

Juliet leaned forward and closed the door, nearly slamming it in her apparent anxiety, and Mona tried hard to get rid of the dismay on her face that bloomed at the memory of what happened the last time Rose went down the basement steps.

"Come on, Rose," Mona said gently, tugging her sister toward the front door in the living room and offering a little smile. "This way."

She was nervous at first that opening the basement door had somehow pulled Rose back a few steps in her recovery, but by the time they'd all piled into Juliet's convertible, Rose's newfound excitement over the day had returned. She beamed as the wind blew her hair all over while she sat on Taylor's lap in the backseat, her legs stretched over Anya and Mona. "Eleanor Rigby" played on the radio as Mom stared blankly ahead, the bag with the hard-boiled eggs and the soda on her lap.

There were balloons decorating the front gate of the

rec center, and several cars were already parked in the lot that stretched around the side. In the distance, a large group of teens played basketball on the cement courts behind the pool. Mom took a while to unbuckle her seat belt once they were parked, and Mona realized that she was nervous about going in. And not because of Rose, either. Mona remembered the woman from the commissary, how clear it had been that she'd been gossiping about Mom with her friends.

"Come on, Mom!" Rose piped up from the back, bouncing up and down on Taylor's lap. She slapped her hands against the back of Juliet's seat, and Mona realized that Rose's giddiness had become almost manic. She felt a stab of discomfort over the sight for a moment, but decided that Rose was just especially excited after being bedridden for days.

Everyone got out and headed to the entrance of the main building, all of them wearing sunglasses except for Mom, who clutched the plastic grocery bag so hard her knuckles were white.

Their entrance to things like this was never subtle or unnoticed; everybody always turned and stared at the Cane pack when they first appeared, the charm of their family's size and togetherness an intriguing combination with the fact that they were both fairly reclusive and the family of a colonel. Everyone always painted the Canes as the embodiment of the American military dream family, but Mona knew that it was only because they were good at playing the role.

"Ashley!" A woman in a yellow-and-blue-striped sundress called to Mom from a table covered in bowls of chips and dip and freshly cut fruit. She shimmied over to the family, her platform sandals clicking over the clinically white flooring. "Now *this* is a surprise!"

"Hello, Rita," Mom said through gritted teeth. "How've you been?"

The two exchanged quick, back-patting hugs.

"Great, great," Rita said, looking down at the plastic grocery bag in Mom's hand. "And what do we have here?"

"Just some eggs and soda," Mom said sheepishly, handing the bag over. "Sorry that it's not much, but—"

"Don't be silly," Rita insisted, taking the bag and turning to the rest of the girls. "Wow, look at all of you! All grown up!"

Mona struggled not to roll her eyes, which Anya did without holding back. They had been in this town for what...six months? And somehow they looked older than before? The look on Juliet's face said what Mona was thinking: Rita was full of shit.

"Anyway, Ashley," Rita sputtered after an uncomfortable silence from the sisters. "Would you like me to get you a glass of wine, dear? Or, ooh, Sarah brought margarita mix..."

Mona saw the alcohol bottles arranged on one of the tables, and immediately realized that she could easily sneak one of them away in her bag and nobody would notice or miss it. She usually got her alcohol by stealing it from the commissary, which was always a heart-pounding risk that left her feeling more alive than she ever had, but the truth was that if she were ever caught doing it, the consequences would be great. Opportunities like this were not to be left without taking advantage of them.

Still, Mona wished that her mother wouldn't drink right now, especially since she already seemed so nervous just to be here. But Mona was tired of worrying about her mother. Rose needed that attention more, anyway.

"Sure," Mom said, her eyes darting from Rose to the crowd to the other sisters. "I'll just have one margarita while the girls hang out."

"Don't worry about us, Mom," Juliet said warmly, flashing a smile at Rita. "You enjoy and relax. We can handle ourselves."

"I like this one," Rita drawled, wrapping her arm around Juliet and pulling her close. "What a blessing to have a pack of responsible, sweet girls like this."

The Cane sisters smiled all together, like they always did when they were out en masse, with their department store catalog smiles. Keeping up with the perceived fairy-tale notions about their family came instantly and effortlessly to all of them, Mona noticed, even though they had never actually talked about how phony it all was. She used to wonder why she went along with it, but then realized that when it came down to it, all they truly had to hold on to on a consistent basis was each other. Why *not* take control over whatever impression they left on the people they'd only know for a short amount of time, anyway? It was none of their business what was really happening behind the family's closed doors. It was kind of nice to pretend that things were as great as everybody else assumed they were. It was one of the few consistent things they had to cling to in life.

"And I heard you turned down a full ride to Juilliard too," Rita continued, a little too encouraged by Juliet's previous warmth. Mona saw Juliet go rigid beneath Rita's arm. "You must really love our little community here if you're so eager to stay."

Juliet's eyes met her mother's. "Oh, yes. I just love it here. Mom just makes it so *hard* to leave, you know?"

It was an innocent comment on the surface, but Mona instantly saw the hurt and embarrassment on her mother's face. All the girls knew that Juliet would be in New York City right this very second if she'd felt like she had a choice in the matter. But Mom's habits kept Juliet locked in, leaving her to take care of the other girls just as she'd been doing most of her life.

"I feel you, honey," Rita went on, unaware of the tremendous tension. "It's her pot roast, isn't it? Mine is the reason why my daughter swears she'll never move out. But don't tell me you still fold her laundry for her, Ashley, we've gotta let them learn to fend for themselves eventually…"

The sisters collectively moved together to the food table, leaving Rita and their mother behind, Rose looking worriedly at Juliet. Mona made a note to come back for one of the six bottles of rum that currently sat unopened beside the giant bowl filled with spiked punch.

They all made themselves paper plates loaded with chocolate-covered strawberries and chips and corndogs, except for Rose, who looked over all the food with her nose slightly crinkled. *She must still be full from the soup,* Mona thought. *Or stressed over Mom and Juliet.* Rose had always been so sensitive to their arguing. In a sick way, Mona was kind of relieved to know that Rose still got especially bothered by it, even after dying. It was just further proof that it really was her that had come back.

The girls grabbed sodas from a cooler and took their food outside to the pool area, where they claimed a row of five lounge chairs that sat in the shade of a large, lazy-branched tree.

"What a fucking bitch that Rita lady was," Taylor said while she opened her orange soda with a crack. "She has no idea what she's—"

"You don't need to stick up for me," Juliet interrupted sharply, looking down at the food on her chair without touching any of it. "I'm fine."

Taylor shrank back, clearly wounded by the tone of Juliet's voice. "Sorry."

"I think you should leave us for Juilliard," Rose said firmly before anything else could be said, and Mona and Anya nodded their agreement. "You're nineteen and it's wrong that you feel like you have to stay."

Mona felt guilty that the youngest of them was saying this, instead of Taylor or even Anya or herself. It was true Juliet shouldn't have had to take care of them. They needed to be able to function for themselves. If only that woman Rita knew that it was Juliet who did *everybody's* laundry, everybody's cooking, everybody's shopping.

And if only Mona could stop relying on that so selfishly and accept that nobody is owed a great mother.

Still, understanding that wouldn't stop the hurt any. If anything, it just irritated it.

"It's not that I just *feel* like I have to stay," Juliet said quietly, poking a strawberry with her finger. "It's that I really truly do have to. I can't leave you guys with Mom. You'd all be fucked."

"We're used to Mom by now," Mona argued. "You and Taylor aren't doing anything noble, staying here for us. You're just holding yourselves back."

You could start your own lives away from all of this! she wanted to scream in their faces. *What in the hell are you still doing here?*

Deep down, Mona knew the answer. It wasn't because Juliet worried about her or Anya, it was because she worried about Rose. Rose had been Juliet's baby ever since she was an infant and their mother admitted that having children had ruined her life. As long as Rose was in the house, Juliet would be, too.

"Shut up, Mona," Taylor said snidely from behind a sip of her soda. "Your ungrateful ass doesn't understand anything."

Anger flared up inside Mona.

"Oh please," Anya cut in. "Don't act like you're the one doing anything noble, Taylor, you just can't comprehend a life where Juliet isn't around for you to worship anymore."

Mona was surprised that Anya stuck up for her, and when she tried to give her sister an appreciative glance,

Anya just lay back in her chair, her plate balanced on her stomach, and retrieved the phone from her pocket to zone out.

"Everybody shut the fuck up," Juliet said, and even though it wasn't hot outside, a chill bloomed in the silence. "I'm sorry, Rose, I'm not talking to you. I just want you to have fun today like you wanted, alright? Can we all just agree to let Rose enjoy her first day out after...the accident?"

Rose squirmed uncomfortably in the chair beside Mona's.

"That's fine by me," Taylor said, crunching on a chip and looking across the pool, through the fence that led to the basketball courts. "But not as fine as that dude in the blue shorts over there."

Mona noticed now that the boys had stopped playing like they were before. A lot of them were looking at the sisters curiously, almost hungrily. An especially tall boy in blue shorts seemed particularly interested in Taylor.

"Don't be pathetic," Juliet laughed, but it wasn't a friendly, jesting laugh, it was cruel, full of resentment, clearly leftover from before. "You're not exactly girlfriend material, Tay."

Despite the comment Taylor had made about her being ungrateful, Mona couldn't help but feel a little bad for her. Juliet laughed again, and Taylor quietly shrunk back and focused on her food instead of the boy.

"I want to go swimming," Rose said, staring at the water without blinking. "It's so hot outside, can't we just tell everybody that the bruising isn't as bad as it looks?

Nobody's going to care if I act fine about it. I'm not in any pain, I feel fine…"

"No," Juliet emphasized, starting to lose her temper a bit. "We told you before we came that swimming isn't happening. It doesn't matter if you're acting fine about it, that bruising is fucking hideous and you're not letting it show in front of all these people, they'll think you're being seriously abused or something, we don't need anyone coming to the house and asking questions…"

"Fine!" Rose nearly yelled, her eyes darkening considerably. An older man a few chairs over looked up from his newspaper for a moment before going back to his reading. "You don't need to be so mean about it, Jules."

"Apparently I do," Juliet said calmly, "if that's the only way to say it where you actually listen."

"Calm your tits," Anya grumbled, and by now most of the adults had started filtering out of the main building and surrounding the pool, jumping in, laughing loudly over one another. Mona realized that it'd be a great time to go back in and take that bottle of rum while nobody was looking.

"I'm gonna go to the bathroom, be right back," she said, not pausing long enough to give anyone a chance to tag along. Luckily, they all stayed put, including Rose, who had her arms crossed over her chest and was looking angrily at a group of kids playing Marco Polo in the pool.

The sight of her so unhappy made Mona wish they'd never come out at all. They should have done something else, something without Mom, away from the post. Gotten ice cream cones downtown again or hit up a swimming pool in the next town over, where nobody knew them and the bruising on Rose's neck wouldn't be as big of a deal.

"Wait," Rose called after Mona, then hopped off her chair and jogged to catch up, her flip-flops slapping the concrete. "I need to go, too."

Shit. How was she supposed to get the rum now? Mona's brain was already working fast to figure it out. Juliet peeked over the top of her sunglasses to make sure Mona saw Rose coming for her, then went back to scowling at the magazine she'd brought along in her bag. Anya was still glued to her phone, and Taylor sulked while she ate her corndog and gazed longingly at the boys playing basketball.

"You doing okay?" Mona asked Rose as they went through the iron fence and down the winding sidewalk that led to the main building. Inside, only a few people lingered, engaged in conversation, and the refreshments tables didn't have anybody around them. "Don't mind Juliet, she's just grouchy over what that lady said…"

"I don't care," Rose said flippantly, waving her hand as if brushing away Mona's words. "I'm so happy to be feeling better that it doesn't even matter to me. I don't need a swimming pool to have fun."

It sounded like she was trying to convince herself more than Mona, but Mona was too busy scoping out the room to fully realize the situation. "Go on ahead," Mona said to Rose, pointing at the restroom sign down the hall. "I'll be there in a minute, just wanted to get one of those sugar cookies first."

"Ew," Rose said, wrinkling her nose again at the sight

of the food. "I don't understand why, but none of that stuff looks good to me. Usually I'd be on my third corndog by now!"

"Well, you had a big breakfast," Mona said, and Rose nodded in agreement and grinned dreamily at the memory of her beloved soup before making her way to the bathroom.

The second she disappeared, Mona beelined for the tables, pausing in front of the one with food for a moment and checking to make sure nobody was watching. Once it'd been confirmed, she did a quick sidestep and smoothly moved one of the bottles of rum into her oversized shoulder bag. She turned away from the table with a satisfied sigh, but then something through the window leading to outside caught her eye: her sisters running for the main building, Juliet in the lead with a look of pure panic on her face.

Mona's heart skipped a beat at the intensity on Juliet's face. *What's going on?*

Her sisters burst through the door, and Juliet sprinted toward the bathroom without a pause. "Hey," Mona called after her, but Juliet didn't stop. Anya and Taylor stopped long enough to look at Mona, and Anya called out the words that chilled Mona's blood and sent an electric bolt of fear down her spine:

"The bathroom mirrors!"

Time felt thick all of a sudden, slow, and Mona suddenly realized that she'd made a stupid mistake, the worst mistake, and when Rose saw herself in the mirror she was going to know that she was dead. There was no way

Juliet would catch her in time. As Mona ran across the room, the bottle of rum sloshing loudly from inside her bag, she half expected to hear a bloodcurdling scream from the bathroom, but the silence that came instead was just as dreadful.

Mona, Anya and Taylor burst into the fluorescently lit room at the same time. Rose was standing squarely in front of the wall of mirrors mounted over the half-dozen sinks that lined the back of the bathroom, and Juliet was behind her, pleading with her in soothing words to *please look away, look away, step away Rose, stop looking, look at me instead, let us help you, let us explain…*

But Rose acted as though she couldn't hear Juliet, or Mona or Anya or Taylor as they surrounded her, blocking her view of the mirror, snapping their fingers in front of her face to no avail. Rose Cane stared ahead, through her sisters, unblinking, as if she was looking at something that she was never supposed to see, something that was killing her all over again.

CHAPTER 9

Juliet turned frantically and checked underneath all the stalls, and thank goodness they were alone in the bathroom. She locked the door, then turned back to Rose, plucking the hot pink sunglasses from on top of her head before placing them gently over her unblinking eyes.

"We're going home now, Rose," Juliet whispered directly in front of Rose's face. "I promise that everything is fine. I promise that you don't have to be scared. Just let us get you home."

Juliet pulled Rose away from the mirrors, toward the door. Rose's nostrils flared and she brought a shaking hand to cover her mouth. "I know where I was," she murmured, and Mona's heart raced with fear. Suddenly, Rose turned her head in one sharp tick. "Mona, you smell different. You smell...like that soup I ate earlier."

"Go get Mom," Juliet commanded Mona just as they were all about to leave the bathroom. "We'll lead her straight to the car so she doesn't have to talk to anybody, everybody's outside by now, it should be fine..."

"I get it," Mona nearly snapped, impatient and riddled with nerves, Rose's words echoing in her mind. *I know where I was.* Did that mean she remembered being dead? If so…what did she remember? "Open the door already."

Juliet did, and like a single working organism, the girls flocked out together, surrounding Rose like they usually did, but this time there was much less space between them than usual. Once they reentered the main room, Mona headed one way while her sisters went the other.

How could we have been so stupid? Mona wondered. Mom had said after enough time it wouldn't have the same effect on Rose, but clearly, it was still too soon for her to see her reflection. If it didn't happen today, it would have happened on her first day back at school. Again, Mona was faced with the awful thought that what Mom had done wasn't miraculous. It was wrong.

But if she hadn't done it, Rose would be gone right now. She wouldn't be getting upset about swimming pools and crinkling her nose at sugar cookies, she'd be *dead*. Mona was slowly coming to understand that she was far more selfish than she ever realized, which just made her feel even more like Mom's little clone, like Taylor was to Juliet, and it made her feel a little sick. Still, despite the terrifying side effects, she'd still choose to have Rose alive.

No matter how wrong it was.

Mona exited the main building and found herself back on the sidewalk that led to the pool. She spotted her mother almost immediately, sitting at a table on the opposite end, laughing loudly with a drink in her hand, surrounded by all the women in her old social circle. She must have gotten over her nerves pretty quick, Mona thought bitterly.

"Mom," Mona said once she reached the table. "We've got to go. Rose is...feeling sick."

At the mention of Rose's name, Mom's face faltered and she stood from the table. "Excuse me," she said to the other women at the table, and scooted out from between the chairs.

"What do you mean she's sick?" Mom said under her breath once they'd stepped far enough aside to gain some privacy.

"She saw herself in a mirror. She looked really upset, Mom, and she said that she remembered where she was when she died."

"Where is she now?"

"Juliet took her to the car," Mona said impatiently, wondering why Mom was standing here asking questions instead of following her outside, scrambling to see if Rose was okay. "She was calm enough, but she needs to go home. We're going to have to explain to her what happened."

Mom's face went white then. Mona realized that explaining to Rose what happened would require Mom to admit that she had lost her temper, got into a fight with Juliet and drunkenly rammed Rose down the basement stairs. Mona hoped, so much, that her mother would somehow find the strength to deal with this head-on, even though she had never done that before. *Just this once*, she pleaded with her eyes. *Please.*

Mom looked over her shoulder, then at the half-empty drink in her hand. "You say Juliet already took her to the car?" she asked, and Mona instantly knew where this was going. "Maybe you girls can just get her home then, and I'll meet you in a few hours. It'd be...suspicious if we all just left so abruptly without saying goodbye to people, you know?"

What a bullshit excuse to stay behind and let the rest of us do the damage control while she stays here to hide out and get drunk with her stupid "friends," Mona thought. The worst part of all was that these people weren't even Mom's friends, not really—she doubted her mother cared about a single one of them. All they were to her was more escape, just like her bedroom usually was, except this type of escape had the facade of being *good* for her, since she was getting out of the *house* and being *social.*

"Wow," Mona nearly whispered, making no effort to hide the disgust on her face. "How is it that you never fail to surprise me?"

"Oh please." Mom rolled her eyes and took a pained sip of her drink. "Rose...she'll be fine. You'll see. It's been a few days since she's been back, just break it to her gently and..."

Mona turned and walked away from her mother midsentence, annoyed that she ever felt defensive to Anya on her behalf. She had always been afraid that agreeing with Anya would mean that there was no hope for her, but now she was ready to accept that there wasn't hope for her *or* her mother.

"Where is she?" Juliet asked shrilly when Mona

hopped into the empty front seat of the convertible without even opening the door. Anya and Taylor sat in the backseat with Rose between them. Rose's arms were wrapped around herself, and there were angry scratches on her face and neck.

"She's staying," Mona said, her face stone. "Let's get the fuck out of here."

Juliet stared through her sunglasses, her mouth dropping open into a fishlike O for just a moment before she gathered herself and went back to her usual cold, calculated demeanor. She turned the key and put the car in drive.

"How are you doing, Rose?" Mona asked after they'd made it to the main road, turning around in her seat to look behind her.

Rose showed no sign that she'd heard Mona. Taylor and Anya leaned in closer to her, rubbing her arms, speaking soft words of encouragement to her. "We're almost home," Mona continued, and she reached back to grab Rose's hand, which was limp and dry. "Just hang in there, you're going to be alright, everything is fine."

"I can smell you," Rose said, looking at the hand that was holding hers, and Mona remembered the weird thing her sister had said back in the bathrooms. *You smell different. Like that soup I ate earlier.* Why would her sense of smell change just from seeing her reflection?

The girls got home and took Rose inside, closed all the blinds and locked all the doors. They sat her down in her bedroom, surrounded her on the bed, and spoke in the gentlest voices they could manage to explain to

Rose that on her birthday, she was accidentally pushed down the basement stairs and died.

They told her that Mom took her body to Danwin Cove, and that Mom's old friend Harlow helped her perform a ritual to command Rose's soul back into her body. They told her about the bruising. They told her about the broken mirrors. They told her how happy they were when they realized that she was alive again.

"But I shouldn't be here," Rose said, her eyes welling up, the thick makeup on her neck starting to wipe away and reveal the dark green and blue beneath. "Dead people aren't supposed to come back."

"But you did, Rose," Juliet said, squeezing Rose's knee. "You got a second chance. We're so sorry we went as long as we did without telling you. We should have been honest with you from the start."

"No," Rose responded quickly, her back straightening. "No, I'm glad you didn't. I don't know how to explain it, but for some reason I feel like if you would have told me too soon…" She paused, swallowed, started crying. "I think something really bad would have happened."

"To you?" Mona asked, heartbroken.

"No," Rose whispered. "To you."

School seemed infinitely less troublesome than it did before spring break. Mona no longer cared as much that she didn't have any friends; it made it that much easier to deal with the secret she was hiding. No one bothered her, nobody asked what was wrong, nobody offered their shoulder or their ear. And for the first time, Mona was happy about that.

After a lot of debate between Juliet and Mom, it was decided that Rose would be withdrawn from her sixth grade class and transferred to an online program that would allow her to work from home.

Initially, Mona felt like it was an unfair consequence of the resurrection, which is what she'd come around to calling Rose's situation to herself. She felt like Mom was taking Rose out of the world after all she'd done to bring her back into it. But then Rose had piped in about how much she loved the idea, since she'd been having such a tough time in school, anyway. She actually seemed excited over the prospect. It was the only thing that reassured Mona in the end, and the same seemed true for her sisters, as well.

But now, sitting in her fourth period art class, Mona felt sad thinking about Rose all alone at home with Mom and Juliet. Since the barbecue, Mom had started slipping back into her old habits again, making the atmosphere at home just as unstable as it was before. Mona hoped that Juliet could find a way to get Rose out of the house for a few hours at least. She liked the idea of the sun on Rose's skin, the sound of her laughter as she saw something amusing downtown, like a funny specials board outside the coffee shop or a corgi wearing a T-shirt.

Mona missed that pre-death Rose, the giggly creative girl with the rose-tinted lenses always on full force, so sweet and loving and painfully optimistic. She almost felt like *that* Rose may not have lived through the accident at all, and wondered what was there instead. Sometimes it felt understandable, like when Rose flinched at loud sounds or stared off into space.

But sometimes it felt...wrong. At night while they were all sleeping, Rose whispered to herself, constantly biting at her nails, leaving bloody little shreds of them on the carpet and in her sheets. She couldn't seem to get them short enough, couldn't stop staring at the ceiling like she was seeing hell, couldn't stop sucking on her bleeding fingertips like they were lollipops. Mona constantly wondered what Rose remembered about being dead, and was so scared by how it appeared to be eating at her, while Rose herself couldn't seem to eat anything anymore.

The soup felt like a false alarm at this point. Slowly, surely, her energy was draining again. Mona asked Mom if she could make more of the soup, but Mom defensively insisted that Rose didn't need any more, that the one bowl should have been enough—*we just have to wait*. Was there some sort of magic spell put on that soup? Some secret ingredient? Whatever it was, Mona was certain that it hadn't worked like it was supposed to. It didn't matter, Mom always said the same thing: *wait, wait, wait*.

The more they waited, the more Mona realized that even though she was surrounded by sisters, they were all becoming more and more isolated, not just from the outside world, but from each other, as well. Juliet doted on Rose, Taylor watched nervously from afar, and Anya turned to Everly.

Mona wished she could turn to Lexa, but Lexa had

never replied to her text about the pretend accident. The more time that passed, the more Mona realized that she'd been a little hasty in her need to throw an explanation out there, and wished she'd come up with something more believable. It was almost like Lexa could tell something was up—she could always tell if Mona was having a bad day and trying to hide it. Why would this time be any different?

Mona thought back to all the unanswered messages she'd sent Lexa since the one about Rose being alive. Maybe it was a little too clear how eager she was to move past the lie.

In their past year of exchanging texts, Lexa had never gone so long without answering. It made Mona feel like she was going crazy. She felt terrified that Lexa was mad at her, but how could she be, it wasn't like there was a way for her to know that Mona had lied.

Now, in art class, Mona's phone vibrated from somewhere inside the purse that sat on the table. She forgot about the watercolor of a bruise-covered figure she'd been working on and checked it eagerly, hopeful that maybe she'd sent some sort of universal brain wave to Lexa and made her think to text. It'd happened before. They'd jokingly referred to it as their psychic connection, one of the things that had helped them become so close so quickly.

Mona unlocked her phone, and the new text was from Lexa after all. Finally!

Hey, the text said, and Mona's mouth slacked open a

little as she read. Sorry for disappearing. Things felt kind of weird before.

When the bell rang, Mona ducked behind her locker door and texted Lexa back. I'm sorry I made things feel weird, she wrote. Are we okay?

She pushed Send and instantly felt ludicrous. She was talking to Lexa as if they were together or something, like they were in a serious relationship and Mona was being the self-conscious girlfriend who was both trying too hard and unwilling to be fully honest at the same time.

I don't know. The reply came almost instantly, and Mona's heart sunk in her chest. I guess. I mean... Tell me more about the car accident. It was just confusing, what you said. I don't think I understand what happened.

Mona stared at the phone screen, willing herself to come up with the right thing to say. The more time that passed, the more upset she got, and the less able she felt to carry on with the lie. Why couldn't she just fix this? Say whatever Lexa needed to hear so that she could continue to support Mona, because this was the time when Mona needed support the most.

You are so selfish. Mona's eyes welled up in frustration over the situation. *Just like Mom.* She didn't want to lie to Lexa anymore. She also didn't want to tell the truth. So in the end, she didn't reply at all, hoping with everything she had that Lexa would assume she was busy and unable to use her phone, while also knowing that she wouldn't.

CHAPTER 10

"I don't feel good," Rose said a few days later, the color drained from her like it had when she had started to fade before. Her skin was the same sickly grayish green color, her eyes surrounded with dark circles. "I think something might be wrong with me."

It was Saturday, and everybody was sitting around the table for breakfast, except for Mom, who had been upstairs since Friday morning. Mona was buzzed, but hiding it well.

"I swear she must have a food stash in her room or something," Anya commented when she came home from school to find Juliet cooking their dinner and pointing out the piles of folded clothing that had needed to be put away since the night before. "How else could she manage to stay up there for so long at a time?"

"What feels wrong?" Juliet asked Rose, putting her fork down and ignoring what was left of her pancakes and turkey bacon. It was the same thing she'd always asked

any of the sisters when they felt sick: *What feels wrong?*
By the look on Rose's face, everything.

"I don't know how to explain it," Rose said. She hadn't
taken a single bite of her breakfast, as usual. She hadn't
eaten anything since the soup days ago. "I'm...hungry."

All the girls stared at their sister, who had a full plate
of food in front of her, who'd been turning down full
plates of food for meals and meals. "What do you mean
you're hungry?" Taylor asked, gawking a little bit. "Eat
your pancakes!"

"I...can't," Rose managed, and her eyes welled up. "I
need to eat something heavier, I think. Nothing tastes
right or makes me feel full. There's a craving. I... I need
to fulfill it."

"How would you know that you can't eat the pancakes?" Juliet asked gently. "You haven't even tried a
single bite of it!"

"She hasn't eaten in days," Mona said softly, stating
what she thought was obvious before. "She hasn't eaten
since that stew."

Rose started crying, her groans dragging on as if they
were taking a phenomenal amount of energy. "I haven't
been eating what you've made for me, it's true. But,
but...I've tried eating...other things."

An awful silence descended upon the dining room.

"What other things?" Mona asked, wondering what
on earth the answer could be that would explain how
ashamed Rose looked right now. The other sisters waited
for her answer, the silence hanging in the air, heavy, lingering.

"A few days ago, I…" Rose covered her face with her hands so she didn't have to look at any of them. "I ate an entire package of hamburger meat."

There was a moment of silence.

"That's…okay, Rose," Juliet offered, reaching across the table to try and reach Rose's hand, but it was too far away. "You may just be lacking iron or something, it might be normal for your, uh, condition."

None of it is normal, Mona thought. *Absolutely none of it.*

Anya's eyes narrowed as she looked at her little sister, who was crying even harder now. "Rose, why are you so upset?" she asked. "The hamburger… You…you cooked it first, right?"

It was obvious by the look on Juliet's and Taylor's faces that neither of them had thought to consider the possibility, but Mona must have picked up the same vibes that Anya did, because she had been wondering the exact same thing. What was left of Rose's composure crumbled.

"I ate it raw," she wailed, full-on bawling now, the inky veins on her neck and chest darkening and thickening in reaction to her body's outburst. Taylor lifted a trembling hand to cover her mouth, but Juliet slapped it back down. Rose continued, her words cut apart by sobs. "And then the next d-day, I ate a package of steaks from the fuh-fuh-freezer downstairs."

Mona thought about Rose's seventh birthday party, when she begged and begged for Mom to take them to a steakhouse, because the last time their dad had been in town he'd gone on and on about how much he missed steak and how it was always the thing he missed most when he was in a tent in the middle of the desert somewhere overseas. When he left, Rose took it harder than usual, begging him to stay, promising him she'd get him steak every day if he did.

But soon he was gone, and Rose spontaneously cried over it for the next week at least. When her birthday rolled around, she started in on Mom, begging her to take them out to a steakhouse for her special day. Fourteen-year-old Juliet had helped convince her, and soon they were all sitting in a massive maroon booth that went up a good three feet above their heads, the elaborately carved wooden frames shining dimly in the dimly-lit restaurant. The waitresses wore cowboy boots and button-up shirts with pearl snaps.

Juliet helped Rose choose which steak she wanted, in the end, a sirloin, since that was cheaper than the other ones. When the waitress had asked Rose how she wanted it cooked, she'd piped up, "medium rare," since that was how Dad and Juliet ordered theirs. When her plate came, Rose's eyes darkened at the sight of the thin red juice pooled around the meat, soaking into her rice pilaf and side of broccoli.

And when Juliet cut it up for her, revealing the bright red muscle, still bleeding, beneath the charred exterior, Rose screamed.

"Why is there blood?" she'd wailed, causing all the other people in the restaurant, men in business suits and couples on first and last dates and other families with far less

than five kids, to crane their necks and lean over from nearby tables to see what was causing all the commotion.

From that point on, Mona remembered, her head light with fear, Rose always ate her meat as well done as it could get.

She ate it raw.

"When did you do this?" Juliet demanded now, and Mona could see the panic lighting up in her eyes at the sudden and swift loss of control. "I was with you all day, we did your homeschooling together, we watched television…" She trailed off, as if remembering something. "You did it when I went to the grocery store. You told me you were going to take a nap."

"I left them out to thaw the same day I ate the hamburger meat," Rose cried. "After you left, I went down there and I ate it in the dark, ate it all like some sort of animal. I couldn't help it but I still can't get this hunger to go away…"

She curled her hands into tight fists and slammed them on the table, causing the plate of pancakes to shudder noisily. "If I can't find something to eat I don't know what I'll do, I'm going to freak out, I can't think of anything else and I feel like if I don't get it soon *something very bad will happen…*"

"What in the hell is all this noise?" Mom's voice demanded suddenly, booming from somewhere up the stairs. "Why do I hear crying?"

At the sound of her mother's voice, Mona slipped into a weird sort of disconnected daze. She was certain it was because of the rum she had taken a few hefty swigs of during her morning shower, warm and buttery on her lips but angry and burning in her stomach. She'd had a feeling she'd need it to get through the weekend, and apparently she was right.

"Something's wrong with Rose," Juliet managed to yell back, her voice ragged. "Why don't you come down here and tell us why she's binge-eating raw meat in order to keep from ripping her own hair out?"

Rose wept into her hands, and Mona forced herself to get up to walk around the table and put her arms around her sister, just like she did that night at the steakhouse after everyone else had just sat around and gawked. "It's alright, Rose, don't worry now, we're going to figure this out…"

"Stay away!" Rose shrieked at the physical contact, flailing her arms to keep Mona at a distance. "Don't get close to me! I don't want to hurt you!"

Mona stood back, terrified. The rage in Rose's eyes was real, tortured, unnatural. She was shaking from head to toe, the whites of her eyes streaked with angry threads of red.

"No," Mom said from where she stood in the living room, her brows knit together in worry, her hands wringing over themselves. "This isn't supposed to happen."

"What do you *mean*?" Juliet finally stood from the table, snapped out of her motionless shock, her cheeks red. Taylor and Anya got up and moved slowly away from Rose, and Mona followed them. Rose hit her fists on the table again and stared at them all, panting, like she was fighting to restrain herself.

"She was supposed to get better after that first dose," Mom said, walking straight for the door leading to the basement.

"Dose of what?" Rose demanded, shivering so hard now that it was causing her teeth to chatter. "Dose of what, Mom?"

"Of your medicine, honey." Mom's voice was gentle and calm, but her eyes shined in bewilderment. "I think I might have some more. Go on up to your room and get into bed now, please. I'm going to make you some soup and mix the medicine in so you…"

"I don't want soup!" Rose screamed, the sound like a solder iron on Mona's nerves, searing. She was crying again, wrapping her arms around herself, rocking back and forth.

"Listen to me, Rose," Mom said, her tone much sharper than before. "Unless you want to see what happens without the medicine."

Rose got up and stormed out, whimpering as she went barefoot through the living room to the stairs. Once she was out of sight, Juliet turned back to Mom, fire in her eyes.

"How could you talk to her like that?" she demanded, but Mom was already on her way down the basement steps into the dark below. "Something is wrong with her, she needs help."

"Then get down here and help me," Mom bellowed, and the girls followed Juliet down the steps. The single bulb that hung from the ceiling shone bright, still swinging from when Mom turned it on. Mona frowned as she watched her mother throw open the door of the freezer and rummage around inside.

"What medicine were you talking about?" Anya said. "You snuck it into that stew you made her before, didn't you? I knew something was weird about that whole thing!"

"You all saw her eat it," Mom mumbled under her breath, digging through the packages of frozen meat, trying to get to the very back corner. Mona wondered what Mom had hidden, and why she felt like she needed to hide it. "You saw how great she felt afterward. That was supposed to be it."

"What do you mean, that was supposed to be it?"

Mom finally stopped digging and removed a small paper-wrapped package of meat—the same type of paper, Mona noticed, that Rose's special stew meat was wrapped in days ago.

"Harlow told me that Rose would only need to eat this once in order to feel permanently better," Mom said, holding the paper package up like it was an unearthed artifact from a tomb. "But she didn't really specify how much a serving really is. Maybe I just didn't give Rose enough of it. Maybe she needed to eat it all."

"What *is* that?" Juliet asked, and suddenly Mona felt a little sick, like they shouldn't be down there, close to where Rose died.

She imagined Rose crouching down here in the dark, whimpering and chewing her way through a family pack of steaks, or handful after handful of gummy pink hamburger meat, and her spine felt tingly beneath her skin and muscle. She knew it was too good to be true—the idea of Rose coming back without any catches or setbacks. *Something is very wrong.*

It smelled weird down there, she also realized. It smelled rotten and metallic and gross. Mona wondered if Rose accidentally left some raw steak out when she was down here before.

"It's special meat," Mom mumbled, already rising to go back upstairs. "And it wasn't easy to get."

"So how do you know that it'll work this time?" Juliet demanded, following Mom back up to the kitchen, the rest of the sisters trailing behind. Mona was happy that Juliet asked. This was madness.

"I don't," Mom said. "That's why as soon as I'm done making this for Rose, I'm going to go back to Danwin Cove to figure out what went wrong."

Mona's first reaction to this was good; let Mom go and find out what's wrong, let her figure out how to fix it. But Juliet couldn't have been more pissed.

"You're seriously going to leave again?" she said, stomping her way up the old wooden steps. "Just leave it to me to handle everything? Why am I even surprised?"

In the kitchen, Mom got out the same pot she had used before, set it on the stove, and fired up the burner. "I don't suppose you want to go find Harlow, then?" She dumped the microwave-thawed meat into the soup pot and it started sizzling and crackling in the oil right away.

"I'm sorry that you're so *inconvenienced* by the small details of your sister coming back to life!"

It was beyond unfair to say, Mona knew, especially
taking into consideration how very much Juliet had done
for Rose for her entire life. Juliet seethed in the corner
as Mom quickly threw the stew together.

Twenty minutes later, it was finished. The stew was
so hastily made, Mona couldn't understand how anyone
would think it looked appetizing. Mom poured it all out
into a big mixing bowl, set it on a tray with a spoon, and
told Juliet to bring it to Rose while she got together a
quick overnight bag for Danwin Cove. Juliet did as she
was told, quietly, which unsettled Mona; it meant the
gears in her mind were turning something over, which
could either be a good thing or a very bad thing.

Upstairs, Rose was sitting up in bed, the empty mixing bowl perched on her lap. She was chewing with her
eyes closed, her mouth lifted into the slightest grin, like
it was the greatest thing she'd ever tasted.

The other sisters sat in Rose's room while she ate,
comforting her and watching in sick fascination as she
went at the stew like Oliver Twist, Mona crept back out
into the hallway and put her ear at their mother's door,
listening to the sounds of zippers and drawers opening
and closing, and, of course, the sound of pill bottles rat-
tling, the sound of liquid being poured into a flask.

I am nothing like her, Mona told herself, remembering
the rum in the shower that morning. *I am everything like
her.* It wasn't fair. In school during drug awareness week,
it was repeated time and time again how addiction ran in

families, how important it was to keep an eye on your-self if you knew of family members who struggled, how important it was to "break the cycle," as if breaking the cycle was something that was easy, when really it was more like throwing a stick into your own bicycle spokes and falling face-first onto the pavement.

When she heard her mother coming for the door, she rushed back to her bedroom, which caused Anya to raise an eyebrow from where she sat on her bed, her arms wrapped around her, her mouth pulled into an ex-hausted frown.

"Better," Rose rasped, breathing heavily from eating so fast. She stuck her dirty fingers into the bowl, wiping every last bit of gravy from it, sucking at them frantically. She made a sad little noise when there weren't any mor-sels left, and in one quick motion that made everyone jump, flung the empty bowl across the room, where it hit the wall noisily and fell down on a discarded sweatshirt.

"Well," she said, turning to her sisters as if nothing had ever happened, working her tongue against her cheek in a way that told Mona she must have been scouring for leftover strings of meat stuck in her teeth. "What are we going to do today, guys?"

CHAPTER 11

Once Mom was gone, Juliet turned toward the other girls where they stood gathered around the front door. Rose was upstairs, taking a shower to get ready for whatever plans they would come up with for the day. Mona remembered how strangely giddy Rose was acting after eating that stew, just like the first time. It almost reminded her of when Anya accidentally smoked too much weed and got super high. What was so special about that meat?

"I'm done with all the bullshit," Juliet said, making her way across the entryway and then the kitchen. "How can we know if anything Mom was on about is even true?"

"That's really weird about the meat," Taylor said softly, crossing her arms as if cold. "I don't get why she won't eat anything else. What was it? Why was Mom acting so strangely?"

"And we're just expected to sit around and *wait* for her?" Juliet was pacing at this point. "This is ludicrous, you all saw how Rose freaked out this morning. It was like she was being tortured! She was terrified. It's so fucked up. We can't let it happen again."

She stopped pacing then, looking over to the basement door. "We should see if there's any more of that meat left. We can keep it in the freezer up here, just in case, you know."

Mona didn't want to go down those basement steps. It always felt so wrong down there, with all the dark and creaking stairs. "But, if what Mom said is true, we won't have to wait that long," she said, remembering how Rose went days without eating before getting to the point where she was that morning. "She'll be back before Rose gets that hungry again."

Juliet looked at Mona, exasperated. "Mona," she said in an awfully condescending tone. "When are you going to learn not to listen to a goddamn word that Mom says?"

Mona's cheeks felt warm. Taylor rolled her eyes in agreement with Juliet, and Anya stared at her shoes. "Whatever," Mona mumbled. "Let's go down there, then."

They went in a single file line, coincidentally by age: Juliet, then Taylor, then Anya, with Mona in the back. Mona was about halfway down the dark staircase when Juliet turned on the dim, dust-covered light bulb at the bottom. The garage was a little more open without Mom's car in there, but the faint smell of spoiled meat was still lingering. Juliet opened the freezer while Taylor looked on with a look of disgust.

"I think Rose left some meat out," Mona offered, looking around for any sign of discarded meat but seeing none. She wondered if she'd ever be able to look at ground beef or steak again without feeling sick. "We need to find it and throw it away, get rid of this smell."

"Ugh," Anya groaned while she held her nose. "What the fuck, why is it so strong?"

"Help me over here, Taylor, Jesus Christ!" Juliet said in frustration, her arms full of frozen packs of chicken and pork chops and roast. "I need to look in the very back, where Mom hid that stuff last time."

Mona wished Juliet would hurry up. She wanted to get out of here as quickly as possible. It was terribly unnerving, with the dull echo of the garage and the dark orange light that made it feel like you were looking through a sepia lens. Plus, she didn't want Rose to come down from her shower, all high and happy only to find them downstairs looking for meat in the freezer.

Anya walked to the opposite side of the basement, where a decked-out tool cabinet stood high, loaded with barely-used tools that Dad had only had the chance to hold a few times. "What the hell?" she said in a low voice, and Mona turned her head to see what the fuss was about. There, in Anya's hand, was a long, curved blade, its serrated edge reflecting the weak light.

The blade was streaked with blood.

"I think this is a breaking knife," Anya said, looking to Mona with wide eyes. "You use it to break down large cuts of meat. When I worked at that grocery store in Dalton, the butcher used to wave his around after hours to freak out the bakery employees."

Mona remembered how raggedly cut the chunks of

meat Mom had used in the stew looked. Had she killed and cleaned an animal herself? Was that a part of the ritual or something?

"Ugh, I can't find shit back here," Juliet said behind them, still wrestling with the contents of the freezer. "She better not have used it all." Neither she nor Taylor had seen the knife yet. Mona was about to call them over when Anya made a soft gasping sound behind her.

"What...the...*fuck*," Anya emphasized under her breath. When Mona looked back, Anya had set the knife back down in the tool cabinet, and was now busy looking at something else inside of it. Mona stepped forward, unable to handle the anticipation, and when she saw what Anya was gawking at, her hand flew over her mouth.

"Oh, my god."

There, nestled amongst the screwdrivers, was an unfamiliar wallet, black with green sequins. An ID card was rubber banded to the top of it. The girl in the picture was unfamiliar, with blond hair and a perky smile. There was more blood smeared across the part that had her information, but you could still see her name: *Jamie Nicole Riley.*

"Guys," Anya said, loud enough for Juliet and Taylor to hear. "Come here."

"Wait a goddamn minute," Juliet snapped, angrily trying to shove everything back in the freezer one by one while Taylor fought to keep everything balanced in her arms. "Thanks for helping, by the way. You've officially proven yourselves to be completely fucking worthless. Why did you even come down here if all you were gonna do is—"

"Juliet," Anya interrupted her. "Forget what you're doing and get your ass over here, now. You need to see this."

At the touch of panic in Anya's tone, Juliet's head perked up, like a dog who'd heard someone say his name. "Put the rest of those in the freezer," she commanded Taylor, who looked nervously over her shoulder at Anya and Mona before complying. Juliet came over to the tool cabinet, saw the knife and the wallet and the ID, and froze.

"No," she said, still staring at the picture of Jamie Nicole Riley, the ID card spotted with drops and smears of blood. "No."

"What is it?" Taylor asked, shoving everything back in the freezer in a single pile and forcing the door closed. She ran over to join her sisters and gasped at the sight of the ID card.

Juliet pawed aggressively through the rest of the tool cabinet, opening and emptying every drawer and tray, spilling them loudly over the cement. *Rose is going to come down any second*, Mona thought wildly, her heart beating a million times per minute.

"There's nothing else in here." Juliet immediately started checking the wooden shelves high on the wall, the area around the freezer, the pantry above the washer and dryer. Finally she went over to the side of the staircase and pulled back the blue camping tarp that hung down like a curtain, hiding the space beneath the stairs.

The smell got stronger than it had been a moment before. In the center of the floor, in the space beneath the stairs, there was a big grated drain, rusty but rinsed clean. Pushed into the corner was a large purple storage container made of heavy plastic, latched shut. Juliet pinned the tarp up, bent down so as to not hit her head, and made her way to the container. With a grunting effort, she pulled it out into the open, sliding it noisily across the concrete, and all of the sisters stared down at it in silence.

"Open it," Juliet said to Taylor, who was physically shivering. "Open it."

"No!" Taylor cried out, her eyebrows low. "I can't, please, you do it."

Without warning, Juliet turned and slapped Taylor, hard, straight across the face. Mona and Anya jumped. Mona's head felt light with fear. She recognized the look on Juliet's face and it wasn't good. She was definitely in her dark place. Taylor was lucky that it was just a slap, and not a punch, or a row of five bleeding scratches. Was it seeing the ID that did it? Mona realized now how Juliet's anger often came out when she was stressed—or scared.

Taylor let out an initial squeal from being slapped, but quieted quickly. Her hands trembled as she unlatched the sides of the storage container. She lifted the lid, and the awful smell was overpowering.

"Oh, my god," Anya cried out, her arm over her nose and mouth. "Oh, my fucking god."

Inside the box was a large, black trash bag, tied shut.

"Open the bag," Juliet said, her voice low, steady. Her

nostrils flared, and her lip curled up in disgust. "Taylor, open the bag!"

Taylor let out a pained moan as she fumbled with the tie on the bag. Suddenly it was open, and the thing at the top of the bag was visible: a tangle of flesh and bone and fat, a severed hand with bright pink nail polish. And, on top of it all, a decapitated head, the blond hair matted with blood, stuck to the head, tangled and snarled. The hair covered the eyes, but the mouth was open, the skin on the face a ghastly dark gray. The teeth were covered in red.

Mom had murdered this girl.

Mom used the breaking knife to cut her into stew meat.

And then she fed it to Rose.

Taylor screamed, and Anya made a horrible wailing sound. Mona stood, shocked silent, paralyzed. Juliet knelt down and retied the bag as quickly as she could, her fingers getting caught in the bright yellow binding, and replaced the top of the storage container. Then she shoved it back under the stairs, breathing so hard Mona wondered if she'd pass out, and unpinned the blue tarp from the side of the stairs. The space beneath the staircase was hidden again; the storage box was out of sight.

But the smell lingered. The terror lingered. Taylor looked down at her hands in panic, a nasty chunk of bloodied blond hair webbed between her fingers, then sprinted to the sink beside the washer and dryer and began frantically scrubbing at them with steel wool and dish soap.

"She…" Juliet managed, bending over while she breathed, on the verge of hyperventilation. "She murdered someone… She cut them up."

"And then she fed her to Rose!" Anya whispered. "The meat was a fucking *person*."

In the midst of the chaos, Mona had a horrible revelation, a memory of something awful.

"I ate it," she said to nobody in particular, struggling to keep her knees strong. "I took a bite."

The last thing she saw before she passed out was Anya, who looked over in time to see her fall, but not in time to do anything about it.

When Mona woke up, she was breathing heavily, lying on her back on the kitchen floor. Her sisters were surrounding her, and Anya had a cold rag resting on her forehead. "How did you get me up here?" she asked groggily, and then she remembered what had just happened.

They'd discovered a dismembered body in the basement. Their mother was a murderer. And Rose…

Rose was a cannibal.

CHAPTER 12

The girls drifted around the house like lost souls. Mona couldn't get the image of the dismembered body in the trash bag out of her head. She thought back to the morning where she'd come downstairs to find Mom cooking the stew for the first time. How tired she'd looked. How dirty and disheveled. She'd probably spent the whole night *murdering someone*.

And not just murdering the girl, *Jamie Nicole Riley*, her name forever burned in Mona's mind. She had murdered her and then hacked her into chunks and bits and smears. She had stuffed her into black plastic, then into a storage container meant for things like Christmas decorations and old baby clothes and out-of-season jackets. She had shoved her into a corner, left her in the dark. How long had Mom planned on keeping her there? Did she think nobody would notice?

It was not like they could call the cops. Not so much because they cared about what might happen to Mom, but because of what might happen to Rose. How would the law handle a situation like hers? Where would they take her? Would they believe them about Rose needing human meat? Mona gulped at the thought. She didn't want to consider what would happen if Rose was in custody and got too hungry.

Mona thought back to a time a few years prior, when Juliet and Taylor were still kids, and Mom was swept away by an especially powerful wave of depression. Anya had pulled Mona into the closet with her, filled with the books and candy and pillow their current closet had, but without the weed smell.

"We have to ask someone for help," Anya had whispered to Mona after the closet door was shut and the only light was the little clip-on reading lamp that was clamped to a nail in the wall. "Did you see how mad Juliet got when she was yelling at Taylor in the kitchen earlier? She was waving a goddamn knife around, Mona!"

"I know," Mona had said, frowning at the memory. "That was so scary. She's always doing stuff like that. Like when she gave you that black eye with the hairbrush."

Anya took a deep breath, raised her hand tenderly to her face even though the black eye was long gone. "Exactly," she said. "When she gets mad enough, there's no telling what she can do. That isn't okay at all. We have to get someone to talk to her, tell her not to do that. Scare her into never doing it again."

The girls whispered and whispered until Juliet found them maybe thirty minutes later, but that was okay, because they had a plan. Mona and Anya had a PE teacher at school that they both loved, who taught them both at different hours, who was young and hip and made all the girls desperately wish they could be as cool as her, or at least be her best friend.

"She'll help us out," Anya had whispered to Mona as they made their way down the stairs. "I know she will."

At the time, Mona thought it was the best plan. The idea of not having to be afraid of Juliet anymore sent an electrical thrill up her spine, the possibility of an apology and a change of behavior too good to be true.

In the end, it was too good to be true. Because despite the intentions they had, the cool PE teacher didn't grin and reveal that she knew exactly what to say to Juliet to get her ass in line. Instead, the teacher sat with her arms crossed over her chest, her expression becoming gradually more grim as the girls tried to explain their request.

Long story short, the law got involved, and fast. Mona would never forget the sound of the knock on the door early in the morning, when they lived in a five-bedroom house that was all on one level. The only ones who'd had to share a room had been her and little Rose, and she didn't mind at all.

Mom had answered the door only to find a police officer and a woman in a maroon pantsuit, her perfume overwhelming, a file folder tucked in her arms.

The questions being asked were freaky. Of course, all the sisters had hid just out of view to eavesdrop, Anya and Mona exchanging horrified glances as they came to realize what they'd done. When the woman in the pantsuit brought up Juliet's name, the oldest sister stiffened from where she was crouched beside Mona.

Suddenly, Mona's mind had flooded in panic at all the potential consequences that could come from their mistake. If physical abuse was suspected and proven, they could be taken away from Mom, put into foster care, separated. What would Dad say when he heard? Just then, Mom raised her voice to call for Juliet, who the case manager wanted to question.

"What is happening?" Taylor whispered to Juliet, tugging at her shirt as if to make her stay. "Jules, what are they going to do?"

"I don't know," Juliet whispered back, the most vulnerable Mona had ever seen her. The look on her older sister's face, scared and hurt and unsure, drove a knife right through Mona's heart. Juliet had broken away from Taylor's grip and entered the living room, her chin high, her demeanor calm as a cucumber, and Mona burst out from where she hid. Everyone looked to her in surprise.

"It was us," she cried, her voice heavy with emotion. "Anya and I are the ones that reported Juliet, but it was just a prank, we didn't know this would happen. We lied! I promise that we lied. Please don't let Juliet get into trouble!"

Next came a solo interview with both Mona and Anya. Mona repeated her new version of what happened, Anya begrudgingly backed it up. After a whole lot of scolding about how domestic violence is never a joke, the woman in the maroon pantsuit left.

At first, Mona had been filled with pure, utter relief—it'd been undone. Nobody would be taking them away and separating them. But when she turned around to face her family, the looks she was getting from every single person made her feel like the family had been ruined anyway, more than it had been before. The face that made her stomach drop the most was Juliet's. It wasn't a look of sadness or betrayal. It was a look of anger, it was a look seeking revenge.

And revenge was had. Sometimes Mona wondered if Juliet was still punishing her, with every little passive-aggressive or aggressive-aggressive remark and action that she peppered through the days, tiny abuses that built up in Mona's heart like plaque. Pinches, insults, spontaneous kicks to the ankle that Juliet thought were hilarious.

She and Anya had never spoken of what they did to each other after that, not again, and only once in a while did Mona let herself remember. It was the beginning of the end for her and Anya, she could see that now, and guilt still bloomed in her stomach whenever she thought about it. Regardless, Mona believed that the lesson of the situation had been made perfectly clear, and it was a lesson she fully intended on applying to this current situation with Rose and the dismembered body of Jamie Nicole Riley:

No outside help.

Now, with all of her sisters out of sight and the house as eerily empty as it was the morning Rose had come back from the dead, Mona continued to wander around. She passed the mudroom, where she could see through the glass of the back door that Juliet and Taylor were sitting side-by-side in the lawn chairs outside. Mona couldn't see their mouths to know if they were talking or not, but she imagined they were. Juliet's foot was tapping ferociously against the edge of the chair, while Taylor picked her armrest with anxious fingers.

Mona walked around the downstairs area a few more times before realizing that she was looking for Anya. She wanted more than anything to know how her sister was really feeling about everything, what she thought they should do, what she thought would become of Mom and Rose. Even if she didn't want to talk, the idea of sharing silence with her was slightly more comforting than being alone with her thoughts.

Anya must have been upstairs. Mona made her way up the steps, chilled at the darkness of the enclosed curved stairway, pushing the visions of the hands below out of her mind. Upstairs, the bathroom door was still shut. Excessive amounts of steam billowed from the crack at the bottom of the door, and there came the sound of feet frantically shuffling around on the other side. Had Rose really not come out since she got in the shower?

There was no way, Mona knew. Rose had gotten in before they'd all gone down into the basement. Discovering the body felt like something that had taken place days ago. While it hadn't really been days since it happened, it'd been too long for Rose to be showering the whole time, at least, not if she was feeling normal.

Again came the shuffling sound from inside the steaming bathroom, so frantic it was almost like a fleshy scuttle. "Rose?" Mona called gently from right in front of the door. The sound promptly stopped. Rose did not respond.

Fighting the urge to tremble, Mona slowly rested her ear against the door and listened.

She could hear Rose, standing directly on the other side of the door. She may have even had her ear up to the door, just like Mona did, because Mona could hear the heavy sigh of her breathing. In the background, Mona could hear something else—a wet, smacking sound. Mona realized what she was hearing, and her hand flew to her mouth.

Rose was licking her lips in a frighteningly intense manner, or at least, that's what it sounded like. The image that immediately sprang up in her mind caused Mona's heart to skip a beat, and she quickly backed away from the door. What in the hell was happening to her little sister?

"Be out soon," Rose said gently from the other side. "Soon, soon, soon."

That was it. Mona had to find Anya, now.

"Take your time," Mona responded, her voice pitiful and cracking. "I just wanted to check on you!"

"Thank you, sister," Rose said. She never referred to Mona as "sister." "Love you."

Mona stepped away from the door, pausing for just a second to see if the shuffling sound she'd originally heard would start back up again, but it didn't. Mona heard the sound of Anya's voice coming from their bedroom, also behind a closed door. She reached for the doorknob, desperate to reunite with her sister in order to survive this stress, but stopped when she realized what Anya was saying.

"No, no," she begged, her voice painfully twisted. "Please, Ev, you've got to trust me. There is a good reason why I can't tell you everything that's been going on with me."

Uh-oh. It sounded like Everly and Anya were in a fight. Mona's heart pained at how much she related to her sister's panicked tone. She felt the same way about the secrets she'd been keeping from Lexa.

"No," Anya urged from the other side. "I do trust you! Don't say that, you don't mean it. Come on, Everly, I'm begging you. *I'm begging you!* You can't leave me over this! I'm doing this *to protect you!*"

Anya had started crying by then. There came a pause, and at first Mona assumed Everly was saying something back, hopefully something good. But then Anya said, "Hello? Hello? Goddamn it!"

There came a sharp, startling sound—the sound of Anya's phone being thrown across the room. Mona heard the battery separate and slide across the hardwood floor. Mona's stomach hurt at the knowledge that Everly had just broken up with Anya. Funny, she'd always imagined that a moment like this would feel amazing.

Before she realized what was happening, Anya opened the bedroom door, still crying, only to see Mona there, apparently spying. Mona put her hands up in defense. "Wait, I'm sorry, I only just came up here to—"

"Leave me the fuck alone," Anya spat, bounding past Mona to head toward their mother's room, presumably to lock herself in the bathroom since the one she usually used was still occupied by Rose.

Mona went back to their bedroom and stepped inside, keeping the door open so that Anya might be encouraged to come back. She sat on her bed, wishing that her rum wasn't stashed in the bathroom, wondering if she would ever talk to Lexa again. Ever since she had decided not to reply to Lexa's text, there had been nothing but cold, hard, silence. Mona suspected that her friend had dropped her, just as Everly had dropped Anya. She crept into the closet, stepping on her tiptoes as if afraid to wake a sleeping baby, and stole a quick hit off of Anya's starglass pipe.

One toke was enough to make her feel different. It didn't make the pain go away, but it sure helped her care less about it. She went over to her bed, plopped down on it, closed her eyes, and waited for the sound of Anya leaving their mother's bathroom. She remembered for a fleeting moment that Juliet and Taylor were still outside... What could they have been talking about for this long?

Before she could consider it further, there came a different sound than the one she'd been listening for—the sound of the *other* bathroom door opening, and slow, almost hesitant steps approaching. When Mona opened her eyes, Rose was standing over her, her hair damp, a mischievous grin causing her mouth to form a funny little curl.

"What's wrong?" she asked.

CHAPTER 13

"So what should we do today?" Rose asked brightly after Mona didn't answer. It was like she had forgotten all about the trauma of the morning, like everything was fine now that she was feeling better, but all Mona could think about was how she'd need to eat again eventually, and again, and again. She never prayed, but now she pleaded with the universe, *Please let Mom figure this out before Rose gets hungry again. Please let there be a way to stop all of this.*

Taylor appeared, her eyes darting around the room as if looking for something. Her eyes were red.

"Should we go downtown?" Rose continued, dragging a comb through her hair. "What do you think, Taylor? Maybe to a movie, or to the science museum, or oooh, how about the zoo!"

It really seemed as though nothing was wrong. Mona remembered the unsettling incident of putting her ear up to the door of the bathroom only minutes ago and got the chills.

"I don't know, Rose," Taylor said hesitantly. "Maybe we should just stay home today." Mona noticed that Taylor wouldn't actually enter the room, like she was afraid to be near Rose. The knowledge that their little sister had turned into some sort of flesh-eater did put a terrible damper on things, even more so than knowing that she'd been raised from the dead.

Still, it wasn't Rose's fault that all of this had happened to her. Seeing her struggle had been so awful. She didn't deserve this.

"Why can't we go out?" Rose stood up and stretched, her bruising vivid and bright, and Taylor actually flinched. Mona caught her eye and mouthed: *Chill out.* Taylor rolled her eyes but looked a little ashamed. "I feel totally better, you guys. Like a million bucks!"

I miss you like this, Mona wanted to say, but held her tongue. *Please don't go strange on me again. Stay with us this time. Stay like this.*

"Let's just wait and see what Juliet says." Taylor went through the shared bathroom to her own room. "I'm gonna get dressed."

Then she closed the door, a little harder than necessary.

Mona looked up at Rose and offered a big, fake-ass smile. "I'm so glad you're feeling better," she said, and she meant it.

"Are you okay?" Rose asked, biting at her lip. "You're acting a little strange. Everyone is, actually. Is it… Is it because I was dead?"

Such a heartbreaking question, Mona knew, because the hard truth was yes, it was because she was dead, but even more so that she'd just eaten a person to keep from losing her shit and had no idea about it.

"Of course not," Mona said with a more serene smile, made a little easier thanks to the buzz she still had going from the weed, although there was an angry, pulsating knot on the back of her head from when she fainted. "We're all fine, it was just a little stressful seeing you so upset down there, when you were hungry."

"Upset?" Rose tilted her head a little, studying Mona's face. "What do you mean I got upset?"

Mona didn't answer at first. The genuine curiosity in her little sister's voice was enough to make her blood run cold.

"Downstairs," Mona said, calmly. "Before Mom made you that stew. When you said you were afraid of hurting us and hit your fists on the table?"

Rose looked at Mona differently now, no more curiosity, but something else, something like disappointment. "Did you drink alcohol this morning?" she asked. "Is that why you're making stuff up?"

"What?" Mona felt like she's been slapped in the face. "What, no, Rose, what are you talking about? Don't you remember—?"

"I've seen you do it before," Rose interrupted, her nose crinkling. "In the bathroom. Don't worry, I haven't told Mom or Juliet or anybody, but I think you should probably try and stop, or you're going to end up just like Mom, with all of her made-up stories and stuff..."

Just like Mom. From Rose's lips. It was devastating.

"Stop," Mona managed, feeling disgusting and fiery

inside. "You did the things I just described. I didn't make it up. Don't you remember freaking out about how hungry you were?"

"I remember feeling hungry when I woke up," Rose said, in a weird little voice that revealed she still thought that Mona was lying. "I went downstairs and breakfast didn't look very good." She trailed off, staring into space, and Mona thought, *Yes! Remember!*

"And then I think maybe I got a little tired," Rose continued. "Felt a little sick. Maybe I fell asleep at the table? Then Mom told me to wait in bed while she made me the stew with the medicine in it." She looked at Mona. "I can smell it on you, by the way. The alcohol. I can smell it on you now."

Mona's eyes were wide, her mouth open just the slightest, her mind in a frenzy. Rose frowned at the sight, and then came forward to wrap her arms around Mona as if some sort of switch had been flipped inside of her.

"Please don't be mad at me," Rose begged, practically clawing at Mona's shoulders. "I don't want to make you mad at me right now, I need you, I need all of you."

"It's okay," Mona said in a hurry, not wanting Rose to get too worked up, not wanting her to expend any more energy than necessary until Mom got back. "It's okay, shhh, I'm here, we're all here for you."

"I just feel so strange all the time," Rose cried, her grip only tightening as she buried her face into Mona's neck. It took every ounce of energy she had not to flinch away, knowing Rose's mouth was mere inches from her jugular vein, but what a silly thing to fear, what a stupid thing to think about. Rose would never bite her, at least, not when she'd just eaten.

"I'm afraid to be dead again," Rose went on, letting out a little whimper. "Please, I can't go back to that place, it was dark and gravity didn't work the same way. It's like you're always falling."

Mona's mind raced to come up with something comforting to say but failed.

"Please don't be mad at me, Mona," Rose whispered. "I love you."

"I love you, too," Mona whispered, closing her eyes and remembering Rose's outburst this morning, how wild her eyes were, how desperate she seemed for everyone to stay away from her, like she might hurt them. And she didn't even remember it.

If that's what happened when Rose got that hungry, if her brain let go of everything to protect itself from trauma or something, what did that mean about the person she became during that time? This tiny little girl who felt as fragile as a bird, with her arms wrapped around Mona like her life depended on it. What would she do if she got hungry but there weren't any dead people around to carve up and cook into a stew? What would Rose do then?

One of two things would happen, Mona thought. *She'd either die again, or she'd do whatever it took to get the food she needed.*

Struggling to keep her composure, Mona suggested they go downstairs and see what everyone else was doing, what Juliet thought about going to the zoo this afternoon. Rose beamed and hopped up with such energy, such liveliness, it almost seemed chemically induced. Mona let Rose go down the stairs first, watched her hair float up as she descended with impressive speed. *One of two things would happen*, Mona tried to convince herself again, even though she was pretty sure that only one of those things would happen.

Which one, she wouldn't allow herself to admit.

The girls settled on the couches with Juliet, who was watching television. Rose talked to Juliet about the zoo until Taylor came downstairs and left them all waiting for Anya. While they were waiting, Mona seriously considered texting Lexa, but what would she say? Things had only escalated since the last time they talked, and Mona hadn't even been able to hold her shit together then. Everything was awful, everything felt nightmarish, knowing that hidden under the basement steps, sealed in a purple storage container, rested the gory remains of a corpse.

You lost Anya forever, her mind whispered cruelly. *And now Lexa, too.*

"Be right back," Mona mumbled, standing, and Juliet shot her a glance as if she weren't allowed to go off without permission. "Gotta pee."

But of course she didn't pee. She went straight to the bathroom, locked the door, and drank her rum, welcoming its warm and burning embrace like a demon dancing in the flames of hell.

CHAPTER 14

That night, after they'd returned from the zoo and were all in their beds, the house dark and dormant and still slightly fragrant of garlic from dinner—spaghetti again, although any meat dish had become considerably less appealing—Mona tried to picture a future for Rose, who'd refused to eat anything, claiming she was still too full from the stew.

She attempted to imagine an adult Rose, working a full-time job or going on dates at restaurants or lying out on the beach, but she only saw blackness. There were just too many things that made it seem unlikely, impossible, even.

Would the bruising ever go away? Would Rose have to cover it up on a daily basis forever, or would she try to make up a medical reason to excuse it? No, Mona knew. If there was anything Rose hated, it was when strangers stared at her for any reason. But maybe she'd get over that in lieu of having to spend thousands of dollars a year on makeup good enough to cover it up.

Or, worse, what if Mom found out while she was in Danwin Cove that the hunger was irreversible? What if Rose continued to have to eat people lest she'd become someone else, someone who was tortured and fighting her impulses until the point where she snapped? Would Rose really ever *murder* someone? Of all of them, she'd always had the purest soul, somehow untainted from the years of familial dysfunction. Hurting others was one of Rose's deepest fears, it was why she begged for forgiveness after bringing up Mona's drinking even though she shouldn't have been apologizing at all.

She'd be more likely to kill herself than someone else.

From the next bed over, Anya let out a long, disgruntled sigh in her sleep. It was hard to tell what had taken more of a toll on Anya in all of this: Rose dying, Everly breaking up with her, or finding out that Rose had come back from the dead as something not quite right. Mona wondered how any of them kept from completely losing their minds, most of all Juliet.

Mona hoped with what little energy she had left that Mom had already found answers, and would come back to them tomorrow with good news. Then, somehow, this would all be over. If it was possible to bring someone back from the dead, why couldn't it be possible to cure the ravenous hunger Rose was experiencing? Mom claimed that there was definitely a way. Mona clung to this desperately, wishfully, absolutely letting herself believe that it could be true.

She suppressed the urge to get up and drink the rest of the rum in order to stop thinking and be able to fall asleep. But Rose bringing up the drinking like that to her, so unexpectedly blunt, had spooked Mona away from the bottle for the time being. Maybe it would end up being a good thing instead of the awful heart-pounding anxiety it currently was in Mona's heart.

Maybe Rose would end up helping Mona to stop turning into Mom after all.

But by three in the morning, she still wasn't asleep, and Anya was snoring, and Mona had become wild with fear from overthinking everything. Suddenly she was wondering what would happen if she were to ever run away from home, just disappear forever like some kids did, only instead of turning up years later at the bottom of a canyon or a river or a shallow grave, she'd be living a different life, a better life, in a new town, under a new name.

But where could she go? She wouldn't be able to choose any of the towns she'd lived in previously, or else she'd be more likely to get caught. Maybe she could figure out a way to win Lexa over. Maybe she could move in with her, finally meet her face-to-face and they could be best friends and roommates, like the stars of their very own sitcom.

She fell asleep fantasizing about it, then felt dirty for the entire next day as a result. How could she ever consider leaving Rose and the rest of her sisters behind? In a perfect world, Juliet would be in New York at college, and Taylor would be out of the house as well, and Mom would be better and taking care of them, and she'd only have to hang on for four more years before she could pick any town she wanted and start living her life under her own goddamn name.

Maybe by some sort of magic, it would all fall into place by year's end. This was the thought Mona always ended her fantasies with, the idea that maybe if she just sat patiently and waited, everything would turn out okay.

But Mom still wasn't back from Danwin Cove by Sunday night.

On Monday morning, Juliet woke Anya, Rose and Mona up by entering their bedroom with Taylor at her heels and announcing that nobody would be going to school until Mom was back. Mom hadn't called once and her cell phone was turned off, but Juliet said it was possible she forgot her charger or hadn't had the chance to use it or that she just didn't want to. Either way, she would hopefully be back that day. In the meantime, Juliet explained, she'd already called the high school to excuse Taylor, Anya and Mona.

By Tuesday, Mom hadn't come back or even called. The girls went on a hike at Thumb Butte in the morning and ordered Chinese food to be delivered for lunch and a pizza to be delivered for dinner, both of Rose's favorites, but she wouldn't eat any of it, even when her sisters encouraged her and begged her, Juliet going as far as to hold a fork loaded with lo mein right in front of her face like she was an infant, all to no avail. Rose had exerted so much energy on the hike, a calculated move on Juliet's part, so how was she not starving?

Nobody mentioned the body. Nobody went into the basement.

The pit in Mona's stomach grew heavier, trembled, screamed to be submerged and soaked and dissolved in rum, but she held strong. She even felt a little sick for the drink, nauseous in her yearning, which scared her almost as much as the fact that Rose wasn't eating and seemed to be growing drastically more tired with every hour.

By the time the pizza arrived for dinner, Rose was laid out on the couch with her pillow and favorite fleece blanket, silently watching *The Virgin Suicides* on television. She cried at the part where Cecilia killed herself but was stone-faced by the end, devoid of all emotion, eager for it to all be over so she could go to bed, gray-faced and mumbling about a stomachache while her pillow and blanket dragged behind her.

On Wednesday, Mona woke up at the crack of dawn hoping a cup of hot chamomile peach tea would settle her stomach. Her sleep schedule had been thrown off by the lack of school and withdrawals from the booze she was trying to avoid. She noticed right away that Rose wasn't in her bed, likely watching TV downstairs, as she always did when she was sick. Mona shuffled through the still-dark hallway, past the other bedroom where Juliet and Taylor were fast asleep, then down the winding stairs and into the living room. Sure enough, Rose's pillow and blanket were set up on the end of her favorite couch, and the television was filling the room with glowing blue flashes of light.

But Rose wasn't there.

Assuming her sister was in the bathroom, Mona continued into the shadowy kitchen, already anticipating the steam from the tea filling her airways. Maybe she could even force herself to eat breakfast or something, like healthy people do. She trudged into the kitchen, rubbing the sleep from her eyes, and went to fill the kettle with water at the sink when she saw that the basement door was open about a foot. The kitchen may have been dark in the pre-sunrise morning, but the darkness that radiated from the narrow rectangle of the open door was so black that it seemed solid. Oh, god, no.

The body.

Her arms wrapped around herself, Mona stalked past the basement door to the hallway where the bathroom was, only to find that it was just as empty as the couch in the living room had been.

"Rose?" Mona called meekly into the vast darkness of the basement. The blackness was so thick she couldn't see further than the second step. She strained to listen and heard what sounded like a shuffling sound, so far below her it was like she was peering down into a pit.

What if she's hurt and needs help? Mona thought, her foot on the first step, then the second, then the third, but as she got closer to the bottom of the stairs and the light switch, her thoughts turned around to *What if she's found the dead girl and is feasting on her rotted remains right now?*

By the time Mona's bare foot settled on the ice-coldness of the cement floor, her heart was pounding so hard she could feel it in her ears. "Rose?" she managed, wondering why her sister wouldn't respond if she was down here in the dark.

She turned the light on, and saw. Saw why Rose

couldn't answer Mona when she called, saw why Rose wouldn't *want* to even if she could have. Squatting over the cement, with her nightshirt pulled up exposing thighs that were streaked with thin rivers of blood, Rose stared at Mona with eyes so wide her irises were entirely visible. In her hands were fistfuls of raw beef, her fingers squeezing it so hard it was dripping down her arms and elbows and on to her legs. It looked to Mona like a family-sized chuck roast, torn apart.

Mona let out a brief scream without helping it, biting down on her tongue in order to stop.

"Rose…" Mona's voice was so weak and full of cracks that she had to take a minute. She breathed a long, shaky breath, shook her head from side to side as if to rattle her fear loose. "Are you okay?"

It was the stupidest question she could've asked.

Rose whimpered in response, looking at the meat grasped between her fingers, and, with trembling hands, brought the meat up to her face and took a big, tearing bite.

"I was hungry," she cried as she chewed, looking back into Mona's eyes and holding her gaze, even as she took another bite. "This was the only thing that sounded good. I think it's good, I think it's helping me a little bit, just like before, and I like how it smells down here…"

Mona's stomach threatened to empty. From behind her came the sound of a loud creak in the wood, somewhere at the top of the steps. "Who screamed?" came Juliet's voice, and sure enough, there she was, standing in the doorway at the head of the basement stairs, her outline bedraggled and ominous.

"I did," Mona called back up, taking a step back. Juliet was here, thank god. She'd know what to do. The oldest Cane sister bounded down, skipping steps, stopping dead in her tracks when she got to the bottom and laid eyes on Rose.

"Oh, Rose," she said, like her heart had broken into a million little pieces.

"I'm sorry," Rose yelled, the half-chewed meat in her mouth falling out onto the floor. She began to weep again. "I'm so sorry, Jules, I was just hungry is all. This is the only thing that comes close to feeling okay, please..."

"Get upstairs," Juliet said coldly to Mona, then rushed forward and gathered Rose up in her arms, bloody meat and all. Mona felt ashamed that she hadn't done the same thing when she first saw Rose. Poor Rose. How pitiful and sick and unfair...

"I said get!" Juliet barked, her eyes shooting daggers at Mona, as if she'd done this to Rose and not Mom.

Mona ran back up the stairs and through the kitchen into the living room, nearly running face-first into Anya and Taylor, who were standing next to the couch where Rose's blanket and pillow were.

"What's happening down there?" Taylor asked, her voice shaky. Mona noticed that she was wearing a set of pajamas that belonged to Juliet. "We all heard a scream."

"That was me," Mona admitted. "I found Rose in the basement...eating meat again. Not the body. It was beef, like she said she ate before."

Mona had never told her sisters what she'd found out, about Rose's memory lapse when the hunger started getting out of control. She'd been hoping that it wouldn't come down to that again. She told herself every day that she was keeping the secret for Rose's sake, not because she was afraid Rose would mention her booze again if confronted.

"Oh, god," Anya breathed, looking like she needed to sit down. "No, not again, not already, Mom's not back yet…"

"What are we going to do about this?" Mona asked, and started pacing in circles around the living room, in front of the still-flashing television. "I don't know what's going to happen. I don't know what we'll do if Mom doesn't come back today…"

"Everybody shut the fuck up," snapped Juliet from the kitchen behind them. She was standing there holding a blood-smeared Rose against her, cradling the little girl's head against her chest, gently walking her through the living room and to the stairs.

"Family meeting in twenty minutes," Juliet said to the sisters as they passed. "I just need to get her showered and into bed."

After the shower, Juliet gave Rose a pill from their mother's stash that would make her sleep. Once she was completely passed out, her damp hair splayed over her pillow on the couch, everyone quietly followed Juliet upstairs to her and Taylor's room. After closing the door and waiting for everybody to sit down on the large circular woven rug between the two beds, Juliet stood over them all, strong as ever in her role as Replacement Mom.

"Clearly we have a very big problem here," she said, in the same voice she used when she would scold the girls about how the house was a mess. "And we don't have a lot of time to figure it out."

"Why won't Mom turn her cell phone on?" Anya said, pulling her knees to her chest. "I have an awful feeling. She said she'd be back by now and—"

"And she isn't," Juliet finished for her. "Thanks for being so fucking on top of things, Anya, you are so *observant*, great job."

Taylor let out a little *heh-heh* like she usually did if Juliet cut Anya or Mona down. How could she laugh at a time like this? Mona could never imagine doing that to her. She narrowed her eyes at Taylor hard enough that Taylor muttered an apology.

"There's really only one thing that we can do," Juliet said after.

"What?" Mona asked, dreading what her older sister was about to say and not wanting to believe it.

"We have to feed Rose."

CHAPTER 15

"No," Anya said right away, raising a hand and taking a small step backward. "No."

"Yes," Taylor retorted with a conviction so solid that Mona knew instantly she'd been in on this plan before Juliet brought it up. She thought back to all the secret little chats they'd been having over the past few days. This was what those chats had been about.

"Where are we going to get access to a dead body?" Mona asked, hushing her tone even though Rose was asleep. It felt so wrong to be discussing this in just the next room over, with only a bathroom separating them. "It's not like we can go grave robbing, the meat won't be fresh. And I'm guessing that even fresh meat from the morgue is too pumped with chemicals. How do we know it wouldn't poison Rose?"

Juliet stared at Mona, expressionless. "We'll...*obviously*... need to get fresh meat."

Anya let out a short burst of borderline hysterical laughter. "Yeah, okay, we'll just hit up the butcher, or

hey, maybe we can just head downtown and pluck someone from the street and murder them!"

Taylor cleared her throat and looked down. Juliet
brought her fingertips to her temples, rubbed them in
small circles. "Don't make me lay this all out for you,"
she said quietly, deadly, like when she told Taylor to open
the trash bag with the body in it. Her eyes shifted back
and forth between them, her stare electrifying. "If you
two fail me now, if you fail *Rose* now, I don't think I'll
have it in me to forgive you, ever. It's important that we
work together on this."

The vague but deliberate threat hung heavy in the air.

"Work together how?" Mona asked meekly, again
knowing the answer but refusing to accept it. "Do you
really think we're capable of killing someone? It's impossible. There's no way."

"I want you to think about what you're saying, Mona,"
Juliet snapped then, lifting her gaze to glare into Mona's. "Mom was able to do it, for Rose. You're not able
to handle something that even *Mom* could manage?"

It hurt, but Mona knew what Juliet was doing. She
wouldn't let herself be tricked using her own feelings
against her.

"You can't be serious," Anya whispered, all hints of
her outburst gone and replaced by terror. "That is impossible."

"It's not," Juliet said. "But I'm not surprised that you
two are the ones having such a hard time accepting reality. Taylor knows what I'm talking about. She knows
it's what's best for Rose, and for everybody. Do I really

need to remind you of how she started acting when she went without food for too long?"

Mona couldn't deny that part. She just couldn't believe they were in this position right now. She hated Mom, *hated* her, for doing this to all of them, for doing this to Rose. It was all so messed up and wrong, beyond comprehension, but here they were in Juliet and Taylor's bedroom talking about murdering someone.

"We'll get caught," Mona tried. "No matter what we do, we are totally screwed. All of us, most of all Rose."

She didn't bring up the most obvious reason they couldn't do this: because it was wrong. Immoral. Evil. But Mona knew that Juliet couldn't care less about that part. What Mona had been wondering ever since the day Juliet threatened to shove her in front of a moving car was being answered now, and it was the worst answer possible: Juliet was willing to murder.

"You're going to help us help Rose," Juliet said, not a question, not at all. Her cheeks reddened a little. "If you don't, I'll feed *you* to her."

"What the fuck!" Anya nearly shouted, prompting a harsh *shhh!* from Taylor. "How could you even say that?"

Mona was too horrified to appreciate Anya sticking up for her.

"I was kidding." Juliet rolled her eyes, but Mona wasn't too sure that she *had* been kidding. "But seriously. If either of you have a better idea on how to fix this problem, let me know now. I'll let you take on the full responsibility of everything that happens."

Neither Mona nor Anya said anything. They avoided each other's eyes.

"That's what I thought," Juliet said. "Now listen."

Rose would do it for you, Juliet had said.

Now Mona was hiding out in the bathroom, the doors locked, the shower on as hot as it would go, slowly filling the room with steam as she broke her promise to herself and got the rum out of the faulty vent above the toilet.

Are you willing to let her suffer? Juliet had asked.

Mona thought about finding Rose in the basement, squatting in the pitch-black and eating the meat with bloody juice running down her hands and mouth and thighs. Mona thought about the scream she'd let out at the sight, how bad it'd made Rose feel, how her baby sister started crying even as she continued to shove hunks of roast into her gaping mouth, gristle and all.

I don't know about you, but I'm pretty sure there are a whole lot of people out there who don't deserve to live as much as Rose does, Juliet had said.

Mona understood the truth of the statement, but that didn't stop her from sobbing against the back of her arm to muffle the sound of her cries. At least Juliet agreed that it was nobody's place to make that call, that nobody could be a real-life Dexter or Frank Castle, that drawing the line on who should die and who should stay alive was something that should never be up to any one human.

Still, Rose's soul had been commanded back against its will, and now they would have to deal with Mom's actions in the best way that they could, just as they always had. It was for that reason, Juliet decided—*It had to be random.*

Getting away with murder might seem impossible, Mona and Anya and Taylor were told, but in actuality it was only easy to get caught if you murdered someone you had connections with. If you wanted to kill somebody and get away with it badly enough, you absolutely could. You just had to pick somebody random. People had managed to keep it up for years or even a lifetime as serial killers, Juliet reminded them, so really pulling off a single incident wouldn't be as hard as it sounded.

We have to do our research.

Research, it seemed, would be true crime shows and documentaries, the ones that told you exactly what the cops were looking for, the ones that revealed how to avoid leaving behind damning evidence. There was zero room for mistakes. It would need to be done seamlessly, masterfully, carefully.

Rose would do it for you, Juliet had said again, and again, and again. *She'd do it for you in a heartbeat.*

To be honest, Mona still wasn't entirely sure she would. Murder. Taking someone's life. They were only teenagers, for Chrissake. Kids!

We owe it to her. We owe it to ourselves.

It was pointed out how important Rose was to the family, how needed, how crucial. She'd been given the gift of a second chance, on the hugest scale fathomable.

She is our baby.

Only, Mona was forced to admit now, she wasn't their baby. She was Juliet's baby. There were no boundaries that could contain Juliet's undying loyalty to Rose. There was no way to break that. Mona wasn't sure what it meant about her that she wished she could. Either way, Mona couldn't deny that she loved Rose very, very much.

We can do this. We will do this. Tell anyone, including Rose, and you're dead meat.

An unfortunate way of wording it. *Dead meat.* Mona wanted so badly to believe that it really had just been a very mean joke. But what could she do? What could she do but nod silently along with Anya and Taylor, who were as solemn as Mona but still nodded their heads, as well. *This is happening*, Mona realized, *this is real life and this is happening and I am going to become an accomplice to murder.*

When the bathroom became so steamy that droplets of condensation were sliding down the sides of the rum bottle and the moisture was making the ends of her hair curl, Mona finally got into the shower, covering herself from head to toe in a thick, frothy layer of the strongest smelling body wash, brushing her teeth as long as it took for the fumes of the rum to stop emanating from her mouth.

She wished she could stay in there forever.

But no, she had to hurry along so that they could gather for their first "research training" session in Mom's room. There was a TV in there with a streaming device, Juliet pointed out during their meeting, and they would go as long as Rose was asleep. If needed, Juliet could give her another dose of the knockout pill. They would sustain Rose on more raw meat and keep her in bed until they were confident they were ready to make the kill.

Make the kill, like they were hunters out in deer season.

They only had a few days. The last time Rose had been driven to raw meat, she'd needed human flesh only two days later. That meant that the day after tomorrow at the latest was going to have to be "go time," as Juliet put it, almost like she was their coach.

Their very own murder coach.

The shower ended, and Mona tried to dry herself off even though the towel was already damp from the steam. Her clothes stuck to her skin, and her comb tangled in her hair as she ripped it through. *I will be a murderer soon*, she thought. *My life will be ruined forever irreversibly, permanently.*

How funny that a few months ago her biggest problem was impatience at the fact that she wouldn't be turning eighteen for three more years. It had felt like the only thing that mattered and the only thing that could ever matter. Her mom's depression was somehow her burden to take on, always weighing on her and upsetting her and causing her to resent her sisters for their apparent lack of ability to care.

Except Rose, of course. Rose always cared. And now Mom had left them all behind without so much as a glance back. Anya had been right about her all along.

Now, standing in front of the steamy bathroom mirror, Mona looked at herself, a completely different person from who she had always been. Mom had gotten them all into this. She had a soul and deserved happiness as much as anyone else, but now Mona was starting to see just how much emotional damage had been caused by the idea that she could help Mom get better somehow. It had never been possible, and it never would be. All Mona had needed to do before was distance herself from it, the one thing she'd never thought to do until now.

Except now it was too late to matter. That revelation would have changed her life completely, but now it wouldn't make a difference. She was about to spiral down to the point of no return and there would be no coming back. There were a whole slew of new problems to deal with, more change to go through, a sick and twisted growth spurt that would lead to irreversible things.

Murderer.

She felt like she'd done it already.

The panic set in again, causing her breathing to quicken painfully in her chest, and she had to lean on the counter to hold herself up. There were no tears, but Mona's lips were trembling as though she was crying. She fought to quiet the tiny gasps escaping them. Only half in her right mind, she shakily reached for her cell phone next to the sink, unlocked the screen, and opened her messages to Lexa.

Can I please move in with you? she typed, hitting Send before she could stop herself. And then she really did start to cry, because she hadn't talked to Lexa in days and days, and had screwed everything up so badly.

What would Lexa say if she knew what Mona and her sisters were planning? Anything Mona had built with Lexa would be gone forever, stripped away like everything else. She couldn't believe how lucky she'd had it before. She couldn't believe how quickly things went to hell.

You text for the first time in ages to ask if you can move in with me? Lexa replied, and already Mona regretted sending the text. You mean, like, now?

I just mean eventually, Mona wrote after a second. And I'm really sorry about that, please believe me, I am. I have some things to take care of in my life first, but I just thought it could maybe work somehow. Do you think your mom would care? Would you?

Mona realized just how sideways she sounded saying all of this after letting the silence between them go on for so long. But she felt so out of control, so desperate for an easy out. She was the worst sister in the world.

Mona, Lexa wrote. What in the HELL is going on with you? Answer me truthfully. Answer me now. Are you in trouble? Is that why you want to move?

Mona's wild thoughts on how exactly to reply were interrupted by a sharp knock on the door.

"Mona?" Juliet barked from the other side. "What is taking you so damn long? We need to get started!"

"Coming," Mona called, pleased with how steady and strong her voice sounded, and after a few moments of silence she heard her sister's footsteps retreat. The last thing she needed was for Juliet to sense her hesitation. Mona could only imagine the berating she'd go through, Juliet commanding her to keep up, get over it, get shit done like everyone else.

I have to go for now, she typed quickly on her phone. I'm so sorry. I'll explain things better when I get an extra minute. I need to be with my sisters now. She waited thirty seconds or so after she sent the message.

Lexa never replied.

Finally, she opened the bathroom door and the steam billowed out into the hallway.

"Jesus," Taylor said from where she was leaning against the wall by Mom's room, her arms crossed over her stomach. "Sauna much? You realize how badly that fucks up the wallpaper, don't you?"

"Does it look like I care, Taylor?" Mona was in no mood for Taylor's shit. "We're about to learn how to *murder someone*, and you're bitching at me about the *wallpaper?*"

"Shut up," Juliet called from Mom's room. "Both of you. Get your asses in here."

Taylor's cheeks reddened, and Mona followed her into Mom's room. Juliet was plugging in a coffeemaker on top of the dresser, and there were plastic grocery bags full of chips and candy and baguettes and other things. It was like they were preparing for a sleepover or something, and not about to start researching how to get away with murder.

"You were in the shower a long time," Juliet accused Mona without turning away from the coffeemaker. "Long enough for me to get to the commissary and back. Are you dealing, or…?"

She asked as though there was only one acceptable answer. Mona knew exactly what she wanted to hear.

"Yeah," she said, letting herself sound just a little irritated. "I was having stomach issues, alright?"

"Must have been that bite of human you ate," Taylor snickered, and Juliet laughed, too. Anya didn't laugh or smile or even look at any of them. Mona fully believed that Juliet's dark place was no longer just for Juliet; everybody had been pulled into it now, and there was no escape.

"Anyway," Juliet said, after the coffeemaker was finally bubbling away with water from the bathroom sink, "let's get this started."

The girls settled into their respective spots, Taylor rushing back to her bedroom to bring some pillows and blankets, and Juliet turned off the lights. Mona noticed that Juliet had a notebook and pen balanced on her lap, like she was planning to take notes.

The screen lit up with the intro to a show all about the stuff that happened in the first forty-eight hours after a murder. This was the best show to start with, Juliet explained, because the entire show was all about people getting caught and how. The intro ended, and Mona felt the change in herself begin.

Killer.

CHAPTER 16

At first, Mona wasn't sure she was going to make it without breaking. On the television screen, a mother screamed and wept as a police officer reached forward to steady her, saying, "I know, I know," over and over again. The cameraman awkwardly fumbled his way around the two of them to get a halfway decent shot. The mother had just been told that the body of her son was found in the trunk of his own vehicle, out in the middle of the forest somewhere. There was a bullet wound to his head.

"Not my baby!" The woman wailed, unable to still herself, like her soul was clawing desperately to get out. "No no no, not my Christopher…"

Mona closed her eyes to calm the sting that had come over them. Everyone was someone's baby, and within a few days she'd be taking one away from their parents, or their kids, or their friends. Watching this wasn't teaching her anything, it was torturing her. A series of photos scrolled across the screen as the narrator rehashed what the viewer knew so far—a car found parked against a thicket of trees, the green of the forest bright and eerily splendid in contrast to the dark music, the car old and beat up and haunted-looking. The next photo was of the slightly ajar trunk, and a pair of pasty man's legs were made visible by what little sunlight shone through the crack.

Then the photos showed some footprints found in the dirt behind the car, distinct and crisp in their style and size. Mona saw Juliet scribble something down on the pad of her paper, nodding as though she was listening to a professor explain a mathematical equation.

The show rolled on, following the police as they tried to worm their way through the puzzle. They followed the victim's cell phone (prompting Juliet to take another note) and found that one number in particular had been called in what would have been just hours before the murder. They found the man whose phone the number was registered to living just twenty minutes away, and brought him in to the police station. They asked him question after question about the victim, at one point dramatically opening the file and strewing blown-up photos of the body over the table. By this point, the man seemed to realize he'd been caught, his lies too tangled and contradictory to ever have hope of being straightened out.

"Why did you do this to Christopher?" one of the cops demanded, standing from his chair and letting his finger drop on a photo that contained a close-up of the bullet wound. "Your shoe prints were found at the scene of the crime, and we know from Christopher's mother that you were angry with him over some ex-girlfriend of yours."

"He was my best friend and she cheated on me with

him," the man said, losing all of the cool if somewhat anxious composure he'd held on to until then. "They were going to run away together without telling me. Can you imagine that, the only two people you've ever been able to trust in your whole life…"

The case wrapped up nice and clean with a big bow on top, and the next one started right away, a body found slashed to death in the bathtub of an abandoned apartment. Up until now none of the sisters had moved, except for Juliet with her sporadic and furious pen and paper action, but now Taylor got up to go to the bags of food and grabbed a can of orange soda and a bag of spicy dill pickle kettle chips. She brought it back to her seat, perched on the recliner by Mom's reading table. Juliet had poured herself some coffee already, even though they hadn't even finished a single episode yet.

Mona refused to partake in snacking, couldn't comprehend how Taylor could crunch and sip her way through the shockingly uncensored images of the dead body in the tub, but as the episodes continued and the hours passed, something strange happened, and Mona started to feel a little desensitized to it all.

After the fifth episode or so, she stopped crying over the reactions of the loved ones, now too ready for what was coming and how normal the whole nightmare actually was. She found herself mentally scolding all the idiots who committed the murders, always leaving behind the most obvious clues directly tying them to their crime.

The more she thought about the whole thing, the more she kind of understood where Juliet was coming from before, when she was insisting that a carefully planned murder could actually be pretty foolproof if you left no loose ends. All of these idiots had never stood a chance, with their incriminating receipts and text messages and call logs. They got themselves recorded on security footage, left behind DNA, had alibis weaker than old cobwebs. These were all things that could be directly avoided if they chose the victim randomly and carried out the task with care.

By the time night fell, the room was dark and hot and smelled thickly of stale breath and cheese crackers, and Juliet suggested they all take a fifteen-minute break to use the bathroom, stretch, whatever. Mona went to put on a fresh tank top, since the one she was wearing was littered with baguette crumbs and smeared with hummus, and looked at her phone for the first time since she'd left the bathroom. There were messages from Lexa there, just like she feared there would be.

You're scaring me.

You know you can tell me anything, right M?

Talk to me. Why can't you just tell me the truth? Do you think I'll judge you or something? Get real!

Mona snuck into her bedroom and put on the clean tank top, careful not to wake Rose, who was still completely laid out on her bed, her mouth hanging open as she snored. There was no time to answer Lexa now, she'd need to wait until tomorrow. She slid her phone into the pocket of her sweats and ran into Taylor, who was returning from the bathroom. Anya was still where she was before the break, but now all the food wrappers that had been strewn around the room before had all been gathered up in a grocery bag, and the window had been opened to replace the gross air with clean, fresh night air.

"Juliet went downstairs to order a pizza," Anya mumbled, hesitantly looking up to meet Mona's eyes. Their gaze was weighed down, stressed by all the unsaid things between them, and Mona wondered if they'd ever get a moment to pull each other aside and talk about everything that'd happened. It was like they both knew they needed to come together again to survive, but at the same time, they were too far gone to go back now.

Mona nodded and offered a faint smile, but it was all she could manage when she remembered what they were doing and what they were going to do next, and she went back to her place on the floor and sat. A few minutes later Juliet came back in, still breathing a little heavily from hustling up the stairs. "Pizza's on its way," she said. "And there are three four-pound chuck roasts in the refrigerator in case Rose wakes up. We'll feed her and then give her another sleeping pill."

Soon, they finished streaming all of the episodes of the documentary show that were available. Juliet already had another one at the ready, with a very different style, much less clinical than the show that followed the police around. This one was different from the start, Mona realized as she cracked open her fourth orange soda.

The music was dramatic and moody, violins and string

basses, sudden outbursts of horns and lone tinklings of piano keys. The camera panned over a wide spread of prairie lands, the grasses swaying gently in the wind.

"Labette County, Kansas, 1871," the narrator said, his voice low and broody, "a well-known family called the Benders lived and worked on their stretch of one hundred and sixty acres of land adjacent to The Great Osage Trail, which was the only open road for westward travel."

The next shot launched into a dramatic reenactment. A group of actors in pioneer garb fed farm animals and tilled land and planted the beginnings of an apple orchard. There were four of them, two women and two men. One of the men and one of the women were older, while the other two seemed to be young adults.

"John Bender Senior and his wife Elvira ran a general store and rest stop for the passing travelers, of which there were many," the narrator continued. "The two people who were originally believed to be their children, John Bender Junior and Kate Bender, both in their early twenties, were later rumored to have actually been husband and wife."

Why are we watching this? Mona wondered. She looked over at her sisters—Taylor and Anya both looked at the screen with big, worried eyes, while Juliet looked on in a sort of excited fascination.

"But by 1873, only two short years later," the narrator said, "there had been enough reports of missing people that travelers began to avoid the Trail altogether. When an investigation led authorities straight to the Bender family's property, it was discovered that they had abandoned it. Animals were left unfed. Only food and personal items were taken. But what was found later in the evening would rock the group of investigators to their very core."

A bright splash of red suddenly splattered across the tall prairie grasses, and a theatrical scream cut over the narrator as the title of the documentary blasted across the screen in big block letters: *Bloody Benders: The Family That Kills Together.*

You have got *to be kidding me*, Mona thought, looking to Juliet in disbelief, but her sister just shrugged at her and continued eating the popcorn she had gathered in the hand that was not holding the pen against the pad of paper.

The "documentary" played out more like a narrated horror movie: the family worked hard on the property, hanging wagon canvas inside to separate the living quarters from the general store area. They planted an apple orchard and a vegetable garden. They invited weary travelers in, offered them a meal, offered them a place to sleep. Some of the travelers left unscathed, for one reason or the other. Others were not so lucky.

The reenactment of the murders showed the Bender family luring people to their dining table, which was placed against a curtain hanging from the ceiling to separate the rooms. They always made sure that the victim sat with his back directly to the curtain, nearly touching it. Then, as the unsuspecting traveler would wait for their stew or conversed with the charismatic and attractive Kate Bender, one of the Bender men, from the other side of the curtain, would hit the victim from behind in the skull using a hammer.

Once their skulls had been bashed in, their throats were cut.

Taylor covered her face during the murder reenactment scene; Anya watched it but looked like she wanted to throw up. Mona couldn't believe that Juliet was making them watch this. How sick and twisted was that? But when she tried to show her distaste to her older sister she was only met with cutting glares and the suggestion to pay attention.

Juliet, on the other hand, looked completely transfixed with the story. She always paid especially close attention whenever the narrator went on about Kate Bender, the young woman with the sweet face and even sweeter demeanor, who had the entire area fooled despite some initial suspicion over the people who claimed to be her parents. Juliet no longer looked like she was learning about all of this because of some duty to Rose, but because she enjoyed it, was *inspired* by it.

It chilled Mona deeply.

When the nightmare on the Bender property was finally revealed, nobody could believe the magnitude of what lay waiting. A trapdoor inside the house led to a dirt room that was stinking with congealed blood. The remains of over twenty victims were found in the dirt of the apple orchard and surrounding area, including the bodies of infants who were believed to have been buried alive.

While some of the victims were of the more wealthy types, there were many who weren't and who offered nothing of value to robbers. For this reason it is believed that the Bender family only killed for their own enjoyment.

The movie finally ended, and nobody moved or spoke as the credits rolled over images of bodies and snapshots from the Bender property replica house, which allowed tourists to immerse themselves in the story by being made to feel as though they were there.

"It's hard to know which is scarier," the narrator added as the screen went black, one last thought to add. "The horrors that the victims of the Bender family experienced, or the fact that the Bender family themselves got away with it for so long."

"What are you watching?" said a voice from the doorway behind them, and Mona nearly jumped out of her skin when she turned to see Rose standing there. "Is this a horror movie or something?"

If only you knew, Mona thought. She understood why Juliet was so insistent on keeping the truth from Rose. If she knew that they were planning to murder someone to feed to her, she'd lose her mind for sure.

"How are you feeling?" Juliet asked in response, jumping up from her spot and rushing forward to meet Rose. "Are you hungry?"

"Yes," Rose whispered, her voice shaking. She didn't look very well, Mona noticed, not at all.

"I got you something downstairs," Juliet cooed, pulling her gently back through the hallway to her room. "You get back into bed and I'll bring it up. We're gonna need you to stay in bed until we can find some more of that medicine Mom was giving you."

"Where *is* Mom?" Rose asked for the first time since she'd left for Danwin Cove. She sounded upset, desperate. Mona wondered for the first time if Rose would even be able to make it to the day after tomorrow.

She didn't hear what Juliet said in return, only turned back to Taylor and Anya. "What was that all about?" Mona asked. "Why did she show us the thing about the Bloody Benders? How was it supposed to help the situation in any way? It was just creepy. As if what we're doing isn't bad enough!"

Taylor narrowed her eyes a little bit. "Doing what it takes to keep Rose alive is bad?"

Mona already regretted showing doubt. She realized that it was essentially guaranteed that Taylor would repeat anything she ended up saying to Juliet later—they did share a bedroom, after all, and Taylor with her endless quest to make Juliet the happiest queen in all the land.

"No, I don't mean that," Mona mumbled, feeling her cheeks get hot. "I just...those people, those Bloody Benders, they weren't like us. What we're doing is different. They buried infants *alive*. They cut people into pieces for fun. Why in the hell would Juliet show us that?"

"Because it's what we're doing," Juliet said from behind Mona, whose heart skipped a beat in her chest. "Maybe if you would sit your ass down and let me explain a few things, you'd understand a little bit better."

"What do you mean it's what we're doing?" Anya asked, shifting her weight uncomfortably while she pulled down on the strings of her hoodie. Her eyes were completely red and glassy.

"The technique the Benders used," Juliet said, pointing to the spot on the floor where she wanted Mona to sit near her feet. Taylor sat right away, and Anya leaned against Mom's bed. After a sticky second of stares and silence, Mona sat down. "With the curtain, and the hammer. It's how we're going to kill our victim."

Mona thought about the reenactment of the murders in the movie they had just watched, how one second the person would be sitting and eating or talking and the next they'd be facedown on the table, with the back of their skulls crushed in like eggshells. Her legs felt weak from where they were sprawled on the floor. Mona brought her knees up, hugged her legs to her chest.

"It's the most humane way," Juliet told them, her voice a little softer. "We can't use a gun, didn't you learn anything from the first show we watched? The hammer will be instant, and then we can just drag them backward from the table straight down the basement steps." She paused, staring off into space for a second, her voice suddenly a little less focused. "I looked up everything about how to properly clean up the blood in the kitchen, from the public library's internet."

"What about in the basement?" Anya said, sounding extremely doubtful. "Whatever we do to get the… meat…is going to leave more blood than you're probably imagining. You won't be able to clean it all up."

"I will," Juliet said. "Haven't you ever noticed the drain on the floor in there, underneath the stairs? Mom had to have used the drain, for what she did to that girl. There's no way she did that outside of the house and then brought the bag of leftover pieces back with her. I'm going to cover the cement with plastic and strip the meat near the drain."

Mona almost threw up her orange soda all over the

carpet when she heard her sister say "strip the meat." She didn't understand how quickly things had come to this, how in just as quick of a time, it would escalate even further. The air was different, she was different, her sisters were different. Nothing was secure and everything was caught in the tornado.

"Who's…" Taylor had to swallow to keep her voice from shivering. "Who's going to be the one with the hammer?"

Silence descended upon the room. Anya and Mona both looked to the floor, either at their feet or at the arms they'd crossed in front of themselves. Even without looking at Taylor, Mona could tell that her sister was absolutely terrified that Juliet would give her the hammer, make her carry out the dirty little task that nobody else wanted. It was what Juliet had usually done with Taylor all through their lives—always making Taylor clean the toilet, or take the trash out in the rain, or unclog the drain whenever the water in the shower would start to gather in filmy puddles at the girls' feet.

And it was Taylor who she'd made open the trash bag in the basement.

But Mona already knew that it wouldn't be Taylor holding the hammer. She was too skittish, too frail, too weak. Juliet would never give anything of real importance to Taylor, and that was the thing that Taylor didn't understand. So here she stood, shaking like a little dog afraid of a thunderclap, while Juliet stared at her and drew the moment on for far longer than was necessary. Mona recognized it as it was happening, and it made her feel ill with anger.

"Don't worry, Thing 2," Juliet said to Taylor finally.

"That'll be my responsibility. I'm the one organizing this whole thing, I'm the one who should have to face it."

Taylor nearly collapsed to the floor with relief. She buried her face behind her hands, shuddering, and Mona couldn't tell if she was laughing or crying.

"There's a role for everybody, though," Juliet said, ignoring Taylor completely and turning her attention to Mona and Anya. "I'll explain it to you tonight and then tomorrow night, it's go time."

"Tomorrow night?" they responded simultaneously, panic evident in their tones.

"I thought we were waiting until the day after tomorrow," Mona said, fear causing her blood to feel like it was electric.

"Rose can't wait that long," Juliet said somberly. "Don't worry. We've got this. I'm going to draw up the most flawless plan. I will keep us safe. I promise. I won't let Rose down."

Mona remembered a moment when she was eight or so, when Mom had a meltdown that had ended with her turning over the coffee table and throwing a glass against the wall. Mona had scurried to the room she shared with Anya and Taylor to hide, all of them like panic-stricken mice. Juliet found them all huddled in the closet together, and wrapped her arms around them and pulled them close and started to cry.

"I will keep us safe," Juliet had told them through her tears. "I will always keep us safe."

CHAPTER 17

The next morning, the plan was laid out:
Anya would distract Rose while the murder was
happening, by watching a movie with her on Rose's bed
with a laptop. The door would need to be closed, Juliet reminded her, and she would need to make sure the
volume was turned up very loud. Anya could feed her
what little was left of the raw chuck roasts to keep her
settled until Juliet was able to cook up the real dinner.

Mona and Taylor would accompany Juliet on the catch,
where Juliet would attempt to talk a random stranger into
coming home with them. How this would be done, Juliet didn't reveal, but Mona figured she'd probably wave
her cleavage in some old drunk dude's face to get him
interested. They'd use a rental car, and park in the alley
downtown next to the ice cream shop, which wasn't
covered by any security cameras, and once they were
parked, the license plate would be covered.

Once they had the person in their car, the girls would
go home, where the curtain would already be hung and

plastic would already be covering the floor from the kitchen all the way down the basement steps and around the drain that sat directly beneath them. If the person asked about the plastic, the girls would say they were preparing to paint the kitchen. They'd even leave a few cans and brushes out in plain sight, to set the victim even more at ease.

Here was where things got precise. Once the person was sitting with their back to the curtain, Taylor would sit across from them and strike up a conversation while Mona stood near the door to guard it in case they tried to get away for whatever reason. In order to make it look more natural, she would pretend to be pouring herself a glass of juice, or emptying the dishwasher. *Just as long*, Juliet reminded her, as *you remain ready to stop them at all times if they try to run.*

Mona wondered how Juliet had decided what each person's job would be. She wished she could have Anya's job, where all that was required was hanging out with Rose and watching a movie, but at least she wasn't doing what Juliet would have to do, or even Taylor. For once, Mona was glad that Juliet lacked faith in her and Anya.

Once the deed was done and their victim was dead, Juliet would wrap the body in plastic and drag it downstairs to the basement to begin the process of stripping the meat. Everything that was left over would be wrapped tightly back up in the plastic, placed into a heavy duty trash bag, and disposed of in the city landfill.

Hopefully, Juliet said, Mom would be back before they had to do it again. Mona was starting to worry, because she suspected that their mother may have straight up abandoned them, ditched them when she saw what a mess she had created. Mona imagined having to kill for weeks or months or years and wanted to die herself.

Why hadn't Mom even *called* yet?

Mona was too used to being let down by her at this point to think about it very hard. Plus, she had enough to worry and stress about with the murder, and wondering how Rose would ever move past this, whether this would all really be for something or if they were all just gonna end up in jail and juvy, leaving Rose to be fostered out. Mona imagined spending decades behind bars, and was saddened to discover that it was much easier than imagining this turning out any other way.

The morning of the murder, Juliet took her car to the next town over, hours away, to buy the plastic covering and the hammer and to rent a car. Taylor went with her, so that she could help drive. They left their cell phones at home. They wore hats and sunglasses and lipstick, like con artists from a melodramatic movie. As two young girls, nobody would notice them in any significant way that could lead to suspicion. With their selfie-ready faces and matching outfits, they were as innocent as it got.

"People underestimate the living hell out of teen girls," Juliet said when she checked herself in the mirror before she and Taylor left. She pulled her lipstick out of her pocket and reapplied it in a smooth, steady motion. "We're *so* going to get away with this."

Suddenly Mona understood exactly why Juliet was acting like she had been, with the research session and the Bloody Benders and all the planning. It was giving her the illusion of full control, *extreme* control, making her feel less at a loss. She was the oldest and she'd always been the one to herd them around and tell them what to do and when to do it. Now, with a plan set in place amidst the chaos that was Rose's death and resurrection, there was an air of power around Juliet that was undeniably stronger than the will of all of her sisters combined.

And when Juliet told you to do something, you did it.

With a final glance at her reflection over the frames of her red-rimmed sunglasses, Juliet turned away from the mirror with her chin held high and whisked Taylor outside with her. "See you bitches later," was the last thing she said before the front door closed. "Start mentally preparing yourself for tonight."

Once the Mustang had pulled away from the front of the house and they were finally gone, Mona and Anya started in on the one task that was given to them today: cleaning the house from top to bottom, and clearing out the space around the drain in the garage in an organized fashion. They were to do a good job, as well as make sure Rose was doing okay whenever she woke up.

After she finished cleaning the kitchen and vacuuming the living room, Mona went down into the basement, where Anya had been moving the drawers of the tool cabinet across the garage and out of the way. It was lucky there was still plenty of space under the stairs left over despite the presence of the storage container with the body in it, Mona realized; otherwise they'd have to move the container into plain view, and that would be a big no-no in the rule book of *Don't Get Caught, Bitches*, written and edited by Juliet Marie Cane.

"I think this is good enough," Anya said grimly after they'd finished moving the enormous tool cabinet, looking at the drain in the cement beneath the stairs. "Where does this drain even lead to?"

"The ocean, probably," Mona said, although she really wasn't sure at all. She didn't want to imagine blood bubbling down the drain while Juliet stood over it, hacking a dead body to pieces with that creepy knife Mom had left behind. "Where's that chain we were supposed to find?"

"I set it on top of the trash can." Anya pointed to a spot behind Mona. "But I couldn't find the lock."

"I know where that is," Mona said, and found it on the shelf above the spot where Rose's bike leaned against the wall. She took the chain, wrapped it through the steel loop on the bottom of the garage door, then through the anchored loop on the ground, and locked it in place tightly. This way, the garage door couldn't be opened.

The two girls stood side by side in silence, looking over the eerily empty garage, knowing that it would soon become some sort of nightmare chamber.

"I can't believe we're doing this," Anya whispered, then cleared her throat and turned away like she was embarrassed. "I love Rose and I know what we're doing will help her, but…that doesn't make it *right*, you know? In fact, all of our souls are eternally fucked."

Despite the awfulness of it all, Mona was at least grateful that Anya was finally opening up to her again, even if just a little bit.

"I know," Mona said. "Whenever I get upset I see Rose's face all over again, after she died. I didn't feel like life was worth living anymore when I saw that."

"I didn't, either." Anya's eyes were glassy. "I don't know what to believe anymore. Or how to feel. It's like the only thing I know is that I love Rose and I don't think our family could take losing her forever without falling apart. We're already so dangerously close."

She looked over to Mona then. They were a year apart, but had always looked the same age. When they were little, they used to pretend they were twins. They even had names that sounded alike, like twins sometimes did. Mona hadn't thought of that in a long time and now she missed it. She loved having Lexa to be able to talk to, but now everything with that friendship was ruined. Too much had happened that could never be explained. Anya knew just what she was going through, Mona could feel it, especially with Everly breaking up with her so suddenly.

Still, it wasn't as though preparing the house for a murder was a great time to try and touch on any of that. They just needed to hang in there. Maybe, Mona thought, they could help make this easier on each other. They could share the guilt. They could remind each other that there was a purpose to it, that there had been an otherworldly intervention to give their family a second chance, that they had to fight for it as hard as they could, even if they ended up in jail, even if they had to carry their sins through this life and on to the next.

"We won't let our family fall apart," Mona said. "We're the goddamn Cane twins."

Anya cracked a smile then, and suddenly it didn't seem so odd that they were doing what they were doing, and they continued cleaning up the house as if it was a holiday and family was coming over.

When Rose woke up, they moved her down to the couch to give her a little variety and let her watch TV. She looked extremely ill, but she hadn't yet started freaking out like she did that one morning in the kitchen, when she'd started to lose control. When Mona thought about how Rose didn't remember any of that, she was suddenly very eager for Juliet and Taylor to get home so they could get this thing done and over with already, to make Rose feel better. She was starting to feel uneasy about the idea of leaving Anya alone with Rose, in such close proximity.

It's just one life, Mona told herself all day, after she'd finished cleaning and was sitting with Rose, braiding her hair while they watched a musical. *It's just one random life in exchange for Rose's. She deserves to be alive. She does. And people die unfairly every single day.*

"Mona?" Rose asked weakly during one of the commercial breaks. Anya napped on the next couch over, her mouth open and her hand on her belly. "What is going on with everybody?"

Mona was careful not to change her expression. "What do you mean?" she asked, not taking her eyes from the television screen.

"Everybody's being so secretive," Rose whined. "Is it because I'm going to die again?"

Mona did take her eyes away from the screen now, so she could look down at her baby sister's face, wide-eyed and frightened. "You're not going to die again, Rose," Mona said. "At least, not until you're old, like the lady in *Titanic*."

"Do you promise?" Rose sat up now, the ends of her short braids only barely grazing her shoulders. "Do you promise me?"

Mona didn't even hesitate. She took Rose's face in her hands, making sure she was listening carefully. "I promise you," she said. "I *promise*."

Whether or not she would be able to keep her promise, Mona couldn't say for sure, but she knew that she loved Rose enough to die trying.

"Thank goodness," Rose sighed, slumping back down onto her pillow that was resting on Mona's lap. "It was so scary being dead."

Mona put her fingers back in Rose's hair, started another braid. "What was it like?" she asked, a little nervous as to what the question may trigger, but too curious to hold it in. "Do you...remember much?"

"Yes," Rose said, her voice flat. "Too much. And it's not something anybody's supposed to remember. I wouldn't have, I don't think, if my memory hadn't been woken up." Her cheeks turned pink despite the sickly sheen she'd taken on. "I mean, I'm glad I'm alive again," she said in a rush. "I didn't mean that I wish you guys hadn't saved me. I'm grateful, I am..."

"Rose," Mona cut her off, too pained to hear her say any more. "Please don't. You don't have to say that."

"But I mean it!" Rose tried, getting more worked up. "I love you, I trust you, please don't be sad because of me anymore. I know you are, don't lie."

Rose was dangerously close to bringing up the alcohol again, Mona could tell. So, like a coward, she kissed the top of her sister's head and pretended like she was watching the show that had just come back on. There was no way she was going to attempt tonight without drinking her way through it. She'd be careful just to let it soften her up a little, not so much that Juliet would ever know.

Hours passed. Mona played Uno with Rose while Anya slept. *She needs the rest*, Mona thought darkly, *although not as much as me.* What if the victim actually *did* try to run? Juliet swore to her that it was extremely unlikely, but still, it could happen.

Mona tried to imagine herself grabbing a person who was scared and running for their life like a rabbit in Mr. McGregor's garden, imagined throwing them down on the floor or shoving them backward into the table. Even though she was the same height as Anya, Mona was a bit beefier, which was probably why Juliet had chosen her for the job, she had always called Mona "the fat sister." Would she be able to do her job if duty called?

When duty calls, her dad would always say when he had to leave them yet again to go back to work, *the only honorable thing you can do is answer it.*

The afternoon passed in a rush. Mona felt like she was stuck in one of those time lapse videos, watching helplessly as the sun got pulled down the sky until finally it was setting. Before she knew it, she heard the hum of the Mustang as it pulled in front of the house, and after a quick glance through the curtains in the living room, Mona didn't see any rental car.

"Where's the other car?" she asked under her breath once Taylor and Juliet let themselves back inside.

"Shhh," Juliet emphasized, her eyes darting nervously behind Mona's shoulder where Rose and Anya were on the couches. "We parked it outside the post. We can park the Mustang in the same spot when we switch."

Mona had to admit, it was good thinking. If anyone ended up seeing their vehicle and reported suspicious activity, the tire tracks wouldn't be able to be traced back to them, and neither would the car, since it'd been rented in a town that was hours away.

"Are you ready for this?" Juliet asked, her eyes wide and wild. "It's go time."

CHAPTER 18

Three hours later, the girls were in the rental car downtown, which was parked in the alley away from any cameras. It had taken them so long to put all the plastic down at home, and hang the sheet in the kitchen, that Mona already felt tired and couldn't comprehend how on earth she was going to make it the rest of the night without disappearing forever into a puff of smoke.

Somebody's going to die tonight, because of us.

Juliet sat in the driver's seat, squinting at the bar across the street, which was brightly lit and packed to the door. People stood outside in groups, smoking cigarettes and laughing loudly while the live music inside played in enthusiastic bursts that grew in volume every time someone went in or out. Mona had to wonder if this was really the best location to choose a random person to pluck, but for some reason Juliet was insistent that they come here.

It just seemed so...public. Even if they were completely hidden in shadow.

"I still don't understand why you didn't get that guy

who peed on the wall," Mona said after another half hour had passed with no activity. She shivered and rubbed her arms, even though the night was warm. "We could have just gotten all of this over with already."

At one point, a drunk guy had wobbled away from the bar to come pee in the alley they were parked in. Mona and Taylor had both been sure that it was the opportunity Juliet would take, so easy, right there and less than fifteen feet away from the car.

"He wasn't the right one," Juliet said, without taking her eyes from a group of women who had just come out of the bar. "I'll know when I see the person, okay? I'll *know*."

A wonderful and horrible thought came to Mona: what if Juliet chickened out? What if they didn't have to kill someone tonight after all, didn't have to stay up all night to wrap up bloody plastic and body parts and clean whatever ended up on the end of the hammer. The idea brought an initial promise of relief, until she remembered what that would mean for Rose. And whatever they would have to deal with if she got too hungry... Mona knew deep down that it would be worse than going through with the murder.

"It's okay, Juliet," she said. "You can do this." She realized how much she'd changed already, even from a few hours ago. She'd gone from being terrified to knowing in a much deeper way than before that they had to go through with this. Her heart rate slowed for the first time since they parked the car. She sat back in the seat, relaxed, a total balance to her previous fidgeting nervousness.

"I know I can," Juliet snapped in response. "What, do you think I'm copping out on Rose? After going through all of this shit to plan everything?" She paused, tapping her fingers over the wheel of the rental car, which was a black Prius. "I'm starting to think you're the one who's going to cop out."

That pissed Mona off, especially since she had finally realized fully that she *wouldn't* be copping out. But there was no point in arguing with Juliet, especially with Taylor in the car. She and Anya had learned this lesson too well when they were younger and just as attached at the hip as their two older sisters. Anya wasn't even here right now, she was at home with Rose. Mona wished she were here.

"So if you're not copping out," Mona cut back, leaning forward and narrowing her eyes at the back of Juliet's head, "what criteria *are* you using, exactly? Show us your balls and put your money where your mouth is. The pissing dude would have been easy."

"Shut up," Juliet said loudly, a stark contrast from the low voices they'd been using. "Just shut up and learn how to be patient."

"Shut up," Taylor repeated, glaring at Mona.

Five minutes passed, then ten, then twenty. *Finally*, the large group of women who had come out for a smoke break before returned, walking in opposite directions from one another as they left the bar. One of them walked across the street toward the alley. Her car must have been nearby. The woman was looking down into her purse, digging through it for keys as she stumbled over the pavement.

"A drunk driver," Juliet said under her breath. "She could kill herself or a whole family on the way home. It's almost like we're doing the citizens a favor."

Whatever you have to say to yourself to make it feel okay, Mona thought. *Just get this shit over with already.*

Juliet told Taylor to get in the backseat with Mona. "See you in a minute," she said, flashing a mad grin and pulling her hood up. She walked up to the mouth of the alley, remaining in the shadows, and Mona had a sudden and petty urge to laugh at how her feet looked wearing men's shoes three sizes too big for her. Juliet had stuffed them with socks so that they wouldn't fall off, and her feet look unnatural and clown-like compared to her long, slim legs.

The drunk lady got closer, and Mona couldn't believe how wide open the situation was. There was nobody else around the alley, and certainly nobody from across the street was watching the woman make her way right past Juliet. Mona saw her hooded sister lift a hand in greeting, and the woman stopped and gave her a hug.

"What?" Taylor said, staring. "Why is she hugging her?"

"I don't know," Mona whispered back, as if the woman could hear her. "That is really weird. She must be wasted, I guess."

Juliet kept talking to the lady, who had stopped looking for her keys in her purse. It was so dark that Mona couldn't see the lady's face to read how it was going. After a few minutes, Juliet motioned back toward the rental car, and the woman followed her into the alley, becoming swallowed by its shadows, and Mona knew that the woman had sealed her own fate by being so trusting.

Oh well, a cold new voice said inside. *One step closer to making Rose better and putting this nightmare behind us forever, one way or the other.*

Whether her new forced impassiveness had been brought on by true enlightenment or the half bottle of wine she'd found underneath Mom's nightstand and chugged before they came, Mona didn't care to explore. She had decided that it was best to stop thinking about things, and just live in the moment instead, take things as they come, be ready for anything.

But then the woman got in the car and she turned right around to look at Mona and Taylor. "Hey, girls!" she slurred brightly. This was when all of Mona's bullshit confidence shattered into a million pieces, because the drunk woman wasn't a random person at all, but Rita from the military post that they lived on. "So lovely to see you all again."

She thought of the last time she'd seen Rita, when they arrived at the post barbecue the day Rose first ate the human meat. Rita was the one who had greeted them, offered her mother a drink, acted so fake-nice it had rubbed all the girls the wrong way. She remembered in horror what Rita had said to Juliet that day. *And I heard you turned down a full ride to Juilliard, too*, she said. *You must really love our little community here if you're so eager to stay.*

"Hi Rita," Taylor said, clearly as shocked as Mona. "How are you?"

Mona saw, in one smooth motion, how Juliet leaned over while Rita was still turned toward them, babbling about her night, and dipped her hand into Rita's purse, which was on the dashboard. She retrieved Rita's phone from the purse. She was wearing leather driving gloves.

Rita didn't even notice when Juliet threw the phone out the window within a few seconds of pulling out of the alley.

Juliet had bought a thing that made your license plate blurry, but as they drove down the street and Mona turned around to see if anyone had seen them, she didn't see a single person and she knew that they'd gotten away with it—so far, anyway. It wasn't like that mattered now, anyway... How could they kill Rita?

What was Juliet thinking? Didn't she recognize Rita when she first struck up a conversation? Why would she bring her to the car? They were supposed to choose someone random, not someone from the goddamn post!

"Juliet was telling me how you're throwing your mom a surprise party tonight," Rita drawled on, completely unaware of the pervasive tension that was slowly sucking all the oxygen out of the car. "Should be a great time."

Mona leaned forward a little, trying as hard as she could not to be suspicious. "Hey, Jules," she said softly, wondering how she could safely imply that they drop Rita off immediately. "I think you missed a turn back there, right?"

"Nope," Juliet said. "I know exactly where I'm going."

"There's only one way back to post, silly!" Rita said and laughed a shrill, drunken laugh. "Don't tell me you're as stupid as your mom." Then, after an awkward pause: "Sorry, I didn't mean to insult her. Or you. I was just kidding."

"I'm sure you never do," Juliet said in a sweet voice, and Rita closed her mouth. "I mean, you just kind of come off as a person who doesn't really think before they speak."

What are you doing? Mona wanted to scream. *Do you want everything to go wrong here? Do you want us to get caught?*

"Rude," Rita said, and turned to look out the passenger window. She crossed her arms over her tanned, bony chest, clearly insulted. "Who did you say was gonna be there again? You said Jackie is coming, right?"

"She is," Juliet said. "We just have to stop and trade cars before heading there. I was helping my friend by picking this one up from the shop before it closed. She works late."

Rita bent down and grabbed her purse, started digging through it for her phone. "I'm just gonna text Jackie to see if she thinks I should come at all," she said. "Maybe you can drop me off at home instead. I've had too much to drink already."

See what you've done? Mona thought as Juliet stiffened and looked at Rita searching for her phone. *It's all ruined now.*

"Don't be so sensitive," Juliet said, playing it cool. "I was just joking with you."

"Mmm-hmm," Rita said politely, still looking through the impressive amount of crap in her bag. "Damn, I wonder if I left it at the bar?"

"Here we are." Juliet pulled into the edges of the dirt parking lot they'd left the Mustang in. "Let's hop in and go back to post. I'll even take you home, if you want."

"Thank you," Rita said in a formal tone. She must've decided that it actually *wouldn't* be so fun to ride with all the Cane sisters to their house after all, where all of her friends would be, much more put together than she was. Mona got into Juliet's car without speaking. Taylor looked like she wanted to throw up.

There's nothing to be done now, Mona realized. *We're just gonna have to go along with whatever Juliet is planning.*

Yes, hadn't she just decided to start going with the flow, no matter what it brought? Mona firmly believed that they'd all have to take their medicine over this, and maybe if she stopped expecting things to go as planned, it'd be easier not to be so damned frightened when it all went to shit. Maybe if she embraced the fact that she would either be in jail by the end of the night, or that Rose would snap and kill them all, she could get ahead of all this dreadful fear.

It's bigger than us now, she reminded herself, *and it has been since the day Mom brought Rose back from the dead.*

"Taylor sits up front," Juliet said as Rita made her way around the front of the car, still looking for her phone. "It's kind of tradition."

"Yeah," Taylor said weakly, and motioned for Rita to climb over the bent-over front seat and join Mona. "Tradition."

"Whatever," Rita mumbled, and sat heavily beside Mona. "Just get me home already."

Mona was so disconnected at this point that she was almost interested to see how this would all go down, if at all. In her eyes, it was all on Juliet at this point. This was her circus, she was the ringleader, and now it was time to sit back and watch the show, like an awful accident on the side of the road that you couldn't look away from no matter how hard you tried.

The car pulled out into the starry night, and Juliet let out a little cheer as the night wind whipped their hair across their faces. The convertible top was up, but the windows were down.

"Hey, Rita," Juliet said when they were almost there, and Mona saw Taylor perk up to attention. "Can you do me a little favor when we get back to post?"

"What?" Rita answered, her tone hard to read.

"Well." Juliet straightened up in her seat. "Apparently my mom is starting to suspect something about the party—"

"Nooo!" Taylor cried dramatically. "After all the planning!"

"I know," Juliet said, a flicker of a smile on her lips as she looked at Taylor. "Anyway, Jackie texted me a few minutes ago to say that my mom is starting to get suspicious and is calling the check-in boys asking if they've let any special guests in with us specifically. We're about to be there. Would you mind hiding back there so they don't know you're with us? They'd totally spill the secret."

"Hide from the check-in boys?" Rita laughed at this, the first time she'd laughed in minutes. "Joseph is always telling us how unreliable they are, especially when it comes to pretty girls. We should sneak me in and then report them. They never even check properly, and we could get them in so much trouble over it."

"Now that's the Rita I know," Juliet beamed, and Rita giggled again. "They definitely don't keep a close enough eye on who or what comes in or out. It'd be a good way for them to learn."

"Totally," Rita agreed.

They pulled into the checkpoint to get into post, and Rita shimmied down to the floor between the seats. She jokingly covered her head with her purse, which made Mona laugh until she remembered that they might actually kill this woman within the hour, and then her smile died away instantly.

The checkpoint was much less intense than Mona expected. They'd been in and out of post in this car together a million times, so much so that the car hardly needed to come to a stop when Juliet was waved on through.

"They didn't even look to see who was in the backseat," Juliet said after they were in, almost as if she couldn't believe it, maybe even like she was a little disappointed. "It was as easy as pie."

"And that's the problem!" Rita squeaked as she popped back up beside Mona, straightening out her bleached curls. "I will definitely report them to Joseph." Joseph was Rita's husband, who worked on post and who came home every night except for the three months a year, tops, that he was called away. Mom would always narrow her eyes whenever Rita humble-bragged about how her husband was able to spend most holidays at home with them. *Thank goodness. I can't live without the man after all.*

Juliet drove the car to the Cane residence, pulling right up to the closed garage instead of parking in the street like usual. If they came around the front of the house from the space in front of the closed garage instead of from the street, Mona figured that would make for less of a chance that any neighbor who could potentially be watching them wouldn't be able to identify that the woman with them was Rita and not Anya.

"I thought you were taking me home," Rita said, sounding a little deflated. "There's not even anybody here."

"Oh, did I say that the party was here?" Juliet answered, and let out another shrill laugh. "Sorry, I meant that it was at the recreation center, but we needed to stop by here first and pick up our present. Want to come in while we get it wrapped up? We have lots of leftover pizza you could scarf while you wait."

She's really going to do it, Mona thought with a shiver. *She's going to try and kill Rita.* So far, everything had gone exactly to plan, except for the fact that they knew who Rita was. But, Mona realized, they didn't really have any distinct connections to her, more than anyone else on the post, anyway. They certainly wouldn't be suspected of anything if she disappeared. She doubted they'd even be questioned by officials.

Juliet must have realized this, Mona knew now.

Mona's heart seized in her chest. Was it possible that Juliet...*purposefully* chose Rita, over a grudge? Somehow learned where she was going tonight and straight up staked her out?

No, no, no, Mona thought. A few snarky comments would not be enough to make Juliet want to literally kill somebody, there was no way. Maybe Juliet really hadn't seen that it was Rita until she came close, and then in true Juliet fashion, just figured, *screw it.*

Yes, of course. Juliet didn't *choose* Rita. It just turned out this way coincidentally. And Juliet went along with it simply because she realized that she could, without it making too much of a difference, anyway.

"Pizza?" Rita repeated. "Oh, god, that does sound really good. And it'll help me sober up a little, too—Joseph hates it when I…" She trailed off, apparently realizing that she was about to share something a little too personal with these somewhat bizarre girls. "Anyway. Let's go in."

"You got it." Juliet opened her door and got out first, quickly looking up and down the quiet, empty street in either direction. She met Mona's eyes and Mona tried to search, unsuccessfully, for any sort of clue as to what her older sister was thinking.

They made their way in through the front door, with the three sisters forming a wall behind Rita to block her from view from anyone who might be watching, even though the street was dark and quiet in the late hour. Mona doubted a single person on their street was even awake, let alone looking out their curtains, but better safe than sorry, she supposed.

Inside, the only light on was in the kitchen, just like they'd arranged with Anya beforehand. Knowing that she and Rose were upstairs right this very second filled Mona with a strange, frantic sort of urgency. If they were really going to do this, they'd need to do it quickly. If they went according to plan, Rita would be dead within five minutes.

Taylor ran ahead of the group and got some pizza out of the fridge. "Take a seat," she said to Rita, casually motioning to the single chair at the table (they'd moved the rest into the living room to avoid the chance of their victim choosing the wrong place to sit). Behind the chair, the brightly patterned cotton sheet looked a little ominous.

"What's with all the plastic on the floor?" Rita looked with her eyebrows furrowed at how much of it there was, covering almost everything and trailing straight down the open doorway of the basement stairs. Regardless, she still sat in the chair. The sight of her in it turned Mona's stomach, made her wish she'd drank just a little more wine than she had, because now she felt like she was going to randomly burst into tears or scream.

"Painting project," Mona mumbled, and Rita cocked her head to the side.

"I'll go start wrapping the present," Juliet announced, her eyes shining in a way that Mona couldn't help but interpret as excited. "Be back in a jiffy. And Rita..." she paused dramatically before running her fingers along the edge of the sheet "...enjoy that pizza."

But Rita wasn't even looking at Juliet, didn't see her slip behind the curtain, where Mona knew the hammer was waiting for her. Before she got all the way in, Juliet shot Mona a look, nodding to the kitchen door, where Mona was supposed to go in case Rita tried to run. Then Juliet disappeared, a rippling wave gently falling through the length of the sheet before it went still.

The microwave beeped, and Taylor opened it to take the plate of pizza. Mona could see from where she stood how badly her hands were shaking. Mona walked to her designated spot and found that her knees felt like they were made of gelatin, to the point where she seriously doubted she'd be able to do anything even if Rita did try to run. Even breathing normally was difficult.

Taylor set the plate of pizza down, nearly dropping it in her nerves.

"Girls," Rita said, looking back and forth between the two of them. "You don't look so good. You look... scared. Is everything o—"

But Rita didn't finish her sentence, and she never took a bite of the pizza in her hand, which dropped violently to the floor once the blurred whoosh of sound came from behind her, Juliet striking from behind the curtain.

The head of the hammer went straight through the back of Rita's skull, like a spoon cracking through the top layer of a crème brûlée.

"Arrrrrmmmmmmm," Rita gurgled, plunging face-first into the plate in front of her. Blood poured in aggressive torrents around both sides of her neck and head, pooling on the table and dripping onto the plastic underneath.

CHAPTER 19

Taylor let out a strangled cry, then clapped her hands over her mouth to cut off the sound. Mona sprinted to the sink, barely making it before she emptied the contents of her stomach into the shining stainless steel.

Rita was twitching, making horrible sounds, somehow trying to lift her head, and Mona wildly wished that she'd just shut up and die already. The sheet was swaying, rippling, the center of it wet with a large blooming splotch of red. Juliet hadn't come out from behind the curtain yet. Part of Mona absolutely hated her for being able to miss out on this part, this horror that was Rita dying slowly and painfully over a slice of pizza that was soggy with blood, even if Juliet was the one who'd had to bring the hammer down.

The girls froze, time froze, *everything* froze except for Rita's twitching arms and legs. Her mouth moved as though she was talking, forming endless silent words, whispers of a poem that none of them would ever be able to understand. Mona thought she could see Rita mouth the words *mommy mommy*, and finally she began crying. Juliet came out from behind the curtain at last, all of the color drained from her, the hammer still in her hand.

"Holy fuck," she said, looking down at Rita. "Is she still alive, or is that nerves?"

"Mlllarrrgh," Rita said, gagging. Her feet jerked against the legs of the chair, over and over again, *thump-thump-thump*. She somehow managed to slide her head off the plate, her cheek flat on the table, and one hand slid heavily across the flat surface, smearing the blood in a long trail behind it. Mona started crying harder.

"She's not dead yet," Taylor squeaked, stating the stupid fucking obvious, and Mona wanted to punch her, punch Juliet, run screaming into the night and never look back, jump off the nearest cliff to stop the endless loop playing in her head like a movie; the hammer cracking through Rita's head as she looked quizzically to Mona, trusting, *concerned* even.

"Close your eyes," Juliet said, and she didn't have to say it again. Both Mona and Taylor desperately flung their hands across their eyes, and there came another sound, a wet popping crunch as Juliet brought down the hammer again. Mona felt something wet splatter across her neck and forearm.

Rita stopped gurgling.

Mona slowly lowered her hands.

"It's done," Juliet said gently, and finally put the hammer down, on the table. There was blood all over the metal head, as well as a thick piece of scalp prickling with bleached blond hairs. "You guys, it's done. We did it. We fucking did it."

"Why did you pick Rita?" Mona nearly shouted, and in a single heartbeat Juliet was across the room and had shoved Mona against the back of the sink.

"Lower your voice," Juliet growled, her tone deadly. "If Rose hears you, if you mess this up after everything we've just been through, I swear to god, Mona, I'll, I'll..."

Mona stared back, aghast, shrinking. She remembered what Juliet said before, about feeding her to Rose. Right now, Juliet looked like she would be willing to do just that. Mona looked over her sister's shoulder, back toward the table, to the hammer with the gore stuck to the end, and her stomach went watery and weak.

"I'm sorry," she managed, her voice shaking. "I just... I don't understand why it had to be Rita. She lives on post. We knew her. Rose knew her."

"You were getting impatient about waiting," Juliet answered, smugly. "Someone walked by and I got them. It just so happened to be Rita."

The way she said it, like *I dare you to challenge me on this*, told Mona that nothing good could come from grilling Juliet about Rita.

"Oh, my god," a voice said from somewhere behind them. Mona turned and saw Anya at the edge of the kitchen, her eyes wide, her mouth open. "Is that...is that Rita Stazenski?"

"Why the fuck are you downstairs?" Juliet turned away from Mona toward Anya, that same awful fire in her eyes, her chest still heaving from the murder. "Where is Rose?"

"She's passed out," Anya said, not tearing her eyes away from Rita. She took a step back, wrapped her arms around herself. "The roast wasn't holding her over anymore. She was starting to act weird. I had to give her one of the sleeping pills…"

"Acting weird how?" Juliet said. Behind her, Taylor was standing still with her eyes closed.

"She was too hungry." Anya looked at Mona, her expression bleak. "She was writhing on the bed and telling me to stay away from her."

Mona wished she could tell Anya every single thing that had happened in this one glance: the stakeout, hiding Rita in the car, the lies Juliet told like it was second nature, the hammer coming through the curtain and cracking Rita's head open like it was an eggshell. She remembered the documentary about the Bloody Benders, how after watching it she'd been so insistent that they were nothing like them, but now she could see that yes, yes, they very much were.

The Killer Canes.

"You did a really good job," Juliet said to Taylor, turning on her heel and offering a thumbs-up. "From the beginning you knew how to go along with everything. Mona, not so much." Now she swung back on the same heel, and her thumbs-up turned down like she was calling a gladiator match. "Don't think I didn't notice how you started to chicken out in the car."

"What happened?" Anya asked, her forehead shining

with sweat, and she looked like she might throw up just like Mona did. "Did she tell anyone she was here? Did it... Did you kill her quickly? Make sure she didn't go through any pain?"

Mona couldn't help it, she let out another sob. How were they all capable of this? How did everything lead to the four of them, standing in the plastic-lined kitchen, the air thick and hot and smelling like the inside of a piggy bank? It was the most blood she'd ever seen, and she should have expected that. *Head wounds bleed a lot,* Juliet had told her once after she rode her bike off a curb and ate shit in the gravel when she was eight. *One little nick, and it's like a goddamn waterfall.*

But she didn't expect it, nobody could have expected the sound of the hammer or the smell of the blood or the way Rita tried to call out for her mother. Mona realized that she never fully believed they would carry out the murder, not in the deeper sense, anyway. They were supposed to get caught, or Mom was supposed to come home with answers, or they were supposed to chicken out and maybe, just maybe, Rose wouldn't turn vicious if she got too hungry, maybe she would just lay down and go to sleep and die again.

Wouldn't that have been better than what you just did?

"No," Mona cried out loud, covered her hands with her face. Ever since she puked, she'd been grotesquely sober, painfully aware. She felt like she'd never eat again.

But Rose will...

There was a pair of cold, clammy hands on her bare arms, pulling up. Mona stood and registered that it was

Anya. Her sister took her hand. If Mona wasn't so out of her mind from the stress, she might be able to appreciate the gesture more. They hadn't held hands in years. *This is what it took*, Mona thought wildly, madly. More tears fell.

"Jesus," Juliet said in disgust. "Taylor's been through the same thing and you don't see her losing *her* shit, do you? You need to remind yourself why we did this, Mona. You need to think about Rose."

Mona did think of Rose. She thought of how when Rose was almost two, she started doing this thing where she'd cup the face of whichever sister was closest and sigh, "Oh, I love you." She thought of how Rose had bawled her eyes out after Dad missed her sixth birthday, how they'd all cried with her, even Juliet, how they promised her over and over again that they would never leave her. She thought of all the times Rose stopped the girls from fighting, with nothing more than a giggle and a suggestion to play a game. She remembered the New Sunday that Rose had so painstakingly set up the day before she died.

If only they had her now, to step in and give out smiles and pour sugar all over everything, but she'd never even know what tonight happened. She'd never know what they'd all just gone through to keep her alive.

She's going to eat Rita.

"Take her upstairs," Juliet said to Anya, and walked over to the sheet, pulled it down. "She needs to go to sleep or something. Me and Taylor got this."

Mona saw Taylor's face as Anya pulled her away, and contrary to what Juliet just said, it would appear that she didn't have her shit together at all. But that wasn't for Mona to worry about, she was tired of existing in this now and desperately wanted to take a shower, to wash away the dirt and the night and the splatters of Rita's blood on her neck.

Afterward, when she was clean and under the covers of her own bed, Mona listened to the sound of Rose breathing heavily in the bed across the room. There was no fear inside of her that Rose would wake up in the night and tear her teeth through Mona's flesh. If that happened, it happened, and then she wouldn't have to worry so constantly anymore, wouldn't have to torture herself with her own thoughts, never-ending, a ring of endless shit. Maybe it'd be nice even, to have that sudden peace, no matter how painfully or violently it was brought about. Peace was peace in the end.

She listened for any sounds from downstairs, but it was quiet, which meant the body must have been in the basement by now. She imagined Juliet squatting over Rita's naked corpse, using the breaking knife to saw away long strips of gristled muscle. In one of the episodes of the crime documentary show the girls had watched for research, a bit of footage had shown a bathtub strewn with an abundance of strange neon-yellow entrails, human fat from a body that was cut up in there. Was that what it looked like now, down there in the basement?

From the bed right beside her, Mona heard Anya sniffling. She was probably crying, but no matter how hard she tried Mona couldn't move a muscle, couldn't will herself to say *are you okay* or *feel lucky you weren't there* or *do you think we've made the worst mistake in the world?* They were beyond the point of no return.

So instead, she went to sleep, dreamed that she was at a pizzeria with Rita and her sisters, and Rita was force-feeding her a soggy, dripping slice topped with pepperoni made from Rose.

"Eat it, you little bitch," Rita snarled, blood pouring from behind her head, one of her eyes pointing straight down, one of them looking right into Mona's soul. "It's the only way, don't you know? It's the only way!"

When Mona woke up, Juliet and Taylor were standing in the doorway of the bedroom. Taylor looked rested enough, but Juliet's skin was sunken and gray, Mona knew instantly that she hadn't slept a wink.

"I have great news," Juliet said, licking her cracked lips. "Mom finally called. She'll be home in three days."

"What?" Anya sat up and rubbed her eyes. "She really called?"

Mona realized that Anya probably assumed Mom had ditched them forever, just like she had. What else could excuse *days* without showing up or even calling? What else could excuse forcing them to murder somebody to keep Rose alive?

"She was doing another ritual with that Harlow woman in Danwin Cove," Juliet said. "One that took a long time. She says there's definitely a way to cure Rose. As in, zero percent chance of failure."

Mona strained her ears. Surely she couldn't have heard that right. The idea of a total cure, an actual end to the nightmare, it almost seemed unreal. Even when Rose was better, Mona would still live forever with the paranoia that someone would catch them for what they'd done, but deep down, she knew that they didn't leave a trace of evidence. There was no way anyone would ever suspect them in Rita's disappearance, just as long as Juliet could carry out the disposal of the body like she said she could.

According to her, it'd be the easy part.

"Thank Christ," Anya said, and turned to look at Rose to see if she heard, but the youngest Cane was still deep in drug-induced sleep. "It's over. It's going to be over soon."

"Yep," Juliet said warily, and turned to go back out to the hallway. "I've got to go downstairs and cook Rose's breakfast before she wakes up. She'll be very hungry."

"You need to rest," Taylor whined. "You've been up all night!"

"What, are *you* gonna do it?" Juliet snapped in reply. "She needs to eat, Taylor. Don't be stupid."

"Is it all gone?" Mona called after them, and she saw Juliet's shadow pause in the hallway. "Is everything cleaned up?"

"Clean as a whistle," Juliet answered, then continued on toward downstairs. "All the scraps are wrapped up nice and tight in my trunk. Plastic and duct tape, baby."

CHAPTER 20

All the scraps.
Mona sat in art class later that week, staring at the painting in front of her.

Plastic and duct tape, baby.

The words repeated in her head over and over as she painted a long, dripping black strip across the huge square of clean watercolor paper. She didn't blink as she watched the paint run down the length of the paper, slowly making its way to drip off the bottom onto the floor.

The old Mona had been sacrificed and spread to the wind like dust. There wasn't a drop of blood in the kitchen anymore, but Mona still saw it, still *felt* it, still heard Rita's last words echoing endlessly inside of her skull, even here, far away from the house.

Girls, Rita's voice said gently in Mona's mind again. *You don't look so good. You look...scared. Is everything o—*

Crack. Crunch. *Smack.*

Deep down, Mona felt a heavy fear that they'd end up having to do it again somehow. Nothing had gone right up until then, why expect for things to go right ever again?

Although, hey, maybe not. Mom was coming home today. Finally, *finally*, the nightmare could come to an end, and Rose could get better, and they could get on with living their stupid little lives that they were never smart enough to be thankful for before. Before Rose's death, the idea of living at home, wherever that would be, for three more years had been torture. Now it sounded like a goddamn cakewalk.

Well hey, looks like kidnapping and murdering someone was at least able to do that for you, Mona thought bitterly. *How sweet.* Her brain was full of all sorts of dark humor these days. It almost felt like a survival instinct, something to cling to desperately while everything else pulsated in chaos. When she stopped and thought about it for more than a second, forced herself to focus on exactly *what* the pulsating chaos was made out of, the white-hot fear that rose up as a result caused her face to tremble.

Rita's disappearance was in the news already. Police had questioned everyone from her friends to her husband to the employees of the bar she was last seen in, with the only lead being the broken cell phone they found discarded on the street outside. Since there hadn't been any activity on her credit cards, and since her car was still where she left it, the police were going forward as if Rita had been abducted.

The girls learned all of this from watching a news report a few days after the murder. Rose recognized Rita almost immediately, gasped dramatically while the other girls sat in eerie silence.

"That's the lady from our post!" Rose said from where she sat cross-legged on the floor, making a pot holder with a square plastic frame and technicolor stretchy bands, back to full energy at last. "Remember seeing her at that barbecue? She was kind of rude."

Mona had looked at her then, tried hard not to think about what Rose would say if she knew that the several pounds of green chile "shredded beef" she'd been consuming steadily over the previous forty hours or so had once been that woman who was rude at the barbecue. Their slow cooker had been running continuously, filling the house with a disgusting meaty smell that was like a rich pork roast, and even after the last batch was prepared and the slow cooker was cleaned and put back into the cupboard, Mona felt like the smell never really went away.

From the television screen, Rita Stazenski smiled at them all, positively *beaming* with her styled hair and expensive jacket.

It was like she was mocking them.

Now, Mona couldn't wait for the school day to end. Every single moment here was about looking busy enough, and being quiet enough, to slither through and around the attention spans of her teachers until the bell rang, and that was about it. She just wanted to fast forward to the part where she got off the school bus and walked up to the house and saw Mom's car parked outside the garage.

She realized that she was painting her own home, all in black, with its two stories and its shutters and its fenced yard. Mona didn't stop painting as she played out a vivid fantasy in her head, *lived* through it:

Mom's car is parked outside. I run the rest of the way in, and everyone is sitting on the couches waiting for me, their hands in their laps, smiles on their faces. Rose is Rose again, and that's not to say that she isn't Rose right now, but here I can tell instantly that Rose has been cured and everything is going to be okay again. Look at how her eyes are lit up. Look how she stands calmly instead of fidgeting until her fingertips are bloody and frayed.

"I found the cure!" Mom cries happily, standing alongside Harlow. Their arms are wrapped around each others' waists. I've forgotten how much I liked Mom's old best friend before. She wasn't so bad, not really, not compared to others in the world. "Harlow forgot to tell me about one silly little thing for the ritual," Mom goes on, "but it's taken care of now. It's done."

"That awful hunger from before is gone, Mona," Rose says, smiling, relaxed, whole. "I feel so much better now." She pauses, casting a sly glance at Mom. "Although, I do kind of feel like I could go for some enchiladas right about now."

Everybody laughs, Harlow, Mom, my sisters. We release all the tension, all the fear, invite our second chance with open arms and open hearts. Rita Stazenski washes down the drain like a long string of hair, slowly eases her way out of my mind forever and ever.

Now, outside of the daydream, Mona Cane shed a tear, quickly wiping it away with the back of her hand be-

fore getting up and leaving the dripping black painting
of her house for somebody else to clean up. She took her
backpack from where it hung on a hook by the door and
slipped out the instant the bell rang. She skipped going
to her locker to drop off the four textbooks, causing her
shoulders to scream from beneath the straps of her backpack, willing her body to hurt, to be punished.

Mona didn't talk to a single person at the bus stop. She
sat alone in the front, looking out the window with a
straight back and a straight face. The bus stopped, went
again, stopped, went. Finally it pulled into post, through
the fence and toward the housing. At the end of her
street, the bus stopped, and Mona rose and exited.

The driveway in front of the garage was empty.

She struggled to breathe calmly, scolded herself for
overreacting before she knew the full situation. The car
could be in the garage. Mom could simply not be home
yet. *How* exactly she couldn't manage to be home yet,
the rage inside Mona refused to dwell on without boil-
ing out of control.

Inside, Rose played video games on a console hooked
up to the television. Juliet and Taylor stood around quietly in the kitchen, leaning against things and taking turns letting out exasperated sighs as Juliet peered
through the kitchen window toward the street, to look
for Mom no doubt. There was an open bag of chips in
front of them, a bowl of salsa beside it, a dollop of red
on the counter that made Mona's stomach turn.

Upstairs, Anya was reading in bed, headphones in, the
room hazy and smelling like skunks.

So Mona drank Mom's gin straight from the bottle, hiding carelessly in Mom's closet instead of in the locked bathroom. She hardly cared about hiding this irrelevant habit from her sisters anymore, didn't understand how it could possibly hold enough water to outweigh everything else they were dealing with, couldn't imagine any of them giving a solid fuck. She remembered with a pained half grin how upset she'd gotten at the idea of Rose tattling on her before about the booze, how positively *fearful* she'd been.

What did I know of fear then?

When she was through with the gin, Mona lay in bed and waited for Mom to come home, or for Rose to come up to change into her pajamas, or for Juliet to call her down for dinner, anything, but nothing happened. Anya had since abandoned her book, leaving it open and facedown on her bed. She must have been downstairs with the others. First it got brighter in the room, a nasty, eyeball-piercing shade of late afternoon orange and red, and then it got darker.

Mom still wasn't home. She promised she'd be home by now and she wasn't. Everything was not going to be okay. Nothing was alright.

Mona's drunkenness was thicker than usual, heavier, and it made it hard to do much more than blink her eyes and swing her face gently from side to side. On the nightstand beside her, her cell phone vibrated loudly, causing her mind to jump while her body stayed slack. After a moment, she lifted a hand and dropped it over the phone, curling her fingers around it to bring it up to her face. The notification told her it was a text message from Lexa. Somehow, some way, after all of the bullshit, Lexa hadn't forgotten about Mona, hadn't deemed her worthy to get thrown out like the weekly trash.

You're going to think I'm crazy, the message read. But at this point, I don't really care anymore.

Mona's heart leaped, and suddenly she was feeling more awake. Her thumbs fumbled over the screen, panic rising in her throat. What do you mean? she typed clumsily, typos riddling the text. Are you okay?

No, the answer said, and Mona began imagining all sorts of horrendous scenarios that may have befallen her only friend. Before she had to wonder for too long, another message arrived: Because you're not.

What? Mona responded, sighing in relief. The idea of Lexa in trouble was shockingly troubling to Mona, had reminded her that she was capable of something other than coldness. I'm fine, really. You scared me.

Lexa responded almost instantly: I'm coming to your house. I'm going to come stay with you.

Mona stared at the text message. She could hear her heart beating in her ears. No, she typed. You can't.

I hope you'll forgive me, Lexa wrote back. Because I'm coming no matter what you say.

Mona willed herself to calm down. It wasn't as though Lexa knew her address…but then Mona remembered. She'd given it to her once, last winter holiday season by request, so she could get sent a gift. She never even returned the favor, that's what kind of shitty friend Mona was, but now she was more upset that she'd given her address away at all.

NO, Mona typed again, all caps this time as if it could somehow make her point come across more than it already had. After a few breaths, Mona regained control, thought for a moment before calculating her reply. I can't believe you'd do something like that even when I'm asking you not to. My mom would freak out if I brought anyone over, and me and my sisters would end up taking the punishment for it, not you. DO NOT come to my house.

Silence, then. Mona stared hard at Lexa's name on the screen, waited for the little dots to appear that indicated she was typing her reply, but the little dots never came. Mona hoped that she succeeded in backing Lexa into a corner about this, but couldn't be a hundred percent sure until she replied to confirm it. Would Lexa *really* ever fly across the country from Northern California, pay all that money just to come make sure Mona was okay?

Mona knew the answer almost instantly. She thought about their past, how whenever she'd been upset about something at home, Lexa was there for her, always there to remind her of her value, an unconditional sort of love that wasn't made to be long distance. But it was. She knew from what Lexa had said about her life that her parents made plenty of money, and apparently they cared about Mona too, somehow. If Lexa told them that Mona needed help, and asked them for the money to fly to her, would they give it?

Fuck.

Mona didn't know if she could handle any more stress.

She fantasized about having a heart attack in her sleep, dying blissfully far away from home, so they'd never find her body, meaning there was no chance her family could move heaven and hell to force her to come back. Not that they would, anyway. *But Lexa would,* was the last conscious thought Mona had, and she fell asleep waiting for a text message that never came.

When she woke up the next morning, Mom still wasn't back.

And Rose was starting to complain that she was hungry.

CHAPTER 21

Mona stood in the kitchen, her hands resting on the counter behind her. Everything was covered in plastic. The door to the basement was wide open, the plastic trailing down the stairs and into the darkness. Taylor shifted her weight from where she stood on the other side of the table. Juliet was out of sight, but not out of mind.

Mona wished this were a dream, or a vision like she had before in her art class, but it wasn't. This was real, and it was happening, and it was too late now to do anything to stop it. When Mom hadn't come home and another day passed and Rose started getting gray, Juliet had called them all in from school again and broke the news that they were going to have to come together once more. Rose was upstairs, refusing soup and water and sleeping on and off from the pills she'd dry swallowed.

This wasn't a life, not for Rose, not for any of them, but it didn't matter now, for the only place they had to go was forward. They were all killers now, forever, it was a *part* of them, as big and relevant as any other mark in their histories, broken bones, spiritual awakenings, memories of their happiest times. They were killers now, and would become killers all over again.

Because now, with Rose ill and Mom missing and everyone delirious from such little sleep, it was time to murder another person, harvest some more of that fresh meat for Rose. The sheet hanging from the ceiling swayed gently in the breeze of the air conditioner.

The man from the bar was big, huge actually. Mona couldn't imagine why Juliet would pick him when he could have so easily taken all of them. At least she actually chose someone random this time. By now, Mona had come to believe that Rita really had to have been a sick coincidence, and that at least brought a tiny amount of comfort to this fucked-up game they'd been required to play.

After careful consideration, Mona decided to go through this murder stone-cold sober. At first she didn't see what the point was anymore, to try and differentiate herself from her mother, but she couldn't deny that the alcohol itself was a huge problem. If she was really doing this for Rose, then she'd better give it her all, and not allow any room for drunken mistakes, even if it meant facing the terror without even a hint of a softened, boozy lens.

Despite her shattered morals, and her soul poisoned forever by Rita's death, Mona wanted what she was doing to mean something. What, she wasn't quite sure. That she was a good sister? That she was purposefully choosing this path, and not simply being scared into it by Juliet? What a laugh, to both.

Apparently this guy's name was Glenn. Mona heard him say it to Juliet as they drove home, his hand sliding up her bare thigh, his fingers grazing the end of her denim cutoffs as he looked at her up and down.

I don't know what's making Mom take her precious fucking time, Juliet had said to the sisters the day before, *but she wasn't lying when she told me. I heard it in her voice.*

She knows a real way to cure Rose permanently.

There's no chance she's wrong, it's a guarantee.

We have to take care of Rose so that she makes it to live past everything she's gone through so far. If she dies again now, all of this would have been for nothing, except for her unnatural level of pain.

"Why did you say all this plastic was in here again?" The man asked, sitting at the table with his back to the sheet hanging from the ceiling. He was drunk, but looked a tiny bit nervous nonetheless as he glanced around. Taylor had offered him the microwavable pizza, but he'd said no, something Mona was embarrassed to admit she didn't see coming.

Apparently Taylor didn't either, because after a few moments of awkward pause, she burst out *well sit down, sit down!* like an anxious little kid and started making the damn pizza anyway, despite the man turning it down twice by now. With Juliet nowhere to be found, Glenn didn't seem so keen on the idea of coming to hang out at their house for a party after all.

"We're painting," Mona said slowly, trying to sound calm and sure and like someone who knew exactly what they were doing. Glenn shot her a look, and she felt him noticing how antsy she was being. As he watched, she took a weird little sidestep to block the doorway out a little bit more, and instantly she regretted doing it.

Suspicious. As. Fuck.

Taylor made a weird coughing sound, and Mona knew she was trying to signal to Juliet to just use the damn hammer already, because by the look on Glenn's face, there was no way he was going to stick around for another minute and thirty seconds while the microwave did its magic.

The impromptu coughing signal apparently worked. Suddenly, the hammer struck down through the sheet hanging from the ceiling, hard, a whirring flash of moving fabric, but Mona never heard that heart-stopping crack of a skull being bust open from behind, never saw blood splatter over the table onto the floor.

That was because Glenn decided to lean sideways at the last moment, to give Mona some serious side-eye as he assessed why this teenage girl would be blocking his exit from their empty, plastic-draped house that didn't have a single paint can to be found.

And so the hammer missed his skull, instead striking him solidly in the shoulder.

"What the fuck?" Glenn roared, turning around and ripping the sheet down with one angry motion of the fist. Juliet stood behind the curtain, holding the hammer, and Glenn stood up so fast his chair went backward and got Juliet in the gut. She leaned over, the wind knocked out of her, as Glenn turned on his heel and made his way around the table in three mighty strides. On the other side, Taylor stood, shaking so hard that she couldn't seem

227

to move out of the way or do anything but stare with wide, terrified eyes.

Glenn grabbed her by the arm and threw her across the kitchen. Taylor flew headfirst into the cabinets, then landed on her hands and knees on the floor. "Taylor," Juliet gasped, and then Mona registered that Glenn was coming for her, full force, ready to throw her aside like he did with Taylor and run screaming into the night.

"*MONA,*" Juliet bellowed, stumbling her way around the chair and the long side of the kitchen table.

It happened so quickly: Mona taking in the drunk man, who was moving a little too quickly from panic and adrenaline, a clumsy giant just asking to be toppled over. Mona acted as though she was stepping out of the way of the door, and the second his pace increased even more at the excitement of having a clean exit, Mona slid down and kicked the man in his ankles from the side, as hard as she could manage, and she was sober and he was drunk, and that, she told herself as she heard the crack of connection between her foot and his ankle, was why she got to win.

Glenn went down hard on his stomach, his face landing on the plastic-covered floor with a sickening slap. A second later, Juliet was upon him, and before he could even lift his head to see what was about to happen to him, the claw on the back of the hammer sunk into his face from behind, hooking itself in one of his eyes and breaking the orbit open like it was a wishbone. His eyeball flew aside and hit Mona in the shin. She cried out and jumped backward, and the small of her back jabbed painfully into the counter.

Glenn let out the briefest bloodcurdling shriek, but Juliet ripped the claw free from his eye in a second and brought it down again, this time in the back of his head, and the screaming silenced at once. Pieces of bone, hair, and brain matter were flung across the kitchen, over Mona's face and arms, all over the wall. Large gelatinous chunks of deep crimson and yellow stuck to the ceiling like strands of cooked spaghetti being tested for doneness. There came the reek of bowels letting loose.

But aside from the horror of the gorefest in front of Mona's eyes, there was something else about what was happening that was somehow more disturbing, chilling, life-ruining. It was Juliet's face. As she beat the already-dead drunk man's noggin into a sopping, squishing pile of bone shards and meat jelly, she was *smiling*.

Her eyes were more alive than Mona had ever seen them, even more so than the time Juliet finally nailed her recital piece half a week before the big show, after it had been frustrating her to tears for months.

And now, with the hammer, Juliet liked what she was doing. She was having fun.

Mona fell into one of the table chairs and buried her head in her arms. She wasn't going to throw up, but her temples were pounding and her hands were shaky and she felt like she hadn't eaten for a week, but the idea of putting anything into her mouth and chewing it and swallowing it made her want to die, actually die right there and then.

"What happened back there?" Juliet demanded, and when Mona raised her head she could see that her sister was no longer high on the glee of the kill, had hidden it well as she looked around sternly between Taylor and Mona. "Why was he leaning away from the sheet like that?"

"It was Mona," Taylor said from where she was still on the floor on her hands and knees, her hair falling forward to cover her face. Still, it was evident from her voice that she was crying. "Mona was acting so weird about everything, he knew something was wrong, and he saw her move in front of the door. She was way too obvious."

No, Mona tried to say, but nothing came out, and anyway, it was true. She had a wild thought that Juliet might kill her too, bash her brains into liquid as punishment since there was already a mess to clean up, anyway.

"Do you want to know what might have happened if good old Glenn had escaped?" Juliet said in the most bewilderingly calm tone. Mona wondered if Anya could hear all of this commotion from upstairs, where she was guarding a sleeping Rose. She thought about how last time, Anya came downstairs, but this time she was apparently smart enough to stay away.

"Yes," Mona muttered, refusing to meet Juliet's eye. "It would have ruined everything."

"Yes," Juliet repeated, gently tapping the blood-slicked hammer handle on Mona's shoulder with every word. "It. Would. Have. Ruined. Everything."

"It was all wrong from the start," Mona burst angrily, deciding that it was a better option to turn the energy racing through her into something less hysterical. "He was here because he thought you wanted to suck his dick, but you disappeared within ten seconds of the front door closing! It's obvious we're not painting in here, he figured out something was up!"

Mona had thought things were bad after Rita. But with Rita, there hadn't been any actual errors in their strategy, in fact, it pretty much passed with flying colors. But this time was rocky from the start; Glenn didn't seem nearly as excited about leaving with Juliet when he saw Taylor and Mona in the backseat, and when they switched from the cherry red rental car to Juliet's Mustang and Juliet begged him to hide from the post guards so that she wouldn't get in trouble, he almost refused. But Juliet strung him along just enough, whispering things in his ear, gliding her fingers down the front of her chest while he watched.

Mona thought about how it felt to kick him in the ankles. She could have easily let him escape, let all of this madness end, went to jail where at least she'd be protected from whatever consequences could come from Rose not getting her meat. But, no, she had instead made the conscious decision to take a direct physical hand in ending someone's life.

"I'm only going to say this once," Juliet said, her tone deadly low, as she leaned close enough for Mona to smell her breath and see how dark the circles under her eyes really were. "Everything that went wrong tonight was because of you."

Mona wondered how much sleep Juliet had gotten, if any, in the past handful of days. Maybe the awful glee she'd spied in her sister before was just the result of being sleep deprived, but as soon as she thought it she knew it wasn't true. All of this, Rose and the hunger and the murder, had revealed something about Juliet that was so deeply buried, and Mona was worried that the change was permanent.

"I'm sorry," she whispered, and Juliet let out an eerie cackle.

"She's sorry!" Juliet repeated fiendishly, her eyes bugging out like a total psychopath. "Well, I'm sorry to break it to you, Mona, but an apology isn't going to be enough in this case."

What could she mean by that? Was Juliet about to kill her? No, she couldn't, this was her *sister* for goodness' sake...

"If Mom doesn't come back, you're not going on the next run," Juliet said, and now Mona understood. "You and Anya are going to switch jobs."

It was supposed to be a punishment, but it felt more like a gift, until Mona remembered the other part of Juliet's sentence.

"But why wouldn't Mom be back by then?" Mona started to cry at the idea. "She promised there's a way to cure Rose so we can stop doing this. Why hasn't she come home yet?"

"Shhhh," Juliet whispered, pressing a blood-smeared, latex-gloved finger over Mona's lips. Mona could taste the salty metal essence of Glenn, and it made her want to die. "You're crying too loudly. Stop."

Taylor finally got up from the floor, and tied her hair back with a band from around her wrist. "Can we clean this up please," she said, more like a statement than a question. "I need to go to bed."

"Is your head alright?" Juliet finally moved away from Mona, walking across the kitchen to check on her mini-me. "That asshole flung you pretty hard."

Because we were trying to murder him, Mona wanted to scream.

"Mom is coming back," Juliet said softly, to nobody in particular as she combed her fingers through Taylor's hairline to check for any significant damage. "We just have to hang in there until she does. She is coming. She *is*."

Of all of the sisters, Juliet had always been the one to most easily know if Mom was lying about something. Even the simplest, most unimportant things, Juliet would call her out right away and that guilty blush would bloom in Mom's cheeks. Juliet told them all before that she could tell Mom wasn't lying when she said there was a cure for Rose. *So what is taking so goddamn long?*

Plus, doing this sober hadn't done a goddamn thing for Mona, except make it clear that the problem wasn't the alcohol, it was never the alcohol, no. The problem had always been *her*. And she'd never be fixed.

Mona imagined a knock on the door while the kitchen looked like a scene from a vampire movie, how screwed they'd all be. She imagined it was Lexa at the door, although that wasn't very easy since she'd never even seen Lexa's real face, her avatars online were all of her favorite fictional characters, Buffy, Loki, Wednesday Addams.

Just coming to check on you, Lexa would say, then notice that Mona was covered in blood and had a shard of skull on the collarbone of her shirt. *What did you do, Mona?*

What did you do?

CHAPTER 22

Once everything was cleaned up and the body had been stripped and Juliet had disposed of all the scraps at the town landfill, the house began to feel haunted. Mona couldn't describe the feeling specifically, but it was like the house now understood that it had become a place of evil, a home of death, and it started existing as such. The hallways were darker. The staircase was scarier, and Mona couldn't go up or down them without sprinting, her heart in her throat at the idea of Rita's and Glenn's hands pulling on her ankles from beneath the stairs, their heads still crushed and wet and glimmering in the shadows.

Even when all the windows and blinds were open, it was like there was dark water over the lens Mona saw through as she looked over the house. At night, she swore she could hear Rita whispering, begging for help from the inside of the closet, calling *mommy mommy mommy...*

Mom didn't return. Juliet continued to deteriorate, physically and mentally, still refusing to sleep for more

than an hour at a time a few times a day, always needing to be awake and cleaning or waiting for Mom to
call or writing in her journal. Mona considered asking
Juliet if she was writing anything that could be used as
evidence against her later, but knew her sister would
become defensive and mean at such an accusation. Still,
Mona couldn't help but wonder.

Juliet wasn't herself.

A few days after Rose polished off the last of the
stringy, gravy-laden "pot roast" from the exhausted and
overworked slow cooker, she asked all her sisters to gather
in her makeshift tent, which she hadn't built since the day
before she died. Mona hoped it was a good sign, a sign
that things could turn around at any minute, because if
Rose's tent was up that must have meant she was feeling
a little closer to herself again. Maybe the cure was just
that she needed to eat more meat than what Mom originally thought. Maybe it was slow-coming, and Glenn
had finally allowed her to meet the required limit.

But after they were all settled in, sitting in the circle
around a few tea-light candles Rose had lit, it was clear
that this wasn't the kind of pillow-fort sister date they
used to have before Rose's death.

"Something horrible is happening," Rose said carefully, looking to each sister's face, clearly desperate for any
sort of read. "And somebody's going to tell me what it is."

"Rose," Juliet started, her unwashed hair hanging in
greasy strips on each side of her face, "please don't worry
about—"

"STOP SAYING THAT," Rose yelled, then brought

her hands to her mouth quickly, as if shocked and ashamed at her own outburst. "I'm sorry, I'm sorry, I'm not trying to sound crazy, but I just don't understand why everything is so different, but I know it has to be because of me, because I died." She looked at Anya, then Mona. "Are you hiding something from me? Like, maybe you all know that no matter what happens, I'm going to die again really soon, and you're trying not to let me find out..."

"What?" Mona said. "No, no, Rose, of course not, it's nothing like that. You're safe. We promised you we'd take care of you, right?"

"Trust us," Anya added grimly. "We have been."

"Uh-huh." Rose nodded earnestly, her skinny little arms reaching forward to pluck a stuffed panda from the floor next to Taylor. She hugged it close to her, so hard that Mona could hear the tendons in her elbows pop. "But then why do you guys make me take those sleeping pills sometimes? When that happens, I feel like I slip away from you again. Days go by and I hardly notice. Is it..." Her eyes welled up, her voice trembled, her face got red. "Is it because you're trying to get rid of me? Is it because none of you can stand to be around me since I died? Are you afraid of me?" A pitiful little sob escaped her lips.

"Jesus," Juliet said, glassy-eyed, and put her hand on Rose's knee. "No, Rose, we are not trying to get rid of you. We would never. I can understand that you're scared and weirded out by what happened, but please, we can get past this, we can, we *will*."

"Then why do I have to take the pills?" Rose demanded. "If you're not trying to get rid of me, what are you doing? Because I'm starting to feel bad in my head, like Mom used to. I'm starting to forget what it's like to laugh and smile and be happy, I'm losing myself."

She was crying now. Anya rushed forward in a crawl and hugged Rose, pulling her close. Mona gently ran her fingers through Rose's hair. Taylor rubbed the small of her back. All of them were trying not to lose it just like she was.

"I can't stop having nightmares about what it's like to be dead," Rose blubbered. "When you make me go to sleep it's like I'm back there, trapped. It's pitch dark, but it's not empty, there are always things moving around in there, they whisper in your ear, they bump into you as they run past." She gasped for air, clutched her arms around Anya as if her life depended on it, the stuffed panda on the floor. "Please stop doing it, I can't take another pill, I won't, *I won't...*"

"It's okay," Juliet cooed, squeezing Rose's knee. "It's okay. You don't have to take any more pills. We'll figure something else out..."

"That's what I don't understand," Rose said, jerking her knee away from Juliet's squeeze. "Why do you need me to be asleep in the first place? It's like you're keeping me in a cage."

Nobody said anything. Nobody wanted to lie to Rose, but they couldn't let her in on the truth, either. If Rose knew she'd been eating people, she'd probably have a full-on mental breakdown, something irreversible. It was like the stakes rose every single minute, with no sign of stopping, and Mona was flailing wildly between being emotionally dead and feeling like she was about to completely lose her shit.

"We just didn't want you to suffer," Juliet said finally, and usually Mona hated when Juliet weaved truths around a lie to make it less of a lie, but now she couldn't be more grateful for the skill. "We wanted you to be able to rest until Mom comes with your medicine."

"But haven't *you* been giving me medicine?" Rose challenged. "You've been putting it in my food. I know you have, because I feel better after eating it. Plus, you told me you were."

Juliet hesitated. "The medicine I give you only works temporarily," she said. "That's why you keep losing your energy and feeling ill off and on. But what Mom has will make you better forever. You'll never feel that awful hunger again, you'll be able to eat anything you want, just like before…"

"Why does it affect my eating so much?" Rose wondered aloud, more to herself than her sisters. "It's like I can only eat if the medicine is in the food. Is it because the dead don't eat?" She paused. "I…I think they do eat. I feel like I understood it at one point, when I was a part of it, but as soon as I was pulled back it all became too scary to know. I've made myself forget."

Already, what Rose had said about being dead filled Mona with unspeakable fear and dread. She'd always believed that death was as natural as birth, and therefore there was nothing to be afraid of, except for anxiety and pain, but even those could only go so far before you died and everything stopped and was at peace again. But to imagine a dark place filled with ravenous, whispering, rampaging souls...it made Mona wonder if that was where we all came from *before* we were born, too.

Would that mean that all humans were inherently evil? That they were all capable of drawing back to that dark, awful place that housed us whenever we weren't alive? Mona thought about the look on Juliet's face when she was ruining Glenn's head with the hammer, and shuddered.

"What you've been through is unfair." It was Anya who spoke up this time. "It's unfair and it's scary and there's no way around that. But you won't feel this way forever, Rose, soon all of this will be such a distant memory, in a different time, in a different town. We just have to make it through this part." Mona could see from how her sister looked around that she was talking to all of them, not just Rose. "We just have to push through this. As a family."

Taylor looked dead-eyed, like she wasn't even listening anymore to what was happening, and Juliet didn't look much better. Mona realized that all of them, even herself, had lost a considerable amount of weight since all of this started. Juliet's under-eye circles were by far the darkest, but they all had them. They looked like the ghosts of their former selves, paler, unwashed, unfed, suffering.

We just have to push through this. Mona repeated the words in her head and did something that even surprised herself: she grabbed Anya's hand. Anya looked down in mild shock, then looked back up at Mona with wide eyes.

After the meeting in the tent was over, Juliet and Taylor went into their bedroom and closed the door. Mona could hear them speaking in hushed tones inside, and she hoped with everything that Juliet was figuring out a way to get Mom back immediately. If they weren't going to give Rose any more sleeping pills, that meant things would get ugly fast the next time she started to get hungry.

She put it out of her mind. Mom would be back by then. *She had to be.*

Mona retrieved her phone from where she left it in the living room and saw that there were new texts from Lexa. Mona hadn't heard from Lexa even one time since she'd tried to force her way into coming over and Mona shut her down. Her heartbeat quickened to see that there were a few in a row. At first she was nervous at the idea of Lexa asking if she could come again, but the first message waiting for her was almost worse than that.

Do you remember when you told me that Rose was dead?

Mona's mouth went dry. She scrolled down, desperate to read the rest.

And then you said that she was safe, and that she'd been in a car accident and her friend was killed. I've been looking through all the news in your area around that time, and there isn't a single report of an accident like that.

The newfound hope and strength that came to life inside Mona after she took Anya's hand in the pillow fort/tent died away quickly.

A young girl dying so tragically would definitely make the news. Why did you lie about something like that? That's when all of this started, with you acting so weird, and you won't even let me come see you, and I thought I was your best friend.

You are my best friend, Mona typed back. Please, please just believe me and trust me when I say, things are just a little hard at home right now, but we are all fine and soon everything will be back to normal again.

She sent the text, waited a few minutes, saw that Lexa had read it. She didn't write back.

I promise, Lex.

Still no answer.

Juliet appeared suddenly, making Mona jump. Her oldest sister had never looked so beaten down and messed up, even during the handful of months after she officially turned down the full ride scholarship for Juilliard. Her fingernails were curled toward her palms slightly, like she had claws, and Mona had to work not to show her fear.

"Mom called again." Her voice sounded like it was bad news. "She got caught up with the police somehow, she was slurring a little bit so I'm wondering if she went on some sort of bender. Either way, she's finally out and on her way."

Something was wrong. It was the way Juliet was talking. For a brief moment Mona worried that she was making all of this up, because if she wasn't, why wouldn't she be happy about it? She just promised Rose that there wouldn't be any more sleeping pills, and that meant that their time was severely limited, you'd think the news of Mom's return would be the best thing she'd heard all week, all month.

Mona's blood went cold then. Maybe Juliet wasn't lying. Maybe she was just genuinely upset that she wouldn't get to murder anybody else.

"That's... That's great," Mona managed. "I'm so happy for Rose. She deserves the peace after everything she's been through."

"Yes, Rose," Juliet said, almost mechanically. "Our baby."

She stared down at Mona without saying anything else, her eyes sweeping slowly over her tangled, alcoholic mess of a sister. "Do you ever wonder why Mom never got her fucking tubes tied?" she asked. "I mean, you think after the second or third one she'd sterilize herself if she hated having children so much."

This was stuff that Mona hadn't thought about in a long time, because she hadn't had an empty moment in time to spare for it. She didn't understand why Juliet was bringing it up now, but the more she thought about it, the more she kind of did.

"I don't know," Mona admitted. "Mostly I wonder if

she's really in love with Dad or if she's just, like, in love with the idea of being a colonel's wife."

"No," Juliet said. "She definitely loves him. That's the problem, actually." Juliet sat beside Mona on the couch, and even though Mona felt her phone vibrate, hopefully a response from Lexa, she didn't look at it.

"Isn't it awful," Juliet continued, "that all of this misery came into existence simply because Mom loves Dad so much? More than she could ever love herself. More than she could ever love us."

Mona thought about how Juliet had taken care of them all since she was young, too young. She'd never gotten to escape in any sense, except when she played her piano, and even now that had been ruined for her, too painful of a reminder of what she gave up. She was a can of shaken soda, a high-pressure tank about to roll off a cliff. She'd been that way for years now, Mona recognized. This was just the first time she'd stopped covering it up with her stern control-freak commands and tendency for mean sarcasm.

What would happen when she finally fell over the edge? Or had she already?

"Mom loves us, she's just really messed up," Mona said, the first time she'd done anything even close to sticking up for Mom since she used to bicker about it with Anya before Rose died. She remembered how upset Mom had gotten after Rose fell down the stairs, how desperate she became for Rose to come back to life.

Mona hadn't been able to imagine a scenario where she didn't at least call them, but if she was caught up with the police, she probably wouldn't have been able to. She would have used her one call to someone who could help her get out, that woman Harlow or some other adult. She must have been desperate to get back to them. She had to be, or Mona didn't know how much farther she could make it without throwing in the towel one way or another.

Juliet looked at Mona, pure disgust on her face. "If you really believe that, you are as goddamn stupid as you've always looked."

And with that, she rose from the couch and went over to the kitchen, leaning her head down and taking a drink directly from the sink. Mona felt her face redden, and slid her phone out to see what Lexa said to her in reply from before:

I'm sorry, but I can't do this anymore.

When Mona tried to reply, she couldn't get through. Instead, she got an automatic reply from Lexa's cell phone provider: This number has been deactivated and is no longer in service.

CHAPTER 23

Rose was riding her bicycle around in the yard, the hood of her sweatshirt raised to conceal the still-vivid bruising that dominated her neck and collarbone. She went in big, sweeping circles, never raising her face to the sun, never attempting a trick like raising the front tire or driving in a straight line with both of her hands raised away from the handlebars. The yard was not filled with the sound of laughter or gleeful shouts or death-defying shrieks as Rose got four inches of air from the makeshift jump she built after first moving here. She just kept riding in the circles, her head down, humming an off-key hymn under her breath.

Inside the house, the other Cane girls found out from the news that Glenn Blackwood was a single father with four children, full custody, and the affinity for the occasional weekend bar crawl with friends. Since he was the second person to go missing after leaving a bar in the area with his cell phone and car found nearby, the police were investigating possible links between this case and Rita Stazenski's abduction only a handful of days ago.

Mona was glad that Rose was outside. If she was watching with them, she'd surely comment on the story like she had with Rita's.

Oh, how sad, she'd say. *All those kids, left behind.* Mona never thought she'd take away someone else's father in a way that was much worse than how she felt her own father was taken away.

As Juliet, Taylor, Anya and Mona watched this piece of news be delivered on the television, Mona saw a variety of other headlines scroll across the bottom of the screen: *Local heroin problem growing out of control, Sal's Bakery to sell their last donut a week from today before closing their doors, severely abused dog found within inches of life underneath Willow Bridge...*

What sort of place *was* this planet, really? Mona took it all in, her head pulsing in pain from her hangover. If bringing people back from the dead was possible, if there really existed a realm like the one Rose kept having nightmares about, what other sorts of things were dwelling within the news headlines on any given day? Were there things that existed beyond rituals? Were there things like underground tunnels full of psychic monsters, or stretches of old prairie lands somewhere that were literally evil, or real haunted houses? Were there vampires? Demons? Zombies?

That's what Rose is, her voice remarked cruelly in her head. Mona shook her head a bit to rattle the thought loose, and Juliet looked at her warily. *No,* Mona thought.

Rose is not a zombie. She's not mindless. She has her feelings and her wishes and her old self to keep grounded. It's not the same.

All through growing up, through elementary school teachers and Disney movies and famous people on TV encouraging their fans, Mona had seen and heard the phrase *Anything is possible!* millions of times. It was supposed to be comforting, inspiring, but now all Mona could see when she thought about it was the endless possibilities of how monstrous the world might have been, in both a literal and metaphorical sense.

The concept of safety was a delusion.

On the television screen, there was a picture of Glenn and his kids, three boys and a girl. Mona wondered where they were today, how upset they were, how much they missed their dad. She wondered about her own father for the first time since before this all started; what he was doing, where exactly he was, what kind of day he was having. She realized something that she somehow hadn't before.

"Why have we not called Dad?" she asked Juliet, and the other girls looked at her through glazed eyes. "Maybe he'd be able to help us somehow, maybe he'd know what to do."

Mona didn't understand why Juliet suddenly looked like she'd been slapped in the face. She stared in silence for a few moments, drowning the atmosphere with her anger, making the air thick with it. She looked at Mona like she was a piece of dog shit on a shoe.

"Why in the *fuck* would we tell Dad what's happening?" Juliet said quietly, in a tone pulled so tight that Mona could feel the inevitable snap coming. "How do you think he, a colonel in the goddamned *army*, would feel at the news that we've murdered two people to *feed to Rose?*"

"What?" came a devastated voice from behind them. The girls turned in one swift movement, to see Rose standing at the far end of the house. She must have come in quietly from the mudroom. "What did you just say?"

Her face crumpled before any of them could say a thing. "You've… I've…*eaten*…" She fell to her knees, letting out gasping shrieks as her chest heaved in an effort to breathe. "You murdered people… *You fed me people!*" she was screaming now, wildly fighting them all away, flinging her arms to hit Mona in the neck and Anya in the nose and Taylor on the head. "What have you done to me, how could you do this, you're killers, *kill me next, kill me next, kill me next…*"

Rose flung away from her sisters, clawing at her face and her hair, making guttural growling sounds that didn't sound human at all. "I've eaten people," she rasped. "I knew I was a monster, I could feel it, I could feel something from the other side stuck to my soul, ruining it, I'm not the same Rose, *I'm not the same Rose…*"

Mona brought a hand to her mouth, devastated. Everything they'd tried so hard to cover up, everything they'd sacrificed to make sure Rose never found out the truth, was for nothing. They'd officially broken her, and all because Mona had somehow thought to ask if calling Dad could possibly help. And to hear Rose insist that she wasn't the same girl, that something permanent had stained her soul, frightened her beyond belief. Of course she was the same Rose, wasn't she? It must have been the trauma, she must have been having a complete psychological breakdown.

Juliet pushed past the other girls, forcibly pressed her palm over Rose's mouth and used her free hand to hold her in place as she tried to pull away. "I'll explain everything to you," she said firmly, her eyes wild as she looked to the open windows to see if any neighbors were out in their yards. "But you absolutely have to stop screaming stuff like that or we are *all* going to jail, and *then what would you do, all alone like that?*"

Rose stopped fighting and screaming, but the tears still fell in endless streams down her face. She sobbed against Juliet's hand, her cheeks a deep shade of red, her hands clawing to grab at the carpet like she was trying to rip it out. Anya moved forward again to hug Rose, and Mona followed. Taylor just looked down at the scene, expressionless, like she was a living video camera instead of a person involved.

"It's okay," Anya said softly, rocking her back and forth, and Juliet lowered her hand to stand over them like Taylor did. "It's okay, it's okay, we are here, you are not alone, you are safe..."

No, Mona realized again. *None of us are.*

It took a full twenty minutes for Rose's body to go slack against Anya, and she stopped crying and allowed herself to be rocked quietly, her eyes staring unblinking into space, a trail of drool spilling over the corner of her mouth. After a while, Juliet leaned down to pull Rose away, lifting her to stand before leading her to the couch. They all sat down around her, and Mona turned off the television.

"We're so sorry," Juliet said, taking Rose's hand and patting it. "You'd gone through enough and we didn't want for you to be scared, or hurt, or—"

"Disgusted?" Rose interrupted. "I don't want to live anymore. I can't live like this. Put me back." Her chin quivered for a moment, but she didn't start crying again. "Even if I have to go back to that dark place, I didn't even realize I was there until I was taken back anyway, you should have just let me stay dead!"

"No," they all said at once, each with their faces twisted into a different degree of pain.

"Please don't say that," Mona said. *We couldn't have ruined ourselves for nothing. It needs to mean something, or we might as well kill ourselves right this very second.*

"It won't be like this forever," Anya said.

"Mom knows how to make it stop," Juliet insisted.

"Juliet has been doing everything she can all for *you*," Taylor said, in a voice much more biting and bitter than her other sisters'. "You don't even understand what we've done for you, what Juliet's done, and now you're just going to give up and make it all for nothing? *Do you know what we've done for you?*"

"Jesus, Taylor," Juliet said. "Back off of her, right now. It's not her fault."

Taylor, nearly panting, finally looked away from Rose

and to Juliet. "I'm sorry," she whispered pitifully. "Of course it's not, I'm sorry, Rose, I'm so sorry…"

Rose didn't say anything at first, but Mona could see that at the very least, Taylor's outburst had snapped Rose out of the despair to some degree. "So it's Mom's fault, then," Rose said. "And she's going to make it up to me."

"That's right," Juliet said. "She knows a way to let you live without needing to…to eat. You'll never have to go through it again. That part of it is over."

There was no way she could know that, but Mona didn't want for Rose to lose it again.

"Never again?" Rose asked hopefully. "Never?"

"Never," Juliet said, and she was obviously holding something back. "I mean, not unless Mom fails to show up again. But if she does," she added at the sight of Rose's face darkening again. "If she does, we will figure it out, Rose, it's not like it sounds, they don't die afraid or in pain…"

False, Mona thought, remembering Glenn and Rita and all the blood and whimpering and screams. *That is straight up false.*

"I want to take a bath," Rose said suddenly. "I don't feel very good after all that. I cried too hard, I think."

"You've got to conserve your energy," Juliet agreed, rising first. "And you just used up a whole lot. I'll go fill the bath for you."

"Thanks, Jules," Rose said softly.

Once they'd both disappeared upstairs, there was a knock on the door. Taylor stared ahead into nothingness, as though she didn't hear it. Mona had a quick flash of panic at the idea that it was Lexa standing on the other side of the door. *No,* she thought desperately, making her way to the door as her hands went cold. *No, no, no, not now, please…*

But it wasn't Lexa, of course. It was some random kid passing out invitations for an event at the rec center in a few weeks, and he was gone as quickly as he showed up as soon as Mona took the little square of neon-green paper from him.

"You look like you were expecting the FBI or something," Anya said, looking at Mona watch the kid ride away on his bike.

"Can I talk to you?" Mona replied, officially at her limit, closing the front curtains and locking the door. "In the yard, or something?"

Anya looked back to check on Taylor, who was sitting silent and still on the couch facing away from them. "Sure," she said. "Let's go."

They walked through the mudroom to the large grassy yard, where Rose's bike lay on its side, looking lonesome. Mona led Anya to the far corner, the one without a neighboring fence right on the other side, and the girls sat cross-legged in the shade of the large tree planted there.

"It's out of control," Anya said. "It's been out of control for a while, but we're getting to the point where everything is going to explode."

It used to be like this far more often, going off somewhere to hang out, just the two of them, usually to get away from being bullied by Juliet and Taylor. They'd talk about anything and everything, good things and bad things and happy things and sad things. Petty things. Gossipy things. All the things you shouldn't talk about because it isn't polite, but when they were together, there were no rules like that, and everything was fair. That sort of sacred bond.

But then came their attempted uprising against Juliet, and the threat of CPS and foster homes, and their disagreements over Mom, and Anya's slow withdrawal from the entire situation, and Mona's drinking. There, now, Mona wanted to start it up again, bring it back. She could start by telling Anya all about the thing she'd been keeping inside.

"I think Juliet likes killing people," Mona blurted, already relieved at the small release of pressure from holding it in like she had. "You haven't seen her doing it, but especially this last time, with…" she swallowed, trying to force the awful lump in her throat down "…with Glenn. Something went wrong, I messed up and he almost got away and Juliet had to…had to…"

"What?" Anya asked, rigid. "What did she do?"

"I don't know," Mona whispered, looking around in paranoia to make sure nobody was within earshot. "I could just tell that she liked getting to take it to the next level. She was… She was smiling. And she kept hitting him with the hammer, for a really long time after he was dead."

Mona remembered the sight of it, and her stomach turned. She began to wonder if they all fell down the stairs that day, if none of them were really alive and they were all just busy scooting their way through the bowels of hell. She wondered how it was possible that their love for Rose and their fear of Juliet had led them here. She wondered if Juliet was on to something with her love-is-poison speech about Mom and Dad yesterday.

"What are you saying?" Anya shivered in the warmth and glanced back to the house. "That she's, what…a psychopath?"

"I don't know," Mona admitted. "It could just be that she's temporarily making herself go to that place to make all of this easier on herself. But when she told me Mom was coming home for real, she seemed legitimately disappointed. I think she wants to do it again. Do you… Do you remember that time she killed the cat?"

Anya nodded, and the girls shared a moment of truly depressing silence. "What are we going to do?" Mona finally asked. "What in the hell are we going to do?"

"I don't know," Anya admitted. "But Mom will be home soon enough and it'll be over, for good. And we'll all be in therapy for the literal rest of our lives," she added with an empty laugh.

Mona tried not to give much thought to the hardships that would come after all of this was officially over and everybody was left to pick up the pieces of themselves that they'd dropped or broken or lost. All she wanted was to get there, and to get away from here, away from a time where they were murderers tending to their cannibal sister.

"That's what I'm saying, though," Mona said, her face grim. "I don't have anything to back this up, but I can't help but feel like Juliet is going to try and delay Mom somehow. Maybe she even has been, all this time. Maybe she's been in constant contact and hasn't been telling us, has been telling weird lies to make the extended trip okay."

"Mona," Anya said, gently. "I think you're over-thinking it too much. Juliet wants Mom back just as much as the rest of us do. Why wouldn't she? You know how much she hates to see Rose suffer."

Mona couldn't deny that. And she also made the dismaying realization that there was no way to really convey what she saw that night in the kitchen, with Juliet and Glenn. There was no way to accurately portray the cold, electric force of evil that Juliet had become in those few brief moments. It was beyond a protective sister pushed to her limit. It was a peek behind the curtain into the darkest recesses of Juliet's mind, that guttural place of ravenous hunger that Rose kept having nightmares about.

"I know she doesn't want Rose to suffer," Mona said. "Just…promise me that if this escalates further, if we end up having to do this again, you'll look out for it. In Juliet, I mean. She told me after I messed up that I wouldn't be able to come again, that it'd have to be you."

Mona was suddenly filled with grief for Anya over the knowledge of how much seeing something like that changed you forever, permanent damage never to fade away.

"It won't go that far." Anya spoke the words but looked terrified. She grabbed Mona's hand, and Mona squeezed. "Juliet told Rose that we were done with that."

Mona looked into her sister's eyes, then leaned forward

to pull her into a hug. They stayed like that for a while, that old familiar love made new again in the embrace, before getting up and quietly making their way back to the house, their arms linked. Mona wanted to believe what Anya was saying so much. She wanted so badly for this to be over, and for it to end as easily as Mom showing up within the next few hours and handing over some sort of magic potion to turn everything around again.

But there was a pit in her stomach, heavy and dreadful and radiating with anxiety, pleading, *insisting* that Mona be prepared in case this wasn't the end at all, in case this was, in fact, only the beginning of something even worse than what they'd already seen.

CHAPTER 24

Twenty times a day, Mona checked to see if Lexa's number had been reactivated, only for each and every message to get sent back instantly, an extra punch in the gut as she was forced to reread what she'd never get to say to Lexa:

Please tell me you're there again.

Lexa, I don't understand how you could just leave me like this.

You abandoned me.

I need you.

I hate you.

Fuck off forever.

Please tell me you're there again.

None of the messages got through. And when Mona tried to email, she got that same awful return message stating that the account had been deleted. She thought about what Lexa would have had to go through just to avoid Mona—change the same number she'd had for years, change the email account she'd had for even longer. Did she have to contact all of her other friends, explaining why she changed her number and email, explaining that the best friend she'd never met was someone she wanted nothing to do with anymore?

Just like that. Mona still could not believe it. Things were sort of getting bad between them, yeah, but not in a way that could have ever led Mona to believe that Lexa would somehow decide that she'd had enough, forever. She remembered the last thing Lexa ever said to her:

I can't do this anymore.

Mona's favorite thing about Lexa was always the fact that she never got tired of Mona, never took it personally when Mona was grumpy or got defensive when she could have (and maybe should have) more than once. Maybe this was just the straw that broke the camel's back. Maybe Lexa had already been feeling more and more fed up with Mona and her nonsense by the day.

She was a loser after all, with all those schools she'd been to and yet not one single person had wanted to stay her friend beyond a friendly smile in class. She'd always been the forgettable girl.

Mona passed the time waiting for Mom to come home by browsing mundane websites online and constantly refreshing her inbox for a message from Lexa. The longer the silence lasted, the more insane Mona felt, and finally, *finally* a new message popped up for her after she pushed the refresh button for the ten thousandth time. "Lexa," Mona whispered aloud, and Anya looked up from her book from the next bed over. "What?" she asked, confused.

"Sorry," Mona said, her voice trailing off as she saw who the email was really from: a spam account advertising fitwear. She exhaled in frustration and snapped her laptop shut. Anya was watching her nervously. "You look upset," she said. "Is everything okay?"

Mona looked back to her sister, flattered in a way that Anya looked so concerned. Before their talk in the yard, she wouldn't have asked after Mona's feelings or appeared to care at all. And now she looked so invested. Maybe they really were on their way back to how things were, after all.

"I'm okay," Mona said with a weak smile. "Thanks for asking."

"Listen." Anya closed her book and sat up, her hands fidgeting over each other. "There's something I need to tell you, I think." She paused.

She's going to apologize, Mona realized. *After all this time, she's going to acknowledge ditching me and say that she's sorry. And then I'll have the opportunity to apologize too, for doubting her, because maybe this could have all been avoided if we forced Mom to seek help, and all of our trust can be fully restored and together we can hold each other up through the rest of this ordeal with Rose. Screw Everly. Screw Lexa.*

"Anything, Anya," Mona said expectantly, and sat with her back straight on the bed. "You can tell me anything."

"I know I can," Anya answered, and wow, she really did look nervous. Apologizing never came easy to her. Mona waited patiently. "I…" Anya paused, looked down at her feet while she said the rest. "I know about your friend Lexa."

It wasn't what Mona was expecting to hear, and it jolted her with a feeling of darkening shock. "What?" she said, her voice caught in her throat. "You've looked at my phone? Or my email?" Or maybe, and Mona hated to imagine the possibility, Lexa somehow reached out to Anya to express her worries?

"No," Anya said, and now there was a tear rolling down her cheek. "I know about Lexa because… because… I *am* Lexa."

Time slowed down, and Mona felt like she was going to throw up. She thought back to the hundreds, maybe even thousands of conversations she'd had with Lexa over the time they'd known each other, complaining about her family, complaining about *Anya* even. How "Lexa" had always known the right thing to say to calm Mona down and get her to laugh it off and "keep on truckin'." She thought of all the secrets she'd told. She thought of all the personal details she'd shared, the types of details that could only be shared with someone who didn't exist beyond the screen.

It was Anya this whole time.

There was no Lexa.

There was no best friend.

Mona's face got hot as she remembered "Lexa" digging for the truth on Rose, pushing Mona to admit that something was wrong, threatening to come over to the house and making things so much more stressful than they already were. What kind of fucked-up game had Anya been playing with her?

"How could you do that?" she managed, and stood on shaky legs. "What is your problem?"

The previously comforting memory of their conversation in the yard soured, turned bad real quick. It hadn't been genuine. Anya had manipulated her way back into Mona's attention, by brushing the Lexa persona off and swooping in in her place. Mona already knew that she couldn't trust Juliet, or Taylor, but now she was faced with the truly upsetting notion that she couldn't even trust Anya, the sister who she used to pretend was her twin. Even before, when they fought and were cold and harsh to one another, Mona still trusted her.

Not anymore.

"I'm so sorry," Anya whispered, and no wonder she looked so worried when she told Mona she had something to say. She looked almost as upset as Mona felt.

"Shut up," Mona snapped angrily, stomping across the room to get to the bathroom. "You are insane. You're worse than Juliet." Anya flinched, just as Mona intended her to, even though it wasn't true about Juliet, but it was close enough and she wanted for Anya to hurt. "What you did is so fucking heartless. I'll never forgive you for it. Ever."

She stepped into the bathroom and locked the door behind her.

"Hey," Anya said from the other side, and Mona could hear her rise from her bed and pad over the bathroom door. "Please don't start drinking right now. Please, come out and talk to me."

Mona's mouth dropped; pure rage surged through her body. *"What?"* she nearly screamed. "Oh, fuck you, Anya, fuck you!" Because, of course, she mentioned drinking to Lexa often. Not framed as a problem, but she had definitely acknowledged being drunk when things were especially hard. And Anya was never supposed to find out.

The room was spinning. Mona sat down and started weeping into her hands. She *had* been coming in here to drink. She was such a fool to believe that she'd been good at hiding it, at gliding by without it affecting anything or anyone else, but Rose knew, and Anya knew, and at one point Mona had become suspicious that her mom knew, too. Why didn't they try to help her?

Because you wouldn't have accepted it. Rose had tried to bring it up before, Mona knew deep down, and "Lexa" had brought up her drinking on occasion as well, both of them shut down with a swift vengeance because it was none of their goddamn business. *You didn't accept the help.*

Just like she knew Mom wouldn't, back when her and Anya argued so passionately about it.

Sitting there, feeling so upset that she wanted to sink into the floorboards and never come back out again, Mona had the knowledge that there was something nearby that had the power to at least help her calm down a little, feel a little less awful about the monster she was growing up to be, more accomplished in the art of evil than most people ever achieved in their entire lifetimes, all at the ripe old age of fifteen.

Mona rose to make her way to the secret spot where she hid her booze, but before she could take a step, Anya's frantic knocks were cut off with an almost startling abruptness. Mona quit crying in order to hear what was happening.

"Mona?" Juliet's voice was there now, quick and stressed. "I don't know what you two are fighting about, but it doesn't matter anymore. Rose is… We need to talk downstairs. *Now.*"

And here we go, Mona thought madly, her head cocked to the side as the last of her tears finished falling. *Here is the beginning of the end.*

She already knew what the issue was. Mom still wasn't home, Rose was starting to get hungry, and they couldn't sedate her even one more time. This was exactly why Mona had been doubtful when Juliet made all those stupid promises to Rose.

This was bad. Things were going to fall apart quickly now.

"I'm coming," Mona said, her voice hoarse, and left the bathroom without so much as a glance in the mirror, she couldn't stand to look at herself right now, so drastically changed and hollowed and doomed.

She didn't even meet Anya's eye as she left the bathroom and headed for the hallway and then the stairs. They followed Juliet silently, the tension coming from downstairs almost staggering.

Taylor was standing with her arms crossed behind the island in the kitchen, looking fretfully to the living room, where Rose was curled up on the couch, moaning.

"My stomach," she said softly. "I'm hungry, I'm *so* hungry, you would not believe…"

"Rose," Mona said, rushing to her sister's side. "Hang in there, we're going to figure this out, we're gonna find a way to—"

"Please," Rose interrupted, begging. "I'm so hungry, Mona, I don't know what I'll do."

So, now was the time when they'd all be punished for their sins. This was the fastest Rose had ever gotten hungry after eating. It wasn't working as well as it did before. Something else would have to be done. But what? Mona had the slow realization that the end was coming, and quickly, either for one or all of them.

"Take one of the sleeping pills," Juliet pleaded, stepping up behind Mona. "Please, just one, it'll give me another day to plan something…"

"No," Rose bellowed, her eyes wide and furious. "You promised me never again. I'm not taking it! *I'm not going back to that place!"*

"Goddamn it," Juliet said, turning away to pace back and forth across the living room. "Okay, okay, we're going to have to make a run tonight, girls, we're going to have to make one right now."

"Yes, please!" Rose cried, and this was when Mona knew that her baby sister's mind was starting to go. Before, she'd been so upset at the idea of them murdering anyone for her to eat. Now she seemed desperate for it. "Go right now, you've got to, *please*, something bad will happen!"

Mona, Anya and Taylor were all looking to Juliet, and

Mona realized too late that they'd once again shoved all of the responsibility off of themselves and onto the eldest Cane. Juliet realized it too, Mona saw it by the look on her face, and she stopped pacing and straightened her back.

"Okay," she said. "Everybody shut up and listen. We're going to make a run tonight, but there isn't any time to rent a car or set up the sheet and the plastic in the kitchen. We have to bring whoever it is down into the basement and do it there. Anya and Taylor, you're with me. Mona, stay with Rose."

Mona never thought she'd want to be the one going to kidnap someone, but the idea of being here alone with Rose when she was like this scared the bejesus out of her, as much as she didn't want to admit it.

"Hurry," Rose groaned, and within five minutes the other girls were dressed in sweats and hoodies and were heading out the door. It was already dark outside, the early evening just settling in. It would have been so much harder for them to do this if it were the middle of the day. *Small blessings*, Mona thought. *A convenient time for a kidnapping and a murder.*

"Let's go upstairs," Mona told Rose, helping her up. "We'll get you comfortable in bed while we wait for them to get back."

"Am I going to hell, Mona?" Rose rasped as they made their way up the stairs. "Because I want to eat a person? Oh, my god, I actually *want* to, I want to really, really bad…"

"Shhh," Mona whispered, her head light with fear as she somehow managed not to drop Rose's arm and flee into the night. "They'll be back before you know it, we just have to hold on…"

She tucked Rose in with gentle care, plugged in the hazy orange string lights that were wrapped around the canopy bed frame, put on a CD of slow classical piano to help them both relax. Rose writhed on the bed a little, moaning. "I'm so hungry," she whimpered, and Mona finally came to terms with the fact that she hated her mother, straight up hated her.

It was her fault any of this had happened, it was her fault it had gotten this far, she promised them the world and gave them nothing, less than nothing, she actually took so very much from every single one of them.

"Sing to me," Rose said. "Sing me the one about the end of the world."

The house was empty and silent around them, also changed, keeping them to simmer in the darkness that had infected it. Mona realized that with how quickly this murder came about, there was little to no chance that they were going to get away with it like they probably would have with the others. But they had started doing this for Rose, knew the risk when they agreed to it, promised that they'd help her for as long as they were physically able. Mona didn't know what would happen to Rose once they'd all been arrested and she got taken somewhere to wait for Dad to come home.

She didn't want to think about it any longer.

"'Why, does the sun, go on shining?'" Mona sang, her voice cracking but on key. "'Why, does the sea, rush to shore?'" Rose leaned back a little, relaxed, a serene smile growing on her pained face.

"'Don't they know,'" Mona continued, "'it's the end, of the world, 'cause you don't love me, anymooore...'"

She finished the song without crying or messing up once. She realized when she finished just how tightly they were holding on to each other's hands. The piano music still played in the background, a delicate piece with many repeating measures.

"Rose," Mona said, and her sister growled in discomfort. "You know how much I love you, right?"

"Yes," Rose managed. "And I love you more."

Mona cried then. She didn't even try to hide it as she leaned over onto Rose's lap and let go, her apology for failing her sister and letting all of this happen to her. She didn't understand how any of them deserved this, with what they'd all gone through up until this point, especially Rose. She felt Rose's fingers comb through her hair as she cried, and against her better judgment, allowed herself to eventually doze off.

"Get off of me," Rose said suddenly, wriggling to get Mona to sit up. Mona could feel that some time had passed. "Get up get up GET UP..."

Mona snapped awake and stood, her heart pounding, and watched as Rose tore off her sweatshirt, wearing only a spaghetti strap tank top beneath. When she did, Mona gasped.

The bruising, all that dark purple and green with black veins...it had spread. And not just a little; before, only one side of her neck was affected, but now it wrapped around her entire front, and her back, making its way down her arms and up her face. It looked like she was decaying, literally decaying, turning into mush from the inside out before Mona's eyes.

"It's so hot," Rose cried, flinging the blankets off and jumping sporadically up. "I don't feel right inside, something is wrong, I've never had to wait this long to eat before…"

Mona jumped as Rose stumbled toward her, her arms outstretched. "Come here, Mona," Rose cried out, her eyes a little wild, moaning in terrible pleasure. "Come here, come here, come here, I want to smell you, mmmm, *you SMELL!*" Mona stepped back and bumped against the dresser with the old CD player on it; the piano music skipped for a brief moment. Rose grabbed at Mona's neck for a split second, but drew her hands away like she'd touched a hot iron.

"No," she said, in a much different voice from before. "Go away, go away and get out of here, get out and shut the door, lock it, I need food, Mona, get me some fucking food *RIGHT NOW OR I'M GOING TO TEAR YOUR FUCKING NECK OPEN WITH MY TEETH!*"

Mona had never heard Rose curse once in her entire life, never seen her look as she did now. The bruising spread to her face now, went about halfway up, was starting to affect the whites of her eyes somehow, made them yellow with angry splotches of red. The thick, black veins crept over her cheeks and up her forehead, slowly, like paint dripping in reverse.

"Come here," Rose said dreamily, different again,

licking her lips, baring her teeth. "Come here and let me do it, you said you want to help me, help me now, take off your shirt and let me look at all your flesh..." She faded away, turned her head unnaturally like she was trying to break her own neck. "Mmm, Mona, I think you'd better run now."

Mona didn't need to be told twice. She sprinted across the room, took the thick and exceptionally long rope that Rose used for double Dutch, shut the door with Rose inside without a word. She tied the rope around the door handle, tightening the knot before she pulled the other end to Juliet and Taylor's doorway down the hall. She closed their door and tied the other end around the handle, eliminating as much slack as she could before doubling down on the knot. Inside the bedroom she and Anya shared with Rose, there was mostly silence except for a quick shuffling sound; the sound of Rose running back and forth over the carpet, like an animal in heat.

Mona was shaking so bad she could hardly function; she had a weird moment where she wished there was a bottle of wine in her hand, to keep her company while she waited for the other girls. She listened to Rose scuttle around in their bedroom, letting out the occasional strained moan, like a woman in labor, for about ten more minutes before she heard the front door slam downstairs.

Her sisters were back at last. Or maybe it was Mom. Mona didn't care. Without a moment's hesitation, she turned away from the bedroom door and ran down to the living room.

CHAPTER 25

It wasn't Mom, of course.

It was Juliet and Taylor and Anya, but something was wrong—there wasn't anybody else with them. Juliet looked spitting mad, standing at the kitchen sink, holding her hand under the water and cursing under her breath. Taylor walked slowly to the table and went down into one of the chairs. Anya just stood at the door and cried, and Mona could see that there was something wrong with her face, like there was a black eye forming, like she'd been punched.

"What happened?" Mona demanded, thinking of Rose upstairs. *There is no time left.* "Goddamn it, what happened?"

"Anya fucked everything up," Juliet shouted from the sink. "That's what happened. Where is Rose?"

Anya cried louder and Taylor stared ahead in a scarily calm sort of way, giving off the look of someone who was truly about to snap. Mona felt overcome with a pure sort of panic, the full weight of everything hitting her at once, realizing how very worried she was for every one of them. This was the point of no return.

"I had to lock her in the bedroom," Mona said. "She's too hungry. She…she changed. The bruising was spreading, the veins…" She stifled a sob, *must keep it together*, mustn't allow herself to fall into hysteria. "They were creeping up her face." She paused again. "She wanted to eat me."

Juliet turned the water off. Silence followed, the air crawling like it was infested with invisible maggots. They were all breaking, going nuts, right this very second. Mona could feel it in herself, could see it in Taylor's impossibly serene face, in Juliet's furious one, in tough Anya's whimpers and tears as she tenderly touched at her massively bruised eye. The thread that had always kept them too closely knit was being cut, slowly pulled out, separating them.

Rose was already gone. They'd all be next.

What now?

"Taylor." Juliet finally broke the silence. Taylor didn't move, kept staring ahead exactly as she was before. "Taylor!"

Taylor finally blinked, turned her head to Juliet gently. "Yes?"

"I need for you to come help me bandage up my hand in the bathroom." Juliet looked to Mona and Anya in disgust. "I can't believe you two. You're both the reason there isn't anybody here tonight for Rose, Mona with your stupid hesitation last time, Anya with your stupid hesitation this time. It's your fault Rose is dying right now."

271

Mona accepted this. She was a murderer and a bad sister. They all were, but there was little point in opening her mouth about that now.

"After everything we've been through," Taylor said softly, nodding as she looked off into space again. "After everything we've done."

"Exactly," Juliet said, cradling her hand to her chest and stepping for the hallway leading to the downstairs bathroom. "It was all for nothing. Taylor, come help me with this so we can take a moment to figure out exactly what we're going to do."

Taylor stood and followed her without hesitation, leaving Mona and Anya alone. Mona heard them go into the bathroom, heard the door click shut. She thought she could hear Juliet speaking in a low voice.

"What's going to happen to Rose?" Anya said, her voice still shaky from tears. "Is she really just going to die again?"

Mona leaned against the wall, resting her hands on her cheeks. She had been ignoring Anya after the Lexa betrayal, but there was little point in keeping that up now. "She could," she said. "But to be honest, I think it's more likely that she's going to become…something else. It won't be her anymore. It'll be a monster that wants to tear us apart." She ignored the horror on Anya's face, kept going. "I guess the only question now is, once she turns, will she turn back to Rose again after she eats? Or will she stay like that forever?"

"No," Anya said, and lowered her head again. "I shouldn't have done what I did back there. I didn't think it'd be like this, didn't think she'd go through so much pain..."

"What do you mean?" Mona asked. She realized she still didn't know exactly what happened when they all went out earlier. "What happened?"

"Juliet took all these backstreets to a random bar. She said it was a different one than the two you guys hit up before. She parked down the street and went and walked closer to the place, leaned against the wall for a while."

Upstairs, there came a single loud banging sound— Rose hitting her fists against the door. Mona's hands went cold. "And then what?"

"She started talking to this older man, way older, like grandpa age." Anya stopped crying, straightened herself as she relived the memory. "I was watching them walk closer to the car, but all of a sudden I couldn't stop thinking about Rita Stazenski, and the stuff we found out about that Glenn guy on the news. They got in the car and when the guy started talking to me and Taylor, I freaked out. I...messed up. Juliet got mad and punched me."

Juliet and Taylor emerged from the bathroom, and Anya went quiet. Juliet's knuckles were wrapped in a thin layer of white bandages. "Taylor and I are going to check on Rose," she said. "Both of you stay down here."

"No," Mona croaked. "You can't open the door. Please, trust me, she's not herself, she'll hurt you..."

"Shut up," Juliet said, so aggressively that Mona did. "I'm not an idiot, but I *am* the closest thing to a mother that she's got, and unlike you, I haven't given up on her yet." Mona's face got hot with shame.

"I have, however, given up on you two." Juliet continued. "Both of you stay down here. Come on, Taylor."

The two disappeared upstairs, and Mona turned to Anya with a newfound burst of energy. "If she opens the door, she's going to be killed. Maybe both of them."

"What are we going to do if what you said is true?" Anya rose to her feet, started pacing around, looking for something. "Should we arm ourselves, somehow? Are we going to have to fight her?"

The idea of fighting off a feral Rose was too much for Mona's heart to handle. "We need to figure something else out," she mumbled, and walked to the foot of the stairs, looking up them. "Maybe we can forcibly sedate her somehow. If we all worked together to hold her down. We should tell Juliet before she does something rash."

Anya said nothing, but joined Mona at the bottom of the stairs. She was holding a heavy brass candlestick in one hand. "Let's go up, then," she nearly whispered, and took Mona's hand with her free one.

"I still don't trust you," Mona said to Anya, disappointed in herself, but grateful for what petty relief saying it brought her. Before Anya could answer, Mona started making her way up.

The girls went up one step at a time, cautiously listening, slower than Mona had ever allowed herself to take these stairs. It was pitch-black, but each of them had memorized the slow curve of the ascending steps, and together they made their way up to the second floor. Soon, there was a soft orange glow that could be seen ahead, cast by the hallway night-light at the top of the stairs. Then they were in the hallway, and Juliet and Taylor were nowhere to be seen.

The jump rope was still holding tight between the doorknobs of the two bedrooms. Inside the bedroom they shared with Rose, there was total and complete silence. Mona's heart seized at the idea that Rose may have just died, like Juliet and Anya thought would happen, but then there was a slow, steady sound coming from the other side of the door.

Fingernails being pulled across the wall.

At the end of the hallway, Mona heard something else, a low giggle of Taylor's coming from behind the closed door of Mom's room. Anya heard it too, and together the two snuck as quietly as they could down the hallway, not wanting to alert Rose to their presence, or Juliet and Taylor for that matter. They went right up to the doorway and listened, their arms linked so hard Mona's was starting to feel sore.

"I know it's awful," she could hear Juliet saying in Mom's room. "But they haven't really left us with any other choice."

Anya and Mona looked to each other in alarm, their eyes glittering in the dark. Anya's mouth slacked open a little bit. Mona wasn't sure either of them really wanted to hear what was coming next. Behind them, there was still the sound of Rose scratching at the walls, steadily growing faster, like she was trying to dig herself out.

"Think about it," Juliet continued. "Who do you think deserves to live more, Rose or one of them? It's not Rose's fault that any of this has happened to her. They put us in this place."

"It's Mom's fault," Taylor said unsteadily. "But, yeah, they are the ones who let the plan fall apart."

Suddenly, a loud crash came from behind Mona and Anya, and both girls nearly jumped out of their skin. For a moment, Mona thought that the door had been ripped open, but when she turned back to check, the rope was still holding tight. The bedroom door closest to them shook as it was hit again, *crash*. Rose was trying to break out.

Mona pulled Anya away from their mother's door, down the hallway toward the stairs again. Juliet and Taylor were going to kill one of them, possibly both, to use their meat. Mona was right—about Juliet and Taylor anyway—that they had all cracked and lost their minds. They were both completely gone, as gone as Rose, and now she and Anya needed to act quick or they were going to die.

"What are we going to do," Anya whispered, shaking with what Mona assumed was adrenaline. It surged through her veins, too, making it hard to think straight. Before she could answer, there came a spine-chilling shriek from the inside of Rose's room, like an animal being cut open while it was still alive.

"LET ME OUT," came a frantic voice, one that Mona refused to believe was coming from Rose's body, it was so

deep and guttural and demonic. "I HEAR YOU OUT
THERE IN THE HALLWAY."

"Shit," Mona whispered. There was no way Juliet
and Taylor didn't hear that. And, just as she suspected,
the door to Mom's bedroom flew open a second later.
The two oldest Cane girls stepped out, their eyes bear-
ing down on Mona and Anya.

The pounding came again on the door to Rose's bedroom, many in a row this time. With each one, a tiny
crack started to open itself over the center of the door.
Before Mona could react, Juliet sprinted down the hallway for them, much faster than Mona ever could have
imagined was possible.

"Run!" Anya shrieked, and the girls let go of each
other's arms and took off down the stairs.

Mona got down them first, dashing for the front door,
screaming for Anya to follow her. She made it to the
front door, got as far as getting her hand on the doorknob, when she heard an ear-piercing screech behind her.
She turned to see Juliet with Anya by the hair, pulling
her to the ground.

Without hesitation, Mona dropped her hand from the
doorknob and ran for Anya, punching at Juliet's arms to
get her to let go, until Taylor emerged from the mouth
of the staircase. Taylor grabbed at Mona's face from over
Juliet's shoulder, poking her viciously in the eye and leaving a stinging scratch down her temple. Mona cried out
and stopped hitting Juliet's arms for a second.

"Block the door," Juliet cried out to Taylor, her hands

still tangled in Anya's hair. Anya was using her nails to scratch angry lines down Juliet's face.

Mona felt Taylor dash past her, tried to grab her, failed. Taylor ran to the door, grabbing an iron fire poker from in front of the fireplace before setting her stance. Mona couldn't believe it; would Taylor actually hit her with that, *kill* her? The feeling of abandonment and betrayal was devastating, but she didn't have much time to dwell on it.

She needed to get her and Anya out of there, fast.

Juliet threw Anya violently to the floor, then shoved past Mona and into the kitchen, where she grabbed the butcher knife from the block on the counter. Without waiting to see what happened next, Mona pulled Anya to her feet and the two tried to run the opposite way, down the hallway that looped around the mudroom and bathroom and eventually the kitchen, but before they could make it to the back door in the mudroom, Juliet was there, pointing the knife at them, her eyes giving away just how mad she'd gone.

"I just need one of you," she said, that terrifying smile that Mona recognized from before spreading slowly over Juliet's face. Mona imagined how upset Juliet must have been when she realized she wasn't going to be killing that old man from the bar.

"If you want to be the one that lives," Juliet whispered wickedly, "say so now."

Neither Anya nor Mona replied, instead turning and running, only to narrowly miss Taylor as she turned around from the other side of the hallway and took a heavy swing with the fire poker. Both girls barely ducked out the way, stumbling over themselves as they made their way to the only doorway that wasn't being blocked: the door to the basement.

Anya pulled the door shut and locked it only a split second before Juliet and Taylor made it there. The door jostled furiously, but it held firm, and Mona knew there wasn't a key for it. She let go of Anya's hand for a second and made her way down the stairs into the pitch-black darkness in order to turn on the light. When she did, she saw that Anya was sitting near the top of the stairs, hugging her knees to her chest while Juliet said a bunch of bullshit to try and get them to open the door.

CHAPTER 26

"Are you okay?" Mona whispered, so Juliet couldn't hear. "They didn't get you with anything, did they?"

"No," Anya said. "I can't believe they'd kill one of us." She stopped for a second as Juliet escalated from her fake, soft pleading to a louder, angrier yell. "Actually, yes I can. Things went too far way before this, especially with Juliet. It was only natural for them to fall apart even further."

Mona scoured the basement quickly, only to realize that the garage door was still chained shut, the key nowhere in sight. With a sinking feeling in her stomach, Mona realized that Juliet had it. They were trapped down here. Underneath the stairs, there was a dip in the concrete as it fell into the wide metal drain, which was still caked with old blood from the murders they'd committed before. This was where Juliet would cut up the bodies, strip the meat from the bones, set it aside while she took measures to ensure that the scraps could be contained within a tight plastic bundle that could fit into a heavy-duty trash bag.

Mona saw what Anya was talking about. At this point, Juliet had not only killed two different people with two different hammers, but was also forced to dismember the bodies herself and dispose of them in the town landfill. She did it all for Rose.

She was still doing it for Rose.

"Rose isn't going to last in that bedroom much longer," Mona said quietly, coming up the stairs to where Anya was. "They're going to have to deal with her themselves." It hurt, to know that there was literally no way there wouldn't come devastation within a minute of Rose breaking out.

Someone was going to die.

To be reminded of how severely they all failed her made Mona's chest ache. She was never going to get over it, never going to move past it, even if she somehow escaped tonight, she'd spend the rest of her life missing out on any sort of happiness because of everything she'd done, whether in a jail or a hospital or wherever, it didn't matter. If she survived the carnage that was to come, she would call the police and tell them all about everything they'd done. They wouldn't get what they deserved in the justice system, but nobody could cause as much pain as they were all going to cause themselves.

Maybe she would hang herself in jail.

"I love you," Anya said suddenly, so defeated and lost and destroyed. "I'm so sorry about Lexa. We weren't the same as we used to be, but I still missed you, I still wanted to talk to you every day."

"You didn't have to lie," Mona answered, her voice devoid of emotion. "You didn't have to put me through what you did, threatening to show up to the house as Lexa, making everything worse. Why would you take it that far?"

"I was trying to get you to tell her to stop contacting you altogether," Anya whimpered. "I didn't want to do it anymore, all the lying and pretending, I was just trying to push you to ditch her completely, make you decide that Lexa was too much trouble to deal with. I wanted you back. It was all so stupid, I should have just come to you. Please, you have to forgive me in case we die, *please...*"

For reasons Mona couldn't understand, she suddenly came to a realization: for too long she'd stayed away, hidden, bending to Juliet's will. For too long she'd held back on what she knew was right, like coming to Anya to talk their problems out so they could be close again.

For too long she'd been like Mom.

Juliet had always faced everything head-on, too head-on, aggressively so. And Mom was always the polar opposite; avoiding, refusing, disappearing. Mona understood for the first time why it was so important that she take a minute to figure out what the third path was. What the balance could offer to their lives, instead of a raging case of fire-against-fire. It was time for Mona to step up for her family, for herself. She had nothing to lose now.

She had nothing to be afraid of.

"I forgive you," she said to Anya, filled with calm. Anya looked up at her in despair, clearly nervous at the sight of the change within Mona, but if she only knew that Mona was about to take back control in a way that she hadn't ever since she took her first swig of vodka.

Without another word, Mona unlocked the basement door.

"NO!" Anya yelled, but Mona was already stepping out, to see Juliet and Taylor arguing frantically in the kitchen. At the sight of Mona, Taylor raised the fire poker again, and Juliet's eyes narrowed.

"Nobody needs to die," Mona assured them, raising her hands to show she meant no harm. "We can still get through this."

"No, we can't," Juliet insisted, taking a step forward, and Mona's heart skipped a beat in her chest.

"Yes, we can." She said it with conviction, sureness, knowing that she was right. Juliet sensed it somehow, and stopped coming for her, put her hand up to signal Taylor to hold on a second.

"What are you talking about?" she asked Mona.

"We can work together," Mona started. "Really work together. No longer leave it up to you to handle everything. You've always taken care of us, Juliet, even when you hated it."

Juliet didn't say anything, continued to stare Mona and Anya down. "Are you trying to trick us so that you can feed one of us to Rose? It won't work," she said, but already Mona could sense how unsure she was at Mona's newfound strength.

More banging came from upstairs. There wasn't much time left.

"You don't have to hold all the weight anymore," Mona went on. "We can work together to force Rose into the basement. We can lock her in there until we figure out a way to get her more meat, until Mom comes home. She won't be able to break out of there, not like the bedroom."

The garage was chained shut, and the basement door could be blocked by boards and the refrigerator. They could command more time, just as Mom commanded Rose's soul back from the dead. "She may not be herself right now," Mona reminded Juliet, "and she may be willing to eat anyone, but make no mistake, when she comes back to herself afterward, she will *never* forgive you for feeding her me or Anya."

Juliet remained silent. Mona could see her digesting what she'd just been told. She knew it was true, Mona could tell. Rose was the only thing that could be used against Juliet at this point.

"How would you feel if Rose killed herself over it?" Mona asked, taking a brave step forward despite Anya's protesting whimper.

Juliet's eyes fell to the open basement door behind them, and Mona knew that she'd won.

"Let's go upstairs," she whispered to her oldest sister, reaching a hand out. "All of us. We'll open the door and handle Rose together. Someone can grab her head from behind to make sure she doesn't bite. Someone else can hold her arms, and someone can hold her legs. The remaining person can use the rope to tie her up. All we'd have to do is carry her down to the basement."

"Okay," Juliet finally said, her shoulders sinking a little bit. "Okay, we're going to do what Mona said, everybody get upstai—"

But her words were cut off by a truly jarring sound: the sound of the front door being jiggled frantically. Before anyone had a chance to react, they all heard the sound of a key being turned, and a second later, the door flew open.

Mom stepped into the entryway cautiously, like she wasn't sure what to expect. When she saw the girls all standing in the kitchen, she nearly fainted from what appeared to be relief. She slammed the door behind her and locked it again.

"Girls!" she cried, stepping forward, dropping her purse on the ground, the contents splaying themselves over the floor. "Girls, thank god you're all okay, I'm back, I'm finally back. Where is Rose?"

The shock of seeing her mother caused Mona's legs to go weak. Was it possible she was really back? After taking so long? Did she have the cure? Was everything going to be okay, somehow, after all?

"Tell us what took you so long," Juliet demanded angrily, and Mona could see the calm that had settled over her just a minute ago was totally gone. She grabbed the fire poker out of Taylor's hands and pointed it threateningly at Mom. "Tell us right now or I swear to god I'm going to kill you and feed you to Rose."

"No, you can't!" Mom squeaked, cowering at the sight

of the poker. "Please, Juliet, you have to let me explain, I may have slipped up a little at first but I came back, I came back for you all, I couldn't live with myself knowing that I'd left you..."

"So you admit it," Juliet interrupted, her nostrils flaring. "You were going to ditch us, leave us to deal with Rose."

"Only because I couldn't find Harlow at first," Mom pleaded. "I... I admit I went on a sort of bender, I was suicidal, I thought that I'd ruined everything..."

"You did ruin everything!" Juliet bellowed, and Taylor nodded in angry agreement. "Just like you always do! Just like you always will!"

Juliet was getting more and more worked up with every second. Mona desperately tried to cut in, to remind them that Rose was upstairs and they needed to handle it *now*, but nobody would listen.

"No, that's just the thing!" Mom pleaded. "I thought I failed, but I didn't. Harlow bailed me out of the police station. She told me more about the ritual. I know what Rose needs to be cured!"

"It's too fucking late for that," Juliet said, much more calmly now, raising the fire poker and bringing it down hard on the top of Mom's head. It went right on through her skull, more sharply than the hammer ever could, splitting Mom's skull in half lengthwise. As Mona watched, her mother collapsed into a gurgling mess on the ground, blood cascading over the floor. Watching in horrified shock, Mona felt a piece of herself die. There was no hope for any of them anymore, not now.

"NO!" she and Anya both screamed, and Taylor backed into the wall, her eyes wide enough to fall out of her face.

"How could you?" Anya yelled, but another sound took over the entire scene, the sound of wood exploding into splinters upstairs. All of the girls froze, unable to move in their terror as there came the sound of furious sprinting from the hallway and then down the stairs, startlingly fast, impossibly fast.

Mona turned to the living room right as Rose tore into the open from the staircase, sprinting toward them while she snarled and spat, her arms outstretched, her fingers hooked and ready to tear into whoever she caught first. All of her skin was a deep, sickly shade of green, with blushes of dark blue and purple in random bursts throughout. The black veins pushed through, the color of rot, like a full-body veil of thick, grotesque spiderwebs. Chunks of hair had been torn from her scalp.

Juliet stepped over Mom's still-quivering body, frantically tried to open the front door, too freaked out to realize that it was locked, and by the time she figured out why it wouldn't open, it was too late. All of the girls dashed for the basement door, slamming it behind them and locking it the same moment that Rose reached it.

The door made a loud cracking sound as Rose ran into it, *hard*, over and over and over again. The sisters headed down the stairs, pushing past one another while trying not to trip. "Maybe she'll find Mom up there and just eat her raw," Juliet said in wonder as she listened to Rose's growls and yelps upstairs. "That is going to be hard, if not impossible, to clean up without a single trace, though."

"You fucking psychopath," Anya cried out, pulling Mona with her to the farthest corner. "You cold-blooded murderer, you killed our mother!"

"She deserved it," Juliet snapped, but even Taylor looked completely doubtful.

"How?" Anya demanded. "She was about to tell us how to cure Rose!"

Upstairs, Rose continued to beat the door. It was starting to crack just like the upstairs one had, but this time it was happening much faster on a much stronger door. The strength it would take to break through was inhuman, impossible for a normal twelve-year-old girl.

"That thing we saw wasn't Rose," Juliet countered, her eyes wild.

"Let us out of here," Mona said before Juliet could say anything else. "You have the key to the lock on the chain. Let us out."

"No," Juliet said, soaked in blood from head to toe. "No, I think waiting her out would be more fun. Every one of you should die. Every one of you is worthless."

Taylor let out a strangled cry. "Fun?" she nearly yelled. "I thought we were in this together!"

"Don't act like it wasn't fun," Juliet sneered, stepping toward Mona. "Don't act like killing didn't make you feel more alive and useful than you've ever felt in your entire life. You're a murderer just like me, you know, all of you are!"

They didn't get the chance to talk about it any further, because at that moment, Rose had burst through the ruined basement door and stumbled down the steps, jumping down them from halfway, bracing herself on the concrete before lifting a bloodshot eye to Juliet.

Before Juliet could so much as scream, Rose flew at her, tackled her onto the concrete floor, and ripped Juliet's throat out with her teeth. Blood sprayed everywhere, and Juliet's gargled shrieks were cut off quickly as Rose ate, filling her ravenous belly at last, the black veins subsiding, the color returning with every bite, as the remaining sisters huddled together in the far corner, shaking, too paralyzed with shock to try and escape.

When Rose finished eating Juliet, she stared down at the torn-up corpse and began to sob.

CHAPTER 27

It was raining the day Dad came home.

By then, Juliet was in the landfill, or at least what was left of her, along with the remains of Rita Stazenski and Glenn Blackwood. But the police didn't know that. They thought that Juliet was somewhere on the run, trying to escape punishment for the crimes she'd committed as a side-effect of the major psychotic break that had driven her to murder their mother in a fit of rage.

Before the remaining Cane girls had called the police, they'd made sure to pull off one last trick as a clan of criminals: they cleaned up the mess in the basement, planted damning evidence against Juliet where they could, and got together to iron out exactly what their stories would be, since they would all be questioned for sure.

It was still up in the air as to whether they'd completely get away with it, but for now, they were all free. Juliet died doing what she'd always wanted to: taking care of Rose. Turned out, the reason why the meat of murder victims only held Rose over for so long was because it was dead flesh. All that time, all Rose had to do to become cured, truly cured, was to eat someone while they were still alive.

The day after the police were called, Rose ate her first normal breakfast since she'd come back to life: frozen waffles, eggs, bacon. She ate it all. The bruising was completely gone. Her veins were back to being delicate and thin and blue.

Within four days of Juliet murdering Mom, the story was all over the news: the Cane sisters had suspected that something was horribly wrong with their oldest, Juliet. She'd been arguing more and more with their mother, and the arguments had started getting violent. After their mother left them alone for days in order to party it up in a faraway town, she had gotten arrested, released and come home to an argument with Juliet.

All the girls had witnessed Juliet kill her in a fit of rage. Before any of them could stop her, Juliet had run off. Police later suspected that she had been responsible for the murders of Rita Stazenski and Glenn Blackwood. Crosschecks with two different rental car agencies confirmed that Juliet had been in the possession of cars that matched tire tracks found at the abduction sites. Detailed notes on how to abduct someone and murder them without getting caught were found in her desk, in her handwriting.

Haunting diary entries revealed that Juliet had been wanting to see what murdering someone would feel like for years and years, as a sick sort of release for all the heartache she'd experienced in her life. She couldn't wait to try it.

The story was a stretch, Mona and the others knew it. But so far, the police hadn't investigated any areas in the house except the scene of the murder upstairs and Juliet's bedroom. The evidence they found had been enough to keep them beyond satisfied. Three murder cases closed in a single day. Mona hoped with everything she had that they wouldn't poke around in the basement too long. It was spotless and unsuspicious, but a simple chemical test on the cement and the drain in the now enclosed space beneath the stairs would reveal everything.

If that happened, they'd deal with it the best they could. Mona was mentally prepared to fight her way out of jail as hard as she could, but if that's where they ended up in the end, so be it. At least Rose would go free—that was the one thing she and Anya and Taylor had promised each other. If more was revealed than what the police currently believed, they'd work together to ensure that Rose would never become a suspect.

They owed her that much, at least.

Now, waiting for Dad's car to pull up to the police station, where the girls had undergone intensive questioning for a few hours each, a caseworker sat between Mona and Anya, none of them speaking. They were all watching Rose standing at the window, looking out at the rain silently, her stature slightly hunched. Taylor stood away from them, her arms crossed over herself, her newly shaved head a stark contrast to her delicate face.

She no longer wore clothes that used to be Juliet's, in fact, she threw them all away the day after Mom died.

Mona and Anya had already talked about Taylor, and what to do about her. They'd all been through a lot, but at the end of the day, there was always going to be that underlying tension with Taylor, the knowledge that at her worst, she had been ready and willing to kill one of them under Juliet's command. They would never be able to trust her, not fully.

It wouldn't matter too much, though; the moment they were all cleared, Taylor would be running away to start her new life somewhere far, far away, and Mona was pretty certain that once she left, she'd never come back.

Mom's funeral wouldn't be until tomorrow morning, because the coroner still hadn't finished examining her body, but Mona was eager to stand over the grave, and whisper everything she'd left unsaid, things like *I'm sorry I didn't try to help you more*, things like *I know what it's like to lose control*, things like *I forgive you*.

If they could make it to tomorrow without raising any additional suspicion, they'd be cleared to leave at last, to start their new life in their dad's hometown, a little place in the wine country of Northern California. It was funny, before Rose died, all Mona wanted in the world was to live somewhere permanent with her dad nearby, and now she was finally getting that. Except this picture was so much different than she'd imagined, and the family would be forever incomplete without Juliet, and Mom, and Taylor.

It would be just Anya, Mona and Rose from now on.

The past few nights, Mona had woken in a cold sweat from the same nightmare: all of the Cane sisters were alive and well, walking together downtown, licking ice cream cones and wearing their matching sunglasses, just like they used to. Except in the dream, the ice cream cones were topped with blood, and fingers, and eyeballs. They giggled together as they slurped them up, walking like a pack down the street, everyone looking on in admiration, Rose in the center of them.

Rose wasn't the baby anymore. She was technically, Mona supposed, but there was something permanently changed about her in the aftermath of all this trauma.

Looking at Rose now, staring blankly out of the water-streaked window, Mona had a horrible realization. She wasn't so sure anymore that it had really been Rose the sisters were thinking of first in all of this. Maybe Rose would have been happier if she'd stayed dead. Maybe they were keeping her alive for themselves, because she was the only one keeping their thin facade of happy and normal and unbroken held together. They all had things to fight through, things to take out, anger to work through.

The reason Mona was sober right now wasn't because of anything she had done, wasn't because she had been especially strong or grounded, in fact, it wasn't even her choice. The problem wasn't the alcohol, and she didn't want to pretend anymore that it was. She was tired of making herself sick in a life where she should have felt like she could do anything.

The reason Mona was sober now was because she really needed to keep a close eye on Rose. Even though

Rose was cured, even though she was eating regular food and no longer got tired and sick from craving human flesh, there was still something off about her. Like she wasn't quite right in the head anymore.

Mona had noticed that when people wore clothing that exposed their legs or arms near Rose, her little sister couldn't seem to tear her eyes away from their flesh, knowing what it had once been to her. And every so often, Mona would catch her licking her lips at the sight.

Mona didn't know if anything would ever come of it, didn't know if Rose had stopped having nightmares about what it was like to be dead, but either way she was going to do her job as a big sister and keep a close eye on her. And to do that, she needed a clear head, a sober head.

A black SUV pulled swiftly into the parking lot. Their father climbed out of the back of it, looking through the window at them, and Mona and Anya stood. After a second's hesitation, they ran out into the rain with Rose, their arms outstretched, and they all tried to hug him at once. He took his time, told them how happy he was that they were okay, told them that everything would be alright somehow, wiped a single tear from his cheek before hardening back up. They all got into the black SUV, and a moment later, they were off.

"Who's hungry?" Dad asked after they'd driven away. "I thought we should probably stop and get something before heading to the hotel. They don't really have much to offer there."

Rose cocked her head to the side at the question, and suddenly Mona remembered something her little sister had said before she was cured: *I'm not the same Rose anymore.* She couldn't have meant that literally, right? Mona thought of the dark place Rose described, filled with ravenous "others." She thought of how Rose insisted something from the land of the dead had "stuck to her soul." Was it possible that the something was still with her?

Rose answered in a strange voice, and Mona met her eyes with fear.

"I'm starving."

★ ★ ★ ★ ★

ACKNOWLEDGMENTS

There are so many people who are to blame for my weird-ass stories. I am deeply grateful for them all:

My dearest readers. Getting to know you at events, signings and online has become one of the greatest joys in my life. You guys are so passionate, and supportive, and wonderful, and inspiring. Love to you all. I hope to keep entertaining you for as long as I possibly can.

Eddie Lukavics, for sending me an article about the Bloody Benders one random day just because you knew I'd be mesmerized by how messed up it was. After reading the article, the half-formed idea that had been simmering for months suddenly became *The Ravenous*, all because of you, my best friend in the entire world and my very favorite brainstorming partner.

My always incredible agent, Joanna Volpe, and the entire New Leaf Literary team. To say you guys go above and beyond the call of duty is an understatement. Thank you for always fighting for me and supporting me as much as you have.

My dear friend and editor, T.S. Ferguson, who I mostly know as my koala. Thank you for holding my hand yet again through the dark, dangerous and exciting path that is writing and editing a novel. I can't wait to continue working with you! Also to Siena Koncsol, my super rad publicist, as well as the entire team at Harlequin TEEN. My experiences with you all so far have been the stuff of dreams.

Sarah Goldberg—there's really no other way to say it: you saved my ass! When I decided that Mona was impossible to figure out, you kindly stepped in and reminded me that she wasn't, not really. Apparently I just had to pay attention to what I'd already written about her, haha! Thank you so, so much for your help with this manuscript. I valued our time working together more than I can say!

The force of nature that is Roxie Blackwood, as always. You are just the greatest, sister-friend, and I love you so very much. I don't know what I would do without you.

Amber Fejeran, one of my best motivators! You were constantly asking me how the manuscript was going, telling me how excited you were for it, and during early reading, telling me that you loved it and couldn't wait for more. I can't wait until I can give you a big high five in real life for it. I owe you a drink or two, my lady! Thanks so much for everything.

Chelsea Stazenski-Ludwig and Alexa Simpson, who

are always willing and excited to talk with me about murder. Hey, what are true friends for, am I right? In extension, thanks so much to my incredible girls who are always able to help me relax in between edits—Cassy Foster, Adie Matthew, Jessica Crocker and Lauren West. Palm Springs was memorable to say the least—"when are we?"

"Two turrr-tle doves," etc. etc. etc. I love and cherish you all with my whole heart!

My online writer group, also known (lovingly) as my hags. You know who you are. Thank you for being there for me always, and beyond. I'm so grateful to have you all in my life.

To my lovely Dungeons and Dragons crew: you have no idea how vital our Friday sessions were to my sanity while I wrote and edited this book! Lux the wizard has the greatest adventure crew EVER—Eddie Lukavics (Fisk the monk), Nick Cristea (dungeon master extraordinaire), Isabel Lindsay (Abbadon the rogue), Madison Burns (Vee the ranger), Chris Hill (Candyman the barbarian) and Jamie Hill (Anya the druid). So many adventures await us, in this realm and the next. "Let's sashay on over there…"

"I'd rather saunter!"

Nickie Culver for answering my incessant questions regarding certain details about army life on post. Any mistakes made in favor of the fiction are my doing, not hers.

Lily and Jude, the lights of my life, and my whole family. I am a very lucky woman to have you all.